BLACK BERRY & WILD ROSE

BLACK BERRY

& WILD ROSE

SONIA VELTON

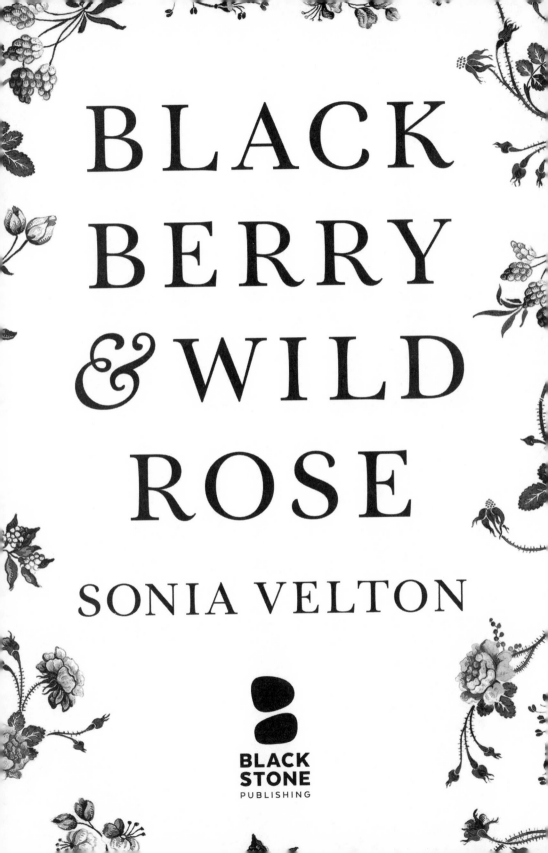

BLACK STONE

PUBLISHING

Printed in the United States of America

First edition: 2019
ISBN 978-1-5385-0775-9
Fiction / Historical / General

1 3 5 7 9 10 8 6 4 2

CIP data for this book is available
from the Library of Congress

Blackstone Publishing
31 Mistletoe Rd.
Ashland, OR 97520

www.BlackstonePublishing.com

For Ron

Umbra Sumus (We are shadows)

—Inscription on the sundial of the
Huguenot chapel in Spitalfields

To scrag: to hang by the neck, or to give evidence that will
see a suspect hanged

—Eighteenth-century London slang

Sara

It was 1768 when I first met Esther Thorel down an alleyway behind the Wig and Feathers tavern. She was on her way to the French poorhouse with twenty newly printed copies of the King James Bible. I was on my way to damnation with a sailor fresh off the East India clipper. But that meeting was my salvation. Before that came my undoing.

When a young girl from the country arrives in London, she is like a caterpillar on a leaf, just waiting for the next bird to pass by. No sooner had I climbed down from the cart that drove me straight into the throng of Spitalfields market than a woman was already pushing through the crowd toward me. It wasn't the London I had been expecting: wide, clean streets lined with tall houses, their windows framing elegant parlors. No, I had stepped straight into a London that was as earthy and pungent as the country, and the shock of it kept me rooted to the spot until the cart moved off and I had to step out of the way.

It was summer, and the heat warmed the market like a stew, and all sorts of noisome odors rose from it. I stood clutching my bag to my chest and reeling from the stink of vegetables rotting among sheep dung, while an unconcerned city busied itself around me. I should have run after that cart as fast as I could, but at the time I saw no threat in an elderly woman picking her way toward me through the old cauliflower heads. When she reached me, she beamed so widely that the skin concertinaed around her eyes. I thought it was kindness, but it wasn't. Her eyes lit up, as if she had spotted a polished penny dropped among the coal.

"Tsk," she said. "I thought he was going to drive right over you!" Then her face fell, and she looked around me in an exaggerated fashion. "Why, you're not on your own, my dear, are you?"

Without waiting for an answer, she grasped my elbow in her bony hand and began guiding me away from the market. "The city's no place for a young thing like you. There's all sorts of nasty folk about." She stopped suddenly as if she had bumped into her own idea. "Perhaps you should come home with me, miss?" she said, turning toward me and bringing out her smile again.

"That is very kind of you, Mrs. …"

"Swann, my dear, Mrs. Swann."

"Mrs. Swann. I am much obliged, but I have an introduction already." I fumbled in my bag and pulled out a piece of paper with a name and address written on it. "My mother said I'm to go here as soon as I arrive."

The smile slid off Mrs. Swann's face and she plucked the paper from my hand. Once she had read it, she looked up and gave a dismissive shake of her head. "This place is miles away. You'll never get there before nightfall."

"But my mother said it was next to Spitalfields market."

"And when was your mother last in London?" Mrs. Swann clutched my arm again and started walking me toward an alley off the main street. "London changes all the time. What was nearby ten years ago is miles away today. Best you come home with me tonight. You can set off again in the morning." Then she folded my piece of paper and tucked it firmly into the top of her bodice.

જી · ટ્રે

At the end of the alley there was a tavern with a wide bay window at the front and a sign hanging over the door. Years ago, the sign must have been brightly painted, but time and weather had turned the paint to faded flakes and curls. Across the bottom, though, I could still read WIG AND FEATHERS. The door was propped open by a cask of ale, presumably because of the heat, and before Mrs. Swann had even pulled me up the step behind her, I was greeted by a rush of warm air full of stale beer and snatched conversations.

We did not stay in the tavern. I stumbled behind Mrs. Swann with my bag, trying to ignore the stares of the men seated at the tables, until we reached a staircase at the back, which took us up to a room above the tavern. It was quite comfortable, with a bed and a washstand in one corner, a chest of drawers in the other. Mrs. Swann left me then, promising to return with a cup of chocolate.

Chocolate! I had seen my mother scrape careful slices of chocolate from a block and use them to make the master's drinks, spiced with nutmeg and cloves rubbed against the back of a clam shell, but I had never tasted it. This must be how ordinary people live in London, I thought, as I walked over to the window. I could see the market in the distance, slowly emptying of people as the stalls were packed up and the sheep herded back into their pens, and I realized how tired I was. Perhaps I slept, I cannot remember, but by the time there was a knock at the door the room was in darkness. Murmured conversation and the clatter of plates rumbled up from the tavern below. The door opened and Mrs. Swann came in, carrying a cup and saucer.

She put the chocolate on the edge of the washstand and busied herself closing the shutters and holding a taper to the candle. "That's better," she said, coming to sit next to me. She picked up the saucer, her hand shaking slightly, making the liquid ripple in the cup. "Here, drink this." She held the cup almost to my lips herself. Her nails were very long, and they scraped against my fingers as I took the chocolate. And what a taste! Bittersweet yet creamy, the rush of the new through my veins. Sugar and excitement made my head spin.

"It's delicious," I said, staring at her over the rim of the cup. She was perched on the bed like a bird, neatly folded in with her hands in her lap. Her eyes were almost black in the half-light and they followed the cup intently as it went from the saucer to my mouth and back again.

"Who were all those girls?" I asked her presently. As we had made our way up the stairs and along the passage, we must have passed three or four.

"They are my daughters," she said, still staring at me with her inky eyes.

"Your daughters?" I was starting to feel confused. I tried to keep hold of my thoughts but it was like pulling eels out of a bucket. "All of them? But they looked so different."

Mrs. Swann gave the bottom of my cup a little tap with her fingernail, nudging it up toward me. "Oh, yes," she said, almost in a whisper. "Every single one. Just like you now."

I wanted to ask her what she meant, but the words seemed to chase themselves around in my head like bees. By the time I could speak, all that came out was, "You're so kind, Mrs. Swann."

She gave me a tight little smile and took the cup from my hands, checking it briefly to see that it was empty. "Good girl," she said, and patted my knee, then stood up. I tried to stand, too, but my legs buckled under me and I fell back onto the bed. I started to laugh so hard that I was folded over with my head on my skirts. Once I had caught my breath, I looked up, expecting Mrs. Swann to be laughing too. But she wasn't. Her face was as set and expressionless as the porcelain cup in her hands. I just sat there and watched as she reached down with her free hand and began to riffle through the folds of my skirts. My shock at what she was doing came out as something between a giggle and a hiccup. Either way, Mrs. Swann ignored it. The tremor in her hand worsened and the cup rattled a jig in the saucer as she pulled out my purse on its string and yanked it from my waist.

She straightened and looked down at me. "You don't want to be carrying money around," she said, cupping the little cloth bag my mother had given me in her hand. "I'll look after it for you. Just like I'm going to look after you, my dear."

I don't completely trust my memory: it offers up snatches of my life in perfect clarity but swallows the rest. Mrs. Swann must have left, but I hardly noticed because the buzzing in my head was so loud that it made me claw at my hair. Then a man came in. I wouldn't recognize him now if I passed him on the street, but I do remember his shoes. They appeared in front of me as I sat on the edge of the bed, staring at the floor, trying not to be sick. They were brown leather with a shiny gold buckle. The ankles and calves that rose out of them might have belonged to any well-to-do merchant or parish constable.

Have I done something wrong? This was what I wanted to ask him, but although I bade my lips to move, they did nothing of the sort. I could only peer at him, watching his image begin to snake and bend, as if I were looking at his reflection in a poorly made mirror.

Then he pushed me back onto the bed. The mattress was lumpy under me and his face was rough against my skin. As he pulled up my skirts, I had the sensation of my whole body falling apart. When he climbed on top of me, I felt as if I was outside myself, struggling to pick up my arms and legs and put them back together again so that I could push him off. But I was like a doll, lying broken on a nursery floor. Then I was hurting, but couldn't tell where the pain was coming from. In my mind, I could hear myself screaming, but the only actual sounds were the creak and thud of the bed and the man's labored breathing.

Once he had gone, a woman—not Mrs. Swann—came into the room and put a bowl of water and a rag by the bedside. After I had cleaned myself, I dropped the rag back into the water and watched as swirls of blood colored it a dirty brown.

The opium, like the pain, came only once. After that Mrs. Swann relied on a locked door and the insistent manner of her customers. I was wrong to think that poor people in London drank chocolate. I never saw a cup of chocolate again until after Esther Thorel, and her basket of King James Bibles, passed by the alley leading to the Wig and Feathers tavern.

Esther

Stepping outside the chilly void of L'Église Neuve—a Huguenot chapel sitting in the shadow of Hawksmoor's grand Christ Church to the west—

and into the sunlight was like being reborn. A time spent in devotion, incubating the spirit, before we were disgorged back into the world, a trailing line of somber-clad, God-fearing folk.

Elias, my husband of four years, stopped at the foot of the chapel's steps and turned back toward me, offering his arm to help me negotiate the stone treads, polished by so many pious feet that they reflected the sunlight like water. I smiled and placed my hand on his sleeve. His jacket was made of silk, a muted charcoal damask for church, but as soft and luminous under my palm as spun cobwebs. As I stepped down toward him, his Huguenot kinsmen filed past in plain black wool coats over neat white collars.

"Ah, Mr. Thorel." Pastor Gabeau stepped toward us, extending his hand for Elias to shake, which he did, vigorously. "And Mrs. Thorel," he said, turning to me and smiling a gracious smile. "I trust you enjoyed the sermon."

There was only time for the briefest of formalities. Behind us, a queue of the devout was forming, snaking right back into the nave of L'Église Neuve.

"Have you heard," continued Gabeau, holding on to Elias' hand for a moment longer, "that a new French charity house has opened in Vine Street?"

Elias knew nothing of the sort. His head was filled with his work. Certainly, he knew which days the silk man received his orders for the finest raw silk from Italy. He knew which throwsters had the nimblest fingers to clean his silk and twist the gossamer strands into yarn, and he knew the journeymen in Spitalfields with the skill to weave those threads into the finest silk that money can buy. But when it came to the concerns of our community, I had learned to leave Elias to the work that sustained him and be the eyes and the ears of the household myself.

"Indeed we have, Pastor," I said, slipping my arm through Elias'. "And we are keen to do all we can to help." It was what Gabeau wanted to hear. There would be endless soup to make and carry to the new charity house. I would do this, along with the other Huguenot wives now milling and chatting behind us. I smiled at Pastor Gabeau. "Perhaps I could sew some shirts."

Gabeau nodded slowly. "That would be very kind, Mrs. Thorel," he said. "But what these people really need, even more than shirts on their backs, is the word of God. Do you not agree?" He did not wait for an answer. "We are looking for …" he glanced upward as if awaiting divine instruction, "… a donation. Perhaps a few copies of the new edition of the King James."

Two weeks later, I was heading toward Vine Street with a basket of Bibles so heavy it made my arm ache. My heart sank when it started pouring with rain—I was certain I would have to turn back. I was just wondering what His plan could be—to thwart my good intentions in such a manner—when I saw the entrance to a small alley off the main street. I had never noticed it before, but the houses there were of the old style, built before the Great Fire, and they overhung the street to such a degree that I could find shelter.

It was a sign, I knew it was: the Bibles, the rain, the tiny alleyway I had never noticed before. I was meant to find her that day.

Sara

I never saw my purse again. I asked her for it, of course, but there was always some excuse. It was locked away in her strongbox and she had misplaced the key. She had lent the money to a friend and would give it to me when they repaid her. Once she even told me that they had introduced a tax on hair powder and she had had to use the money to buy a certificate from the justice of the peace. But she always said that she would give it back to me, just not then.

There was a pound in that purse. My mother had worked as a servant all her life to save it. When I had left home, she had pressed the purse into my hand and told me to use the money to set myself up in London. I could not go home nor move on without it. At the time I was most desperate to leave, I was stuck. I tried to find the piece of paper my mother had given me with the address on it, but it would have been easier to delve inside Mrs. Swann's bodice than get into her bedroom or the cellar where she kept her ledgers and accounts.

She had probably tossed it into the nearest fire. I pictured it sometimes, curling and blackening in the grate, while I tried to read the disappearing words. Phoenix Street became Peacock Lane and number six was sometimes number eight until eventually I could recall none at all.

Then an odd thing happened. I stopped spending all my time thinking about how to find the key to Mrs. Swann's strongbox. I stopped trying to sidle past Nathanial, the Wig and Feathers' houseboy, and out onto the street. I just did what Mrs. Swann expected of me and the months slipped into a year or more, until I could no longer be sure how long I had been there. I only remembered the day I had arrived, the heat of the summer as I stood in Spitalfields market and the pungent stink of the life I had been dropped into.

My name is Sara Kemp. It is a good, short name, serviceable and no fancier than it needs to be, and in this regard, it suits me well. I worked hard at Mrs. Swann's and made no fuss. And why not? I was the daughter of a servant, after all, and no stranger to drudgery. I had been taught to accept my fate by a mother who had accepted her own with the silent fortitude of the widow. I was too young to remember my father, a cook on *Baltimore* sloop, who squandered the money he brought home on petty wagers and gin, before he had the decency to leave for the New World and never come back. She told everyone he had died at sea, which was a noble enough end for a man who had sold her shoes for the sake of a threepenny bet.

The Quakers helped us. They found a position for my mother in a country house and sent me to the Quaker free school in the village, where they taught me about the wretchedness of vice and the dangers of drink, as if the tales of my father hadn't taught me that already. I learned to read and to sew, but when they told me I had to learn a trade, that I would go into service just like my mother, I never went back, and my mother let me follow her around the kitchen instead: learning to cook was all I wanted to do. It seems I was my father's daughter after all.

Mrs. Swann must have thought me the most biddable of all her girls. After a while, I found that Nathanial no longer barred my way at the door and I was allowed small freedoms. I was not happy exactly, but I suppose I was happy enough. Except for this: for every shilling I earned Mrs.

Swann took sixpence. I came to understand that if I ever wanted a future away from the Wig and Feathers, I would have to earn it elsewhere. So, from time to time, I would stand on the edge of the docks at Billingsgate, watching the ships come in, their white sails snapping in the wind, like sheets hung out to dry. When they docked, their crusted and slippery hulls yawned open and the sailors rolled out barrels of tea from Bengal and Ottoman spices. Once the cargo was unloaded, they would stride out onto the docks and stand, their hands on their hips and their shirt sleeves rolled up to the elbows, sniffing the air's salty tang, as needy as the seagulls wheeling and screeching through the fog of the city.

But I was no twopenny strumpet, lifting her skirts among the piles of old ropes and the dogs nosing through the scraps of fish guts. There was an old woman, Mrs. Hughes, who lived opposite the back entrance to the Wig and Feathers. She was deaf as a post—or pretended to be—and you might have thought blind too, for all the goings-on she must have seen from across the alley. She would let me use the little room above hers in return for the occasional measure of gin siphoned from one of the bottles hidden behind the empty ale barrels in the cellar at the Wig and Feathers.

But there are no secrets in London. Even the houses lean across the narrow alleys toward each other and offer up their scandals in the blink of an opened curtain. One of the girls must have told Mrs. Swann what I was up to because I saw her come out of the Wig and Feathers from the window as I was getting dressed. It was raining at the time, but she seemed not to care. She stood on the step with her nose in the air, like a rat on its haunches sniffing for trouble. In a moment, she hoicked up her skirts and splashed through the puddles until she disappeared under Mrs. Hughes' jetty.

Don't let anyone tell you that sailors are a brave breed. He took off at the first sight of Mrs. Swann, a woman no taller than the average cabin boy. Still, she was a sight to behold, her face twisted with rage, telling me what she thought of me in language that made me grateful Mrs. Hughes was stone deaf. Then she grabbed my arm and yanked me out of there so fast that it was all I could do to snatch my overskirt from the bed and stumble after her. Once we were outside, she couldn't even wait to get back inside the Wig and Feathers before she started on me again. So I stood there, in the rain and my petticoats, listening to her tell me what she would do to me. Then she boxed my ears so hard my head reeled.

࿐ · ࿐

A woman had been sheltering under one of the jetties near the main street. I saw her out of the corner of my eye, while I was listening to Mrs. Swann's colorful language. After Mrs. Swann hit me, the woman became agitated and hovered about, like a concerned bee. When Mrs. Swann grabbed hold of my ear and tried to tug me back to the Wig and Feathers, the woman stepped out in front of us.

"Madam," she said, in a voice that wavered slightly, "please let this poor girl go."

"Poor girl?" repeated Mrs. Swann, pinching my ear even harder. "There is nothin' poor about her. She's a thief and a liar, that's what she is."

The woman blanched. I felt quite sorry for her, standing there arguing with the likes of Mrs. Swann, while the rain plastered her neatly curled hair to the sides of her face and darkened the pale blue silk of her dress.

"To be sure, I don't know the circumstances," she continued, "but whatever she has done, it cannot be right to hit her in the street. Why, she is barely dressed!" She gestured toward my petticoats.

Mrs. Swann let go of my ear, as if it were a hot coal, and rounded on her. "Indeed, you do not know anything, and I'll thank you for staying out of matters that do not concern you." She paused and looked her up and down.

"What are you even doing round here?" she asked, as if the woman were as strange and unexpected in that alley as the King himself.

"You'll forgive me for sheltering from the rain, madam," she said, her voice tart, like lemon cakes.

"Well," said Mrs. Swann, "the ribbon shop is that way. Good day." She gave a dismissive nod in the direction of the main street and even I couldn't stop a smirk creeping into the corner of my mouth. She took hold of my upper arm and made as if to walk back to the Wig and Feathers.

11

As we turned the woman said, "I know what you are."

Mrs. Swann stilled and rotated back toward her. "Do you really?" she said, but the woman had spoken to me.

She regarded me earnestly, her pale face stained pink with indignation at the cheeks. Slim, smooth hands fingered the delicate lace of her cap as it stuck wetly to her forehead over a sweep of copper hair. "There are other things you could do," she said pointedly to me.

I looked at the ground. She must have mistaken my reluctance for shame or self-doubt, as she then said, "Plenty of young girls like you are needed in service," in an encouraging voice.

I found her rather sweet. She seemed naive, assuming I did not know that I could spend my days doing someone else's laundry, up to my elbows in lye, scrubbing out the stains with brick dust until my skin split.

A window in the Wig and Feathers opened and one of the girls called out to us. Mrs. Swann drew in an impatient breath. "Get inside, Sara," she said, giving me a sharp push toward the tavern.

We left the woman standing alone in the alley, shifting her basket from one hand to the other, a grim expression on her face.

Esther

I delivered nineteen Bibles to the charity house the day I met the girl called Sara. When I got home, I took the final one into the withdrawing room, sat at the desk and opened it, smoothing back the front cover so that the spine cracked. I had not been able to stop thinking about the kind of life she must have. Surely her need for the word of God was every bit as great as that of anyone at the poorhouse. Of course, I had no idea whether she could read, but I picked up the quill anyway and wrote: *From Mrs. Esther Thorel of 10 Spital Square.*

I thumbed through to Corinthians and placed the ribbon among its pages. Although I hated to mark a book, I could not resist drawing the tip of the quill alongside a certain passage. Then I pressed the Bible shut.

I had no desire to go back to the tavern, so I told our cook to take the Bible to the Wig and Feathers and ask them to give it to a girl there called

Sara. "The Wig and Feathers?" he said, with a lift of his eyebrows. Indeed, I insisted. Then I pressed a sixpence into his hand for his trouble and told him not to dally.

I went to find Elias. I knew where he would be. Though it was already six o'clock, he was still in the room at the front of the house, which he used to conduct his business. When I opened the door, he was bent over a wooden counter laid out with pieces of paper painted with stripes and scrolled shapes. He looked up at me, slightly confused, as if he couldn't fathom what I was doing there. Then he looked out of the window to the square, as if he needed the emptying street and dwindling light to tell him that the workday was over.

My husband is one of the finest master silk weavers in all of Spitalfields, as was his father before him. His grandfather had learned the craft on the famous looms of Lyon, but when Huguenots could no longer live in peace in their homeland, his grandfather had escaped, bringing nothing with him save this exquisite skill. Many Huguenot weavers did the same, and when they settled in Spitalfields, the beauty and craftsmanship of Spitalfields silks began to outshine even those of Lyon.

"These are lovely," I said, joining him at the counter and idly picking up one of the patterns.

He nodded slowly, still staring at them. "But which one is best, Mrs. Thorel? This is to be a very fine silk indeed."

I looked down at them, all variations of elegant designs. Geometric shapes, tiny Chinese temples, and one with a dainty repeat of shells. "I like this one," I said, gesturing to one that had a pattern of flowers in an Oriental style.

"Ah, the India plants," said Elias. "Yes, I like it too."

I put it back on the counter and began to ask him about supper, but he stopped me, reluctant to leave the subject of his silks. "There is a journeyman silk weaver," he said. "He is extraordinarily talented, and I believe he could become a master. I have said he can use one of the looms in the garret to weave his master piece. They are just standing there empty after all."

"Our looms? But why can he not weave his master piece on his own loom?"

Elias clicked his tongue. "He still has to earn a living! His loom is full of my work. This he will do in his own time, for his own purposes. I will give him the silk and pay his fee to the Weavers' Company."

Sometimes my husband surprised me. It was a generous act from a man usually driven by his commercial success. "That is very kind of you, husband."

He gave a slight smile. "Not at all, wife. I shall get a figured silk to sell of unprecedented complexity, woven for me for nothing. One of these, in fact." He indicated the patterns scattered over the counter. "For his part, if he is successful in being admitted, he will be a freeman and I will help him set up as a master on his own account. A fair exchange, do you not think?"

"But a journeyman, in our home, it seems …" I struggled to find the words. I hardly knew what I thought of the idea. Was I horrified or excited?

"I am letting you know, that is all. He will use this door," Elias nodded toward the door from his workroom onto the street, used by the mercers, dyers, and silk men who visited him to make deals over the wooden counter, "and the back stairs, so you should not see him at all. I mention that he will be here only because you may hear the noise of the loom in the attic."

"The noise!" The whole of Spitalfields echoed with the movement of a thousand looms. "Oh, Elias, not in our house, surely."

Almost immediately I regretted my outburst. Elias lifted his head from where he had returned to studying the patterns and faced me again, expression intent, daring me to challenge him. "This is a weaving household, Mrs. Thorel. The house was built by my grandfather with the money he made from nothing but talent. My father spent seven years as his apprentice on those looms and I myself spent seven more as *my* father's apprentice, just to carry on the business I was born into. The only reason this house's looms stand empty is that I have no son to follow me. So, if I do not complain about the want of a child, then you should not complain about the noise of a loom."

He turned back to his designs, reordering them on the counter, moving one on top of another, the favored and the shunned. For once, I was glad that the silk drew his attention from me. He did not see the sting of his words.

I was a good wife, that much I know. I was diligent about my sewing and I ran an efficient household. We cooked for the poor and entertained the rich. At church I sat beside my husband, pretty enough to please him but somber enough to satisfy the Low Church. In the bedchamber, I conducted myself with neither complaint nor unseemly enthusiasm. Only the Lord knew why we had not been blessed with the child that my husband's community considered a duty and a necessity.

In bed that night I pictured the looms above me, barren and empty, as unproductive as I had proved to be. Elias had no son to teach and mentor so now this man was coming into our house.

A stranger to me—an extraordinarily talented stranger.

Sara

My life was like one of my own petticoats. It just got grubbier and grubbier, and I was in it every day, so I scarcely noticed. At least, not until something so bad happened that it couldn't be ignored, like a blot or a stain that could not be gotten out.

The day he turned up at the Wig and Feathers, Mrs. Thorel's Bible had lain unopened on top of my chest of drawers for weeks, slowly becoming hidden by a pile of fans and wigs, growing dusty with face powder. I had known who it was from as soon as it arrived. Esther Thorel was not the only well-meaning woman to think that words in a book might change my life for the better. But what she, and they, didn't understand was that I had no desire for a different life. Why would I when, after ten years in service, my own mother's life had been worth just a pound? It was bewildering to me that Mrs. Thorel would think I might prefer getting up at dawn to scrub steps to what I had to do at the Wig and Feathers. It was half the work for twice the money. Or did she think that servants never got their ears boxed?

I had grown used to the men. I saw all manner of them at the Wig

16

and Feathers: the bakers and butchers, the tanners and tallow chandlers, the merchants and magistrates. The men who tipped their hats to ladies as they passed and stepped to one side to allow them through the door first. The men you went to if you were sick, or if a street urchin had lifted the purse clean out from under your skirts. But they were not those men when they came to me. They were urgent and selfish. They cared nothing for pleasantries or the doffing of a hat. They say that whoring is a rage that comes upon a man and this was never truer than for that particular man.

He was not known to me or even to Mrs. Swann. Usually, Nathanial would stand outside the door when a man was new. He had been a slave and had seen things that would be unimaginable even to the residents of the Wig and Feathers. Something about his silent presence outside the door was enough to temper the extremes of most men. But that evening Nathanial had been sent out on an errand and the man walked in unchecked.

The preamble was typical enough. He had barely closed the door before he started shrugging off his jacket. He was a large man and his waistcoat strained under the pressure of his belly. Still, the fabric of it was very fine; I remember it well. When I sat back on the bed, it was level with my eyes and I concentrated on the beautiful sheen of the cream silk and the tiny mulberry trees repeating across it, rather than on the bulk of the man who wore it.

He bade me take off my dress. I started to protest that it was hardly necessary, but he fixed me with a sharp stare and I found myself loosening my bodice. When I was in my petticoats and stays I went to lie back on the bed, but he caught my arm with his hand, pulled me up and said, "Take it all off."

I opened my mouth to complain, but he took an extra shilling from his pocket and tossed it down by the bed. The thought of a shilling that had not passed through Mrs. Swann's hands first was enough to close my mouth for me. I undressed completely and lay back on the bed.

The room was cold. My arms crept across my body for warmth and to shield myself from his gaze. But he sat down on the edge of the bed and firmly took hold of my wrists, parting my arms and laying each one alongside my body.

"I want you to be cold," he said softly.

And he did, as cold as a leg of mutton lying on the butcher's block. He seemed intent on taking me there himself as not a minute after he had begun, he had his hands around my neck. A burning sensation started in my chest, as if I had inhaled hot coals from the fireplace and they lay smoldering in my lungs. Then stillness. I was aware of the man on top of me, but he was blurred around the edges, like the first man at Mrs. Swann's had been.

I truly thought I had died, but when I came around the pain in my throat was so intense that I surely could not have been in Heaven. And if whores do not go to Heaven, then surely there is something worse for us in Hell than a room at the Wig and Feathers, which was plainly where I still was. The door was ajar and I could hear one of the girls clattering down the stairs screaming for Mrs. Swann.

She came up, in her own sweet time, and stared down at me. "Got a bad 'un, did you?"

I tried to speak but the words passed through my throat with all the ease of an apple stuck with pins. Mrs. Swann handed me a shawl to cover myself and a glass of water to ease my voice. After I had told her what happened, she shrugged and said, "He's just a man that likes to bake his bread in a cold oven." Then she left, but not before she had bent down to pick up the shilling lying on the floor.

I pulled the shawl tight around me and lay back on the bed. I closed my eyes because I could not manage anything else and let myself sleep. When I awoke the next day, I opened new eyes—eyes he had given me. I saw the shabby coverlet and the stained washstand. I saw the streaks on my thighs and the jut of my bones under my skin. I dressed in my undergarments, but I could not bear to put on the same dress, so I walked over to the chest of drawers to look for something else. Then I saw the corner of Esther Thorel's Bible, almost covered by my tawdry ornaments. I pulled it out from underneath them and held it in my hands. It fell open at the pages she had separated with the ribbon and I saw the inked lines marking a passage:

II CORINTHIANS 5:17

Therefore, if any man be in Christ,
he is a new creature:
old things are passed away;
behold all things have become new.

Esther

It was not easy to climb up into the garret. The stairs were narrow and spindly, leading to a trapdoor in the floor. I had been up there once before. When I was first married and exploring my new home, I had been fascinated to see the looms and to imagine my husband as little more than a boy, strong and determined at the weaver's bench, learning the craft of his forefathers.

But now my fascination had altered. Someone else would be there to pick up the dormant shuttle and throw it through the warp threads. I wanted to see where he would spend his time, where he would sit and what the rooftops of Spitalfields would look like to him as he gazed out of the window.

It was late afternoon and the light was fading, but when I pushed up the trapdoor, I found that the garret was still flooded with light. Built into the attic of a weaving household are long lights: huge wall-to-wall windows facing south to illuminate the looms with as much light as possible, for as long as possible. They made me squint so it was a few seconds before I could make out the looms.

Two of them, angular silhouettes against the long lights. I could see that one had already been strung with warp threads, strands of cream stretched across the wooden frame and hung with weighted pulleys that would become the ground. The weft was cobalt blue. I walked over to the loom and ran my hand over the worn wood, pitted and grooved by three generations of silk weavers. Handles and treadles jutted from the sides and bottom. To me it was a structure of unanswered questions: what to pull, wind, lift, and throw, and when to do it. I had sought to answer those questions once, but Elias had snapped shut, like a book of secrets closing. Weaving was the work of men: go back to your sewing, little girl.

It was not a surprise that I married a silk weaver, a creator of art. I started drawing when I was a child. I took coal from the fire and marked any paper I could find with it. My mother would catch hold of me and turn my palms face up. If she found them blackened and dusty she would cuff me around the ear and tell me I was no better than a chimney sweep. When I was thirteen, she bought me a set of watercolors and I began to paint. As I grew older, I would wander on my own to Spitalfields market and walk through row upon row of flower stalls, piled high with carnations, geraniums, tulips, or roses, depending on the season. English fruits, like apples and pears, sat alongside pomegranates from some exotic faraway land. I would paint them all.

Then there were the old silks. Cuts of fabric that had been stitched and unstitched a hundred times, still shabbily radiant, hung above stalls or folded on tables. Styles from bygone days, which no lady of quality would ever wear again, left to be picked over by the masses, haggling for a good price on a piece of a life they would never have. The fruit and flowers of Spitalfields market had been woven into those fabrics with a clarity that made my heart race.

And what of the men who made the silks, who designed the patterns and choreographed the endless dance of warp with weft? I did not have to go to Spitalfields market to see them. There was one on my street, just across the road from my father's house in Spital Square. Elias Thorel was always in his workroom when I walked past, draping a bolt of fabric over his counter for a mercer to consider or sitting alone with his ledgers. I stole glances at him from time to time, as if they were candied cherries. Then one day he looked up and saw me too.

The walls of the garret were lined with shelves, boxes of shuttles and bobbins among silk thread wound onto spindles and spools. There were the pale cream and intense blue they were already using, but also other colors, greens, grays, and frost silver, which would become the color changes of the weft. The laborious process of mounting the loom must have gone on for days without my knowing he was up here. The sight of the loom being clothed with thread in readiness for weaving was a poignant one for me. In the early days I had thought that Elias and I were well matched in every respect. I had imagined that the union of his talent for weaving and mine for art would be a fruitful one.

As the wife of a master silk weaver, I painted with new enthusiasm. I was not just painting flowers, I could almost feel the finished silk live and breathe beneath my brush. When I had something I was pleased with, I took it to Elias. He was upstairs in the withdrawing room, bent over his papers with his quill in his hand. His wig was on its stand beside him and his head was resting on his hand, fingers scratching at his shorn hair.

"Mr. Thorel?"

"Is something amiss?" he said, frowning slightly and putting down his quill.

"Not at all," I said, enjoying the flutter of anticipation in my belly. Foolish, I know, but I felt like a child seeking approval from a parent. "I just wanted to show you this." I put the watercolor in front of him and walked around his desk so that we could look at it together. Suddenly I felt nervous, wondering what he might think of the flowers curling up the page.

He picked up the pattern, then twisted round to face me.

"What is this?" he asked.

I could not help but smile. "It is a design, husband. Perhaps for the next silk you weave."

He looked at the painting, perplexed. "But you jest, of course," he said.

"Jest? No, I do not." I reached out and traced a finger along the meander of foliage. "See how I have made the flowers into a repeating pattern? Imagine it made in silk, it would be—"

I looked up at him then and saw that his mouth had a strange twist to it, hooked up at the side. The words I had thought I would say faded to nothing in my throat. Elias gave his head a slight shake as if dislodging his thoughts. "Why do you concern yourself with such things?" he said.

"Because I want to be part of what you do. Think of it, I could paint the designs for the silks you weave. Not the heavy geometric styles we have now, but something more natural and realistic. I have watched you and learned—"

"Learned! You presume to learn in a few months what my family has learned over generations?"

"Not at all. I just thought it was something we could do together." My voice was starting to waver, but I tried desperately not to cry in front of him. He stared at me a moment, then his face softened and he pulled me down onto his lap, crushing the painting into my skirts as he did so.

"You do not need to be part of what I do," he murmured into my ear. "You do plenty already, organizing the servants and planning the meals. If you want to do more to help, ask Pastor Gabeau—there are always shirts to be sewn for the poorhouse. But silk? No, you cannot do that."

Of course, more sewing. "You are right, husband," I said, trying to keep the disappointment from my voice. Elias tugged the pattern out from underneath me and smoothed it on my lap, studying it properly. Then he laughed. "What is a dezine, Mrs. Thorel? You must know, surely, if you are to be a pattern designer." I swallowed hard, wishing I had not opened myself up to his ridicule. I freed myself from his arms and got up, but he had not finished. "Perhaps it was you, not Mongeorge, who brought the secret of creating luster in silk taffeta from Lyon to Spitalfields!"

There was a brightness to his eyes as he searched my face for a reaction. I thought it was misplaced humor, but it wasn't. It was the first spark of a fire within him that would later consume us.

⁂

Before I left the garret, I went back to the trapdoor and reached down to retrieve what I had left on the stairs. It was a birdcage with a pair of linnets inside, fluttering against the white metal bars as it swung in my hand.

I took it over to the long lights and hung it from a hook in the ceiling, stilling it with my hands and whistling gently at the birds as they fussed on their perches and eyed their new home.

"There, there, sweet things," I whispered. "You'll be happy here. There is not a Huguenot weaver in Spitalfields who does not love a songbird."

Sara

I found Mrs. Swann in the tavern downstairs. She was drying glasses from the night before with a rag and placing them upside down on the many shelves that lined the wall behind.

"Feeling better, my dear?" she asked, as I climbed onto one of the stools in front of the bar.

My throat tightened again, but it was not because that man had throttled me. Instead, it was the inevitable twisting of my gut and stilling of the air in my lungs that happened every time I tried to talk to Mrs. Swann about anything. I shook my head.

"Ah, well," she said, unconcerned, "you will soon get used to him." She turned her back to me and stepped lightly onto a footstool so that she could reach the highest shelf. "You've got a good customer there now," she announced to the row of pewter pots in front of her. "It's always the ones who like that kind of thing who keep coming back. I must say, he seemed happy enough when he left. He tipped me an extra sixpence!"

When she turned back to face me, she picked up the rag and tossed it toward me so that it landed damply on my hand. "Here, make yourself useful instead of just sitting there." She reached under the bar and brought out another cloth. Her hand twisted briskly in a glass while she stared at me expectantly.

I picked up the rag and dragged it off my hand, dropping it into a crumpled pile on the polished wood of the bar. Mrs. Swann's hand paused inside the glass. "Like that, is it?" she said, her voice quiet. "Too good to dry glasses, are we?"

I looked up at her. I had always thought that her eyes were black, but with the morning sun streaming in through the tavern window, I saw that they were not. It was her pupils, which were strangely dilated, even in the light. Around them was a thin margin of green so intense it was almost catlike. Now that Mrs. Swann had stopped her purposeful drying, the glass began to shake slightly in her hand. She put it down abruptly on the wood, so hard I thought it might crack.

"Spit it out, then," she said crisply, "whatever it is that's on your mind."

"I can't do this anymore."

"Do what? Dry the glasses? Help me a little? All right then, be off with you to your room, and I'm only saying that because of what happened last night. I won't be so kind tomorrow."

"No, I mean I can't do all *this*." I raised my hand and waved it above my head, indicating the floor above the tavern and everything that went on there. "I'll never lie with that man again."

Mrs. Swann narrowed her eyes and leaned both hands on the bar in front of me, one a bony claw clutching the wood, the other still wrapped in the cloth. "What do you mean?" She spoke each word deliberately.

"I am leaving the Wig and Feathers, Mrs. Swann. I should like my purse back and all the money that was in it. I'll not wait for him to kill me next time."

"I wish he'd done the job last night!" exclaimed Mrs. Swann, rearing up from the bar and shaking her hand free of the cloth. She folded her arms across her chest. "No, no, no," she said, furiously shaking her head, "this will not do at all."

I slipped down from the stool and stood in front of her.

"Mrs. Swann, you cannot keep me here. I am free to go whenever I choose. Now, please, just give me my money back."

"But why would you want to leave, Sara? What's out there for a girl like you?"

"I intend to find a position in service."

"In service!" screeched Mrs. Swann. "You'll be a street miss before the week is out, you foolish girl. You'll be poxed and clapped by Christmas!" Mrs. Swann wrinkled her face in distress. "You just don't understand how well I look after my girls. Have you ever wanted for anything here? Have you?" she insisted, her expression both angry and confused. "When have you gone to bed without a full belly? When have you lacked for coal in the grate or clothes on your back? Never, you ungrateful wench, never!"

"I have earned my keep a hundred times over, Mrs. Swann, and well you know it."

Mrs. Swann's expression suddenly altered as if the wind had changed. She became wide-eyed and innocent-looking.

"Have you indeed, my dear?" she said, her head bobbing like a children's toy. "Then you must have your money back, mustn't you?"

For a moment I was wrong-footed, so I just stood there, gaping, the fear and anger I had summoned to confront her still fizzing round my veins.

"You just wait there, my angel, while I go and get it." She disappeared through a door and I heard her shoes tap-tapping down the stone steps to the cellar. I waited nervously, unsure who, or even what, might reappear. Mrs. Swann was as unpredictable as the weather.

When she came back, I was almost relieved to see that she was simply carrying a leather-bound book. She returned behind the bar and placed the ledger heavily on the counter between us. Then she gave me an odd sort of smile, something between sympathy and triumph, and said, "I'm afraid you cannot leave just yet. At least, not until you have settled your account." Then she opened the book and thumbed ostentatiously through its pages. "Here we are," she said, twisting the book round so that I could see it and tapping on the page with her long fingernail.

My name was written at the top and beneath it were long columns of figures. A penny here, sixpence there, sometimes a whole shilling. And by each amount was a date and the item to which it related: food and ale, board and lodging; the laundering of shifts and petticoats and the darning of stockings; the supply of fans and wigs and face powder; coal and wood for the fire; a poultice for this or that. Even a contribution to Nathanial's keep was recorded against my name. I turned the page and kept on turning. Page after page of debt going back to the moment I'd first set foot in the Wig and Feathers, all recorded in Mrs. Swann's own spidery hand.

"So you see, my dear," said Mrs. Swann, staring at me intently, the rim of green round her eyes all but disappeared, "there's nothing left of your money. In fact," she flicked on a few pages to where the writing stopped, ending with two-pence for a draught she had given me the night before to ease my throat, "you owe me money."

I stared at the page. A slightly wavering line had been drawn under the last entry and underneath it was a final tally: four pounds, eight shillings and sixpence.

Mrs. Swann closed the ledger and walked around the bar so that she could stand next to me. The twisted fury of earlier had left her face and her expression was kindly, almost needy. She reached up and began to stroke my cheek. "My daughter," she murmured. Then she laid her head against my shoulder. "No, no, no, you shall not leave me," she said, into the gaudy folds of my whore's frock.

Esther

"There's a girl to see you, ma'am."

I looked up from my sewing. Moll, our scullery maid, was standing by the door, hands clasped in front of her, gazing at my feet as if she was not quite brave enough to look at me directly. I set down what I was doing and followed her out to the landing. From the top of the stairs I could see down into the hall. The girl was standing by the door, and at the sound of our approach she raised a pale face to look at me. I didn't recognize her at first, but she clutched a book to her chest and when she saw me appear, she held it up and waved it at me. I could see that it was one of my King

James Bibles and an image flashed into my mind of this girl standing in the lane behind the Wig and Feathers.

"What shall I do with her, ma'am?" whispered Moll, who looked ready to shoo the creature out of the door along with the cat.

"Just a moment," I said.

I have a box in the parlor full of buttons, scraps of material, and ribbons wound round bodkins. I keep a few coins in there too, for just this kind of circumstance. I pushed the buttons around with my finger and picked out a sixpence. I was about to go downstairs, when I opened the box again and poked around for a shilling instead. That old woman really had been most objectionable, and the poor girl needed as much help as I could give her.

I dropped the coin into Moll's hand and nodded toward the girl. Moll glanced up at me, but she knew better than to question my charity. At the foot of the stairs, I saw Moll try to give the coin to the girl, but she shook her head and pushed Moll's hand away. Then she looked up at me again and said, "Beg pardon, madam, but I should like to speak with you, please."

I took her into the parlor where she sat on the sofa, sinking a little awkwardly into its soft cushions. When I settled myself on the chaise opposite her, she fixed me with an earnest gaze.

"Mrs. Thorel," she began, chewing briefly on her lower lip, "you were kind enough to suggest that there might be … *hope* for me." She glanced at Moll, who hovered at the doorway dressing up her curiosity as usefulness. I flicked my hand to dismiss her. When we were quite alone, and the door was shut, I told the girl that she could speak freely.

"Madam," she went on, more purposeful now, "I want to have a new life, the one you said I could have. A position with a good household."

"And I do believe you can find one," I replied, nodding in encouragement. "Even girls like you can work in service. I could ask at church if anyone has need of help. And, please, take this." I held out the coin Moll had given back to me, but again she shook her head.

"You are so kind, madam, but you see, my situation is rather difficult."

I knew what was coming next. I had heard it ten times or more. She was going to ask for more money. There would be an elderly mother afflicted with any manner of ills, or perhaps a baby to feed. I stood up to indicate our meeting was over. "I cannot help you any more than this," I said firmly, placing the shilling on the table next to the sofa.

Had I not seen for myself the viciousness of the old woman in the alley the day I had first met the girl, then I might not have believed what she told me next. But the fact was, I had seen her. I had seen the swipe of her hand when she boxed the girl's ears and I had heard the spite in her voice when she spoke to her. I could well imagine that this girl was now in exactly the predicament she claimed to be in.

"But it's almost five pounds!" I said.

"No, madam, just three pounds, eight shillings, and sixpence. She already has the pound I brought with me."

"Even so, I cannot possibly spare that much. Have you thought of going to the charity house?" Even as I said the words, I began to feel uncomfortable. I stared down at my hands because I did not want to look at the elegant curve of the velvet chaise I was sitting on, or stare into the mother-of-pearl face of the grandfather clock standing by the wall, measuring my reluctance with each swing of its shiny brass pendulum. But even my hands told their own story, smooth and delicate as if they had never had to lift anything heavier than a needle to my sewing.

The girl nodded. "Forgive me," she said, standing up. "I had thought that the Christian kindness you spoke of was your own, not someone else's."

We stood there for a moment, each eyeing the other. Me, caught in the web of my own well-meaning words; she, silent yet strangely defiant, as if challenging me to be the woman I had suggested I might be.

If any man be in Christ, he is a new creature.

How could those words not be true in my own household? Did the word of God that I took to the poorhouse mean nothing to me? Every time I step out of church, I am reborn. How could I not allow her to be made new as well? Even if it would cost me three pounds, eight shillings, and sixpence.

"I shall expect you to work, to pay it back," I said sternly. Her face broke into such a radiant smile that it was almost worth four pounds just to see it.

From the parlor window I watched her leave. I'll own that when I saw how she skipped down the street with my money in her pocket, I wondered whether I would ever set eyes on her again.

Sara

Mrs. Swann's face puckered when she saw me. By then I had become an annoyance to her, like a comb in her hair that wouldn't quite stay where it was put.

She was down in the cellar, sitting behind her desk, the place where I now knew she had recorded her inventory of charges, with every entry spinning a web from which she thought I would never escape. I clutched the coins Mrs. Thorel had given me and approached her. "I have your money." I placed them in a neat pile on the desk, with the sixpence on the top.

Mrs. Swann's eyes grew wide and black as coal in the half-light. "Where did you get that?" she snapped.

"That is not your concern," I replied. "I have paid my debt and now I am free to leave."

Then she laughed. Proper threw back her head and chortled as if I had made a great joke. Then, as abruptly as she had started, she fell silent. There was a dank feeling in the cellar. It was cold and poorly lit, and something about the exposed brick of the walls made me think of a prison. I half expected Nathanial to loom behind me, his towering bulk blocking the door.

"What's in your bag?" she asked.

"Nothing but what I brought with me."

"Show me."

I shook my head. "No."

Mrs. Swann drew a deep breath and released it slowly so that it came out as a long sigh. "He must have been right, then."

"Who? What do you mean?"

She got up and walked round her desk to stand beside me. When she was as close as she could get without actually touching me, she said, "That man you lay with last night. Do you know who he was?"

I did not because I did not care who any of them were.

"He was the new parish constable," she continued. "He came to me after and said that his pocket watch was missing. I didn't want to believe it of you, I really didn't. One of my sweet girls a common thief? But it's in that bag, isn't it?" She poked at it with a finger, making it swing around my legs.

"Of course not," I said.

"Ah, then you sold it, didn't you? That's where the money came from." She jabbed toward the coins on the desk.

"This is nonsense, Mrs. Swann. I haven't done anything wrong." I realized then that I just had to leave. Her words, like the numerous entries in her ledger, were little strings she tied me with.

I was halfway up the cellar steps when she said, "Did I never tell you about young Biddy Armstrong?" I stopped but did not turn.

"One of my best girls, she was, the Lord rest her soul." Her voice was strangely disconnected, coming from the gloom of the cellar below. "Pretty as a daisy and sweet with it. Then one day she started talking about leaving me, and the next thing we knew, the local magistrate walked out of here one night five shillings the lighter. Well, what to do? I tried to help her, but she kept insisting she was going to leave. Strung her up, they did. I'll never forget the sight of her swinging from the Tyburn Tree, her little feet kicking out from under her petticoats. Problem is, when something like that happens, who do you think they believe? The magistrate or the whore?" My whole world seemed to shrink to the step I was standing on. I clutched at the wall to steady myself as my heart clattered in my chest. Mrs. Swann appeared at the foot of the stairs, her face as stony as the walls around us.

"Just go back upstairs, Sara, and we'll forget all this unpleasantness."

And I truly believe that she thought I would do it. But instead I gripped my bag even tighter and placed one foot steadily in front of the other, climbing the steps away from her.

"You'll never get away from me, you wretched girl!" she screamed. She even tried to run after me but stumbled on the first step and fell heavily on the stone. She cried out in pain and frustration, but I did not look round.

"You wretched, wretched girl!"

It was only when I was at the very top that I felt able to turn and look at her. She sat crumpled and sobbing at the bottom of the steps. Then she turned a bitter, tearful face toward me. "If I ever see you again, I'll call the constable and you'll hang for what you have done. D'you hear me? You will hang!" I did not reply. I just left her sitting there, an old woman crying like a little girl.

Esther

The first pulse of the loom above me was like the quickening of an unborn child. It made my hand still as I turned the page of my book and knotted my belly with excitement. The muffled *clack-clack-boom* announced a new presence, resetting the rhythms of our household to its strange meter.

I tried to ignore it, concentrating on my book, then picking up my sewing, but it was like a constant tapping on the door. I fretted about disturbing him if I went up there but felt rude not to have welcomed him to our household. Finally, curiosity got the better of me.

He didn't notice me at first. The noise of the loom masked the creak of the trapdoor and he was concentrating so hard on guiding the shuttle through the warp that I was nearly beside him before he saw me.

"Ma'am," he said, standing up, flustered. The shuttle clattered against the loom, dangling forlornly from the weft.

"Here," I said, bending to pick it up and handing it to him. "I didn't mean to startle you."

"I thought it was the master," he said, taking the shuttle from me. "I was not expecting …" His words tailed off.

"But you are not French!" I said.

"No," he agreed. "I'm English."

I laughed. "I brought you flax for the linnets. But perhaps you don't want the songbirds?"

He smiled then, glancing at the cage hanging by the window. "Did you put them there? No, we're enjoying them, aren't we, Ives?"

A small head peered up from behind the weaver's bench. A boy of about twelve, sitting cross-legged on a straw pallet alongside the loom.

"This is Ives, my drawboy," said the weaver, "and I'm Bisby Lambert, ma'am." He bowed his head and I inclined mine in return.

"Mrs. Thorel," I began to say, but he nodded before I had finished, leaving my words redundant. It felt a little odd to think that this man I had never met knew who I was. Had he seen me as he came and went from my house? He looked at me with intense blue eyes, their color made almost translucent by the long lights.

"So, you are here to weave your master piece, Mr. Lambert?"

"Yes, ma'am. I'm very grateful to Mr. Thorel for letting me use his loom."

"What are you weaving?" I walked round the loom, inspecting the threads as if they were as familiar to me as the stitches of my own embroidery. The drawboy shifted on his pallet, retracting like a snail as my skirts brushed past him.

"Figured silk, ma'am. A brocaded lustring."

"Well, I am sure it will be beautiful." He said nothing, just watched me as I went over to the birdcage. The linnets hopped on their perches, cocking their heads as I clicked my tongue at them and sprinkled the seeds through the bars.

The weaver stood awkwardly by his bench until I had left, while the boy knelt by the loom and took up his bundles of threads. When I was back in the hallway, I heard the noise start up again, the slow resonance of the working man.

I have a memory from my life before everything changed. It is like a trinket to me, something treasured to be taken out occasionally, then put back in its box. It is Elias asleep beside me, the weight of his arm across my waist and the warmth of him behind me through my shift. Even when I turned over he did not stir. For a moment I looked at his face in a way that I never could if he were awake. When he is dressed, with his wig on and his brow set into its permanent furrow, Elias appears older than his years. He likes it so: he is able to conduct his business with the gravitas of a man twice his age. But in that moment, he looked like a boy, smooth-skinned and vulnerable, still sleeping peacefully as the light and the birdsong streamed in through the gaps between the shutters. It was a moment of absolute tranquility, like a still pool before a pebble is thrown into it.

6

Sara

Flicking her fingers with the dismissive confidence that only the privileged and wealthy have, my new mistress almost laughed when I told her about Mrs. Swann.

"Well, did you take the watch?" she asked.

"No!"

"Then what have you to worry about?"

I tried not to sigh in frustration. I had been in my new position of maidservant for only ten minutes and it would not do for me to be squabbling with the mistress already. But, really, she was infuriating. Or, at least, it infuriated me to be sitting in front of my betters explaining how the world really worked.

"Madam, the point is not whether I took the watch or not. If the constable says I took the watch, how can I gainsay it?"

"But why would he, if you did not?"

I stared at her, thinking that she would come to her own realization. She did not.

"He is a man of standing, of good repute," I explained. "Once a man like him spends time at Mrs. Swann's, she has something over him. If she tells him to say that I took the watch, he will say it rather than risk the trouble Mrs. Swann could make for him."

Esther Thorel gave a slow nod. "But you are here now," she said. "She will not find you here."

I nodded back out of compliance, not agreement.

It would not have been polite to talk about money. Mrs. Thorel busied herself showing me the house and introducing me to Moll, the maid, who smiled pleasantly, then threw me a furious glare as soon as Madam turned to peer into the scullery as if she might actually know what was in there. I wanted to ask Madam how much I should be paid and how long it would take me to pay back the money she had given me, but there never seemed a chance, between the detailed explanations of their daily routine and the instructions on how long to boil her egg in the morning.

I wanted to return to my mother. I wanted Madam to wipe my slate clean, to brush over my past life with her respectability and status. It was not just Mrs. Swann taking my money that had stopped me going home. Who would want to return to their mother a whore? I would earn more than just an honest wage in Mrs. Thorel's household: I would earn back my reputation.

❧ · ☙

"And what shall my wages be, madam?"

I decided to ask her later that afternoon, as she was reaching for the silver candlestick on the mantel, no doubt about to tell me how to bring out its shine. She paused fleetingly before turning to face me with it in her hand.

"A crown," she said, neither asking me nor telling me. I was a little taken aback. I would now be earning in a week what I could have earned in a night at Mrs. Swann's.

"And you will have your board and lodging, of course."

At least there would be no inventory of charges as there had been at Mrs. Swann's. At least no one's hands would be tightening around my neck.

"My mother showed me how to clean silver," said Madam, flourishing the candlestick at me. "You must rub it from the bottom to the top, not crosswise." She was looking at me to check that I was listening. "And never, ever use salt or sand. Do you understand?"

"Of course, madam." But I wondered how Madam's mother might have learned that skill. I had assumed that such women scrubbed at nothing more than their own faces. She must have known I was wondering, as then she said, "My mother was not always a lady, you know."

I said nothing, wondering what this had to do with cleaning silver.

"She worked in a tavern." Madam caught the lace fringe of her sleeve between her fingertips and the bottom of her palm and started to rub at the candlestick. "A little like you, perhaps." She clouded the silver with her breath then worked the lace slowly upward, from the bottom to the top. "Then she became a singer and an actress and married my father." Madam beamed at the shiny candlestick as if it were personally responsible for her mother's success, then turned to me again. "So, you see, with God's help, there is always another path to take in life."

What did she mean, a little like me? Was she implying that her own mother had done more than polish the silver at that tavern? Yet she had not done so forever. I looked around me at the arch of carved marble over the hearth, the richly embroidered upholstery and the elegant sashes. Madam was standing there now, with a pound or two of solid silver in her hand, only because her mother had left the tavern she worked in.

She replaced the candlestick, then reached over to pick up its twin from the other end of the mantel. When she offered it to me, I took it with a smile.

From the bottom to the top.

Esther

If you pick up a pot of honey then, sure as eggs are eggs, the wasps will follow.

That is what happened when Sara Kemp came into our household. I behaved as if her concerns about Mrs. Swann and the constable were trivial because I didn't want to worry the poor girl. The truth was I had heard of girls much younger than Sara hanged for the sake of a loaf of bread. The world she had left seemed to trail behind her, like straw caught under the hem of her dress. If they ever found her, I was not sure I would be able to protect her from what would follow. She was right about the constable, of course. What man would not think his reputation worth the life of a harlot? "You are here now," was all I could say to her. "She will not find you here." But the Wig and Feathers was only streets away from Spital Square. Just a few streets, but a whole world away.

I tried to make her feel welcome. I told her all the little details of our lives—hot rolls in the morning, toast at supper—so she would feel part of it, even if she was only to be here for a short time. Perhaps I told her too much because at times she seemed overwhelmed, looking almost tearful when I said that I preferred chocolate at breakfast, not tea. I supposed it was because she had not had to remember much in her previous position. I even wondered whether she could be taught, such was the glazed look on her face, so I took a candlestick from the mantel myself and showed her how to polish it properly. When I told her she could earn a whole crown with us, she looked quite taken aback. I suppose she wondered what she might do with a crown to herself every month.

There was a reason I felt drawn to Sara and could not stand by and watch her ears boxed by Mrs. Swann or turn my back on her when she came to ask for my help. My own mother had come from the same place she had. Not the Wig and Feathers, of course, but there were a hundred bawdy houses just like it, all offering the same mix of desperation and opportunity. If no one had given my mother a chance, she would have stayed doing it until too old, or pox-ridden, to carry on. I felt it my duty to pass on to Sara a few skills: knowing how to polish the silver or darn a shirt would mean she had another way to earn a living for the rest of her life. I was struck by the smile she gave me when she took the candlestick from my hand, such was her gratitude for the opportunity to do some honest work.

Then there was Elias. The man whose affections had frozen like ice when he heard tell after we married of what my mother had been years before. It was as if he had discovered it had been me, not my mother, who had sold sweet favors to sailors. But then she had stumbled past Drury Lane and stopped in the gush of warm air from inside the Theatre Royal and smelt the chemical burn of the stage lights. It wasn't long before my mother persuaded someone to allow her inside. She must have looked well, standing under the dazzling lights, because they began to let her sing to keep the audience quiet before the curtain went up. Soon she was all alone up there, singing and dancing among the boards painted with colorful scenes sliding on and off the stage. My father fell in love with her elegant step, as she moved round the stage, and the sweet voice she cast out to her audience, as though she was scattering petals. When they married, the sailors were left far behind her. But my husband does not believe in redemption: Elias thinks that people are molded like jelly by their choices and, once set, they can never be anything else.

If Elias abhorred the thought that such a woman could be connected to his family, what would he think if he knew one was living under his own roof? I told myself he would never find out, that she would stay just long enough to pay back her debt and earn a few skills. But the world turns on a sixpence and our lives shifted the moment she walked through the door. She was like a cat sidling in uninvited and looking about. You don't want to turn it out straight away, so you offer it a scrap of food. The next thing you know it's curled up on your favorite chair, watching you with unblinking elliptic eyes.

Sara

It was a beautiful thing: delicate white porcelain with a large scroll handle on one side, covered with a whimsical painting of lovers frolicking in a garden.

"Well, go on, then," urged Moll, her hands on her hips and a cocky expression on her face.

It was perfectly clear to me that Moll was giving me all the worst jobs. I had already scrubbed the scullery floor until my hands were raw and scraped so much coal dust from the hearths that my tongue felt like leather. Now she wanted me to empty the mistress' chamber pot.

"It won't bite, you know," said Moll. "Or have you never emptied the slops before?"

The truth was, I hadn't. Mrs. Swann prided herself on never letting any of her "daughters" go. Once they were all used up she put them to work doing the tasks that went unseen to everyone else. As my hand closed around the elegant handle, I'll own that I wondered why I had given up that life to stand, chamber pot in hand, at the edge of a privy pit.

It was relentless. No sooner had one pot been emptied than another was being filled. While one grate was being cleaned, the coal in another was burning to ash. Once the outdoor steps had been scrubbed, the wooden staircase needed to be swept, then buffed with linseed oil. And while I did all this, that snip of a girl sat and watched me, sucking marzipan she'd stolen from Madam's epergne.

Unless Madam was watching, of course, in which case her smile was so sweet you'd have thought the marzipan was still stuck in her mouth. She'd pluck up her skirts and kneel beside me, as if the hearth was an altar and we were joined in mutual devotion. Once Madam was out of the room, she would sit back on her haunches and watch me as I scrubbed the floorboards with sand, throwing out occasional questions about who I was and where I had come from, which I tried to ignore, along with the aching in my knees.

Once, when she came in and saw me using vinegar on Madam's washstand, she rushed at me as if I was about to set a torch to it. "What are you doing?" she exclaimed, grabbing the cloth from me.

"Cleaning, of course."

"She'll not thank you when she puts her face in the wash bowl and it smells like a scrubbed-out slop bucket! Didn't you think of how it would stink?"

I had not. I had been told to wash down the kitchen with vinegar and castile soap and had thought to do the same in Madam's bedroom. Moll tipped her head on one side, eyeing me silently while the sharp tang of vinegar stung our nostrils.

"I cannot fathom," she said softly, "how a maid-of-all-work would do such a thing. Did the last house you worked in stink top to bottom of vinegar?"

"You are the maid-of-all-work, not me," I said, taking the bottle of vinegar from the washstand and trying to get past her.

She stepped in front of me and blocked the door. "But you said you was a housemaid before you came here?"

"Yes, and a housemaid is above the maid-of-all-work, so please stand aside as I have work to do."

"Why don't you know you shouldn't use vinegar in the mistress' bedroom, then?"

"Because the maid-of-all-work did it!" I thrust the bottle into her hand and pushed past her to the door.

⁂

I lasted a couple of weeks before I went to Madam. I knocked, but perhaps she didn't hear as when I opened the door she was sitting on her embroidered stool with her skirts up around her thighs, trying to tie a garter round her stocking. She started when she saw me and dropped the ribbon on the floor. She must have expected me to excuse myself and walk straight out again, but instead I closed the door behind me and approached her.

"Here, let me," I said, kneeling beside her and picking up the garter.

"Thank you," she said, sounding uncertain. I ran my hand up her stockinged calf, smoothing the wrinkles where the stocking had begun to sag back down her leg. They were a fetching green, matching the silk of her dress. I tied the pink garter round the stocking, just above her knee, then reached for the other stocking lying on her dressing table. She seemed tense at first, flinching when I touched the stocking to her toes and almost shrinking from me as I rolled the sheer material further up her leg. But she seemed to relax into my touch and did not demur when I fixed the other garter. When I had finished, I smoothed her skirts down, although it seemed a shame to hide such prettiness. I had thought her rather odd-looking when I first saw her, with her unusual complexion and features too strong to be dainty, but now I had come to know her, I found her quite beautiful.

"You were right, madam," I said.

"About what?" She was almost blushing. I suppose she wondered what I might be about to say.

"You really don't need another scullery maid. Little Moll does such an excellent job keeping the house clean, there is no need for anyone else."

She nodded slowly. "Are you leaving us so soon?" If I had not known better, I might have thought she sounded a little disappointed. Or perhaps she was just wondering how I would be able to repay my debt before I left.

I turned away from her and busied myself picking up a shift lying discarded on the floor. She watched me intently as I folded it and placed it on the bed. Then I said, "The house is well looked after, but you, madam, are not."

She was taken aback, as if she had no idea what I was referring to. I smiled to reassure her. "A lady's maid, madam. You need a lady's maid."

She laughed. "Are you suggesting yourself?"

"And why not, madam?" I returned to her side and sank to my knees. "How could I better repay you than by that?"

In that moment, I felt truly grateful to her, as if I actually wanted a life serving her every need. I surprised even myself with what I did next. I clasped the hand resting in her lap and brought it up to my lips. I felt the chill of her wedding ring press across my skin as I kissed her hand. She tolerated it for an instant, then snatched it away, busying herself with a wisp of hair come loose from under her cap.

Esther

I spoke but my husband barely looked up. He continued to spoon the soup into his mouth, as diligent and single-minded in that task as he was with everything else. A drop ran down his chin and disappeared into the beginnings of his beard. He sat back and swiped a cloth across his face.

"What did you say?"

I straightened in my chair, responding to Elias' attention.

"I was talking about the girl staying with us, Miss Kemp. I thought I might keep her on to help me. As a lady's maid, perhaps."

Elias picked up his wine glass and eyed me over the rim. My own husband, yet his thoughts were as inscrutable to me as the columns of figures with which he filled his ledgers. We were a modest household, given my husband's wealth. We did not need another housemaid—servants for whom there was no need would have been an intolerable extravagance for any Huguenot household—but the more I thought on it, the more Sara Kemp seemed to be right. I did have use for a lady's maid. And if that would mean a new life for someone else—a way for Sara to repay her debt—then I was made doubly happy by the thought.

"Do you agree then, husband?" I said, my voice cautious. I had not wanted too detailed a conversation about Sara, so I had mentioned her over supper when his head would be full of that day's business and preoccupied with the tasks of the next.

Elias finished his wine. "Who is this woman?" he asked.

"Well," I began brightly, "Miss Kemp used to work in a tavern—"

"A tavern?" Elias' words cut through my own. "Have we not had enough of women who used to work in taverns?"

I swallowed hard and ignored his reference to my mother.

"She was a cook," I continued. "Well, a kitchen maid, really, but she is skilled in the kitchen and has been a great help to Monsieur Finet, I believe."

He looked down at his plate. "I thought the pie tasted better than usual. I think she should stay in the kitchen."

"But we do not need a kitchen maid and she has worked in a household as well. I need help with my toilette and my wardrobe, bathing and dressing."

"What's she going to do? Cover you with egg wash and stick pastry on you?"

"Do not mock me, husband."

"My point, Mrs. Thorel," he said, tilting the wine jug toward him and peering into it, "is that she is not qualified for the job." He let go of the empty jug and turned his gaze back on me.

He was right. Sara did not fit into our household and trying to put her there was like hiding a cow among the sheep, but I could not give up so easily.

"She has need of help and sanctuary," I said. "You of all people should understand that."

He fell silent, his reply, if there was one, stopped by the history of his own people.

When we had finished the meal, Moll brought in a gooseberry tart. Its sticky sweetness seemed to mellow him as then he said, "The girl—Kemp—she can stay, if you like. These domestic matters are for you to decide."

Sophia Courtauld. I saw her sometimes, gliding across Spital Square with her basket of good deeds swinging from her arm. The woman my husband would have married, if he hadn't married me. The one chosen for him by his family. A good Huguenot wife for the Thorel heir. Elias Thorel had slipped into the same house and profession as his father as though they were a pair of perfectly fitting shoes. And he was about to take the wife who would have joined the Courtaulds to the Thorels when he looked out from his workshop one day to see an English girl passing.

I was his one rebellion, the single way in which he pushed against the expectations of his community, and they punished him for it. In small ways they made him an outsider. He no longer had first choice of the best patterns or the new malachite shades from the dyer, and for a time the best Huguenot journeymen weavers filled their looms with silk from other masters. Even then, I don't think he ever questioned whether I was worth it. He was able to reestablish himself in Spitalfields simply by the force of his own talent and acumen, helped by the more pragmatic attitude of the English suppliers and weavers.

I was not a poor match: I was the daughter of a well-known surgeon. We lived in Spital Square in a house worthy of any master weaver, and my father often attended court to purge and blister the nobility. Then a girl died, the daughter of a duke or earl, and suddenly all the bloodletting and evacuations that had earned my father his fortune made him a quack or worse. He was not told to go: they forced him out with whispers and tittle-tattle. Rumors started, first about my father, then about my mother. Elias had married me knowing full well that my mother had been a singer, but it was only then that it came out she had started her career singing ballads from chapbooks in taverns. After they left a lawyer moved into their house in Spital Square and I have seen neither my mother nor my father since.

Sophia Courtauld became Sophia Marchant and not three years later, little feet pattered after her when she walked across the square. I wonder what Elias thinks when he looks at her.

Sara

It is the job of a lady's maid to make her mistress as fair as her God-given assets will allow. My own mistress had a bewildering array of daubs and ointments on her dressing table. It was she who was the respectable one, but the vials of paints, creams, and patches she owned could have come straight from a harlot's toilette. Indeed, their house seemed full of contradictions. They were supposed to be Calvinists, Puritans almost, yet their home was full of wealth. It scattered the mantel with silver trinkets and lined the walls with wood paneling from floor to ceiling, painted tasteful shades of gray and palest ocher. I asked her once whether such a comfortable life sat well with the austerity of the master's religion. She replied that wealth earned with a good heart through honest toil was always godly. I was glad to hear that, if only for the sake of the girls at Mrs. Swann's.

One morning, when I came into her room, she pulled the cloth cap from her head and sat at her dressing table, waiting. The sight of her hair uncoiled down her back was a silent summons, so I placed the clean linens I was carrying in the cupboard and stood behind her. She had become particularly concerned about her appearance of late, even while at home, and I watched her reflection in the mirror as she drew her teeth over her lips to redden them. Mrs. Swann would have called Madam an *unusual beauty* and put her in front of the widest clientele possible, in the hope that at least some would find charm in her angular limbs and the freckled imperfection of her pale skin. Fortunately, once the powder was on, no man would know the difference.

"That's enough, Sara!" she exclaimed, among genteel little coughs as I dusted over her face.

"But you can still see them, madam," I said.

"See what?" She sounded hurt.

"Nothing," I mumbled, putting the lid back on the powder and picking up the tortoiseshell brush. I busied myself untwisting the rope of hair. It was the color of autumn, shades of red and amber turning to gold where the light caught it, and for a moment I was engrossed with brushing it out so that it fanned across her shoulders. When I looked up she was studying me intently in the looking glass. "Madam?"

She smiled at me benignly. "You must be feeling so happy, Sara."

I looked down at her hair, finding a little knot and pulling at it. "Yes, madam," I said.

"And I am so happy to have helped you," she said, praising her own reflection in the mirror. "To think that I have saved a woman like you from having to do what you did at Mrs. Swann's, well ..." She fell into a reverie, the beatific smile still on her face.

I plucked at the knot. A woman like me? What had I become under the patronage of Mrs. Thorel? Even as a lady's maid, I still rose at dawn and emptied her chamber pot. I bathed and dressed her and looked after her clothes and wigs. For this I was promised a crown a week and given a room at the top of the house, which she made me share with Moll. It was two yards wide and three yards long. In it there was a bed and a washstand. Only one floor below, her bed was stuffed with feathers, while mine was stuffed with straw. She drew linen up to her chin at night while I lay under a rough coverlet. Only the water we splashed on our faces was the same. This was the life she had given me, and she expected me to be grateful. So it is, when you exist only to serve another. It is an enviable transition from whore to lady's maid, but both are a life of forced intimacy serving the needs of others.

"Tsk."

"Ma'am?"

"You're hurting me."

Her eyes were wide and surprised in the glass as they flicked up to mine. I must have been tugging at that knot too hard, imagining the bronze finery of her hair turning withered like autumn leaves and falling to the floor. I left the tangle and went back to brushing, stroking the hair from her face so that she could see herself more easily. And she took full advantage of that, staring at her image as if pride were not a deadly sin. I had not realized what vanity lay behind that godly exterior. How gratifying it must have been for her to glance up from studying her own delicate features and see me standing behind her. As if her face was the picture, and mine the dull, sturdy frame.

"Madam, may I remind you that I have not been paid my wages these past few weeks?"

"Your wages?"

"Yes, ma'am. A crown a week, you said."

Madam flushed somewhere under all that powder. "A crown a month, Sara, not a week."

I let go of her hair as if it had turned to snakes in my hand. Five shillings a month! It would take me years to pay her back the money I owed. I turned away from the mirror so that she would not see the helplessness in my face. The room seemed to close in on me. How could she have misled me with dreams of bettering myself, then pay me a crown a month? I was as trapped in Spital Square as I ever had been at the Wig and Feathers.

Madam twisted in her chair to see what I was doing. I stepped over to the washstand and tipped a little water from the jug onto my hands as if to clean them.

"I need to teach you the value of honest hard work, Sara," she said to my back, as I shook the water from my fingers. "That is the best thing I can give you—better than money."

I forced myself to walk back to her, drying my hands on my skirts as I did so. She settled herself back round to face the mirror and I lifted the lid of the glass pot on her dressing table and ran my finger round the inside. I rubbed the pomade round my palms to soften it, then raked my greased fingers through her hair. She leaned her head back slightly and half closed her eyes. As I worked, the smell of the lavender became stronger and she breathed deeply as if she welcomed the heady scent and the steady rub of my hands. Once I had pulled and teased her hair on top of her head, I had any number of silver pots to choose from to powder over the pomade. So I patted and preened her, covering the person she really was under a thin layer of dust.

That night I climbed into bed with Moll. Her feet were blocks of ice against my calves and as she shifted to get comfortable, sharp elbows dug into my sides. I jabbed her back. She had barely spoken to me since I had become Madam's lady's maid and risen above her in the household. So we played out our little spats there, in that tiny bed, with digs and pinches as we jostled for space.

The only other person I had ever slept with was my mother. We would curl up together in her little bed and she would sing me to sleep while she stroked my hair. I had not seen her since the day she had thrust a bag into my hands, containing little more than a loaf of bread, a farthing's worth of cheese and *The Art of Cookery*, the only thing my father had left us. My mother had used the knowledge in it to persuade the Quakers to find her a job as a cook instead of a scullery maid. I read it while she cooked so I would know why she pressed the onions with studs of cloves and sweetened her cakes with rosewater and sherry. That day—the day she told me to leave—is preserved in my mind, like pickles in a jar. She gave me the pound she had saved and wrote out the name and address of her cousin, who lived in Spitalfields. It was to be my introduction to London, but it had gotten no further than the top of Mrs. Swann's bodice.

In the early days, I used to cry every night, wondering why she had sent me away, what I could possibly have done wrong for her not to want me anymore, but after a few months at Mrs. Swann's it became hard to know what I was crying about. I knew my mother loved me, so there must have been a reason she had sent me into all of this. I just couldn't work out what it was.

I must have dozed off. When I awoke, I looked for the gray silhouette of Moll sleeping beside me and listened for the gentle rasp of her breath, but when I patted the bed next to me, I found she was gone.

Esther

I tried to persuade myself that my husband was a good man. That he had given up the approval of his community to have me as a wife and I had rewarded him with whispered gossip at church. And with each month that went by without a child, I sensed his simmering disappointment. He began to turn away from me when I spoke to him. He barely looked up as I entered a room and left without bidding me goodbye. I accepted that he was always somewhere else, even when I was in the same room as him. It was in those moments of isolation that I turned to my painting.

It was my sanctuary. When I painted, I had something to cherish and nurture, in the way that other women might have turned their thwarted affections on a lapdog. Or a child. I captured the swell and bloom of those flowers even as my own belly lay flat and empty. And if my husband's attention was invariably on the artistry of what he created, rather than me, then it was not my place to complain. After all, even a wife cannot compete with the beauty of silk.

I was painting in my room when I heard it again, like a strange melody thumped out by a child. A single refrain, over and over.

"The Lord preserve us," said Sara, clutching the shift she was folding to her chest, "what is that noise?"

"A loom in the garret. You will get used to it. There'll be a journeyman up there from time to time."

"But I thought the master sent his work out?"

"He does, but Mr. Thorel is allowing this journeyman to borrow a loom to weave his master piece. If the silk he weaves is good enough, he will be admitted to the Worshipful Company of Weavers and become a master himself. My husband says he is one of the most talented weavers in Spitalfields."

"I see," said Sara, doubtful. She eyed the ceiling suspiciously, as if the loom might fall through it, then continued folding my fresh linens. "It seems an imposition on you, madam," she suggested, to the neat pile, when she had finished.

"Not really." I concentrated on my brushwork, giving a tinge of blush to a pale petal. Sara loved to find slights and injustices where there were none. I would not allow her to draw me into her web of bad feeling. "This household was built for weaving, Sara. The floor of the garret is packed with silk waste to deaden the noise of the looms. A weaver in this house is as natural as a baker in a bakery. Besides, he seems pleasant enough."

"You've met him?" Sara seemed both shocked and intrigued by the thought.

"Just once," I said. "I took some seeds for the linnets I put in the garret."

Sara bent to pick up my dirty linens from the floor but not before she had cast me an odd look. Then she left me to my painting. I found it comforting somehow to listen to him as I worked. As the light faded, I began to think about asking Sara to arrange some supper. Almost as soon as I had put down my brushes the noise stopped, as if we were linked in some way, the daylight our mutual taskmaster.

I looked at my painting. Another pattern for a silk that would never be made. Elias had not stopped me drawing my designs, I just painted when he was not about, contenting myself with imagining what the finished silk might look like. But something about the weaver's presence above me—the thought that a design was slowly turning from paper to silk in my house—was tantalizing, like not realizing how much you have missed someone until you hear the sound of their voice. I picked up my watercolor, damp from my afternoon's work, and left my room.

I waited on the landing, listening for any sounds from the garret. When I was sure he had left, I climbed the ladder to the trapdoor.

The room felt different. The late afternoon dimmed the long lights to panels the color of pearls across the wall, and the inside of the garret was full of shadows and unexpected edges. Close to his loom I could smell the silk, woody and nutty, laced with sweet woodruff.

I took my watercolor to the other empty loom and laid it over the heddles, which would hold the warp threads, trying to imagine it as a real silk, a tabby or a lustring, brocaded with silver-gilt foliate. I left the pattern on the loom and went to the shelves on the wall, holding spool after spool of silk thread. The linnets began to flutter and chirp, hoping for flax seeds, as I stood considering the colors, weaving one into the other in my mind, wondering which might show the other to its best effect. Then I chose a porcelain blue, a pretty burnt orange and a dark green. The spools were as big as melons in my arms as I carried them to the loom. I arranged the silk on top of the heddles so that they overlapped the edge of my pattern. Then I took a small step back to try to imagine the colors in the murky daylight, merging on the loom into the shapes I had drawn on the paper.

The trapdoor of the attic lifted as someone came up the stairs. I started, thinking it was Elias, feeling guilty although I was not sure why. My first instinct was to cover my pattern as if it were something shameful, so I moved to stand in front of the loom, grateful for the width of my skirts. I was facing him then, as he stood on the top step, confused and squinting. Because the last of the light was shining on him, I could see him clearly, but to him I must have been just a shadow by the loom.

"Forgive me," I said. "I didn't think you would still be working."

The weaver stepped inside the garret but hesitated to come any further. "I forgot something, ma'am," he said, indicating a cloth bag by his weaving bench.

"Please, take it," I said, smiling but reluctant to step away from the loom. He approached the bench slowly, but instead of bending to pick up his bag he came over to me and the unused loom. Such was his height, it was easy for him to see behind me to the spools sprouting, like cabbages, from the heddles.

He almost smiled. I knew it was there in the background, behind his perplexed expression. "Can I help you with something, madam?"

I felt foolish. What had I been thinking, coming up here? I should have left my pattern where it belonged, drying in my room.

"No." I gave a little shake of my head and turned away from him to take the spools off the heddles. Once I had removed them, the pattern slid from the loom and floated to the floor at the weaver's feet.

"May I?" he asked.

I wanted to snatch it up, but could only stand there helpless, my arms full of silk. The weaver bent down and picked up the pattern. He laid it back on top of the loom, then offered, arms outstretched, to take the spools from me. Once my hands were free, I reached out to take back my watercolor.

"Did you paint that?" he asked, as I folded it firmly, not caring now whether it was dry.

I glanced up at him. It was a bold question from a journeyman. "Yes," I said.

"It's beautiful. You have a gift, Mrs. Thorel."

I blushed as if he had complimented me on my hair or my dress. His comment seemed shockingly intimate, there in the darkening garret with no one else around.

He walked over to the shelves and began replacing the spools. I watched him for moment while his back was turned. His hair was a sandy brown, tied with a neat black ribbon at the nape of his neck. His shoulders were broad under the thin linen of his shirt and I could see the muscles flex as he reached for the highest shelf. When he turned back toward me I lowered my eyes to his shoes and followed them across the room, back to the bag he had left behind. Once he had picked it up, he inclined his head to me again to take his leave.

"Could you weave this?" I asked, brandishing my watercolor at him. The question came out before I had a chance to decide to ask it. He seemed so taken aback that I immediately wished I could snatch it back and make it unsaid, just as I now wished I could make my painting unseen by anyone but me.

"What I mean is … would it even be possible to weave it?" He must have sensed my discomfort, as his face became kind. "Of course," he said simply. "You can weave anything. Birds, flowers, fruit, even shells. It's not easy to make curves and shade the fabric, but it can be done."

"So you could weave this?" I opened the paper again, revealing my hopes and secret desires on the page, made bold by his confidence.

"Well, not that exactly, no." I snapped it shut again.

"Ma'am, please understand, your drawing is lovely, but it means nothing to a loom. You need to translate it into a language the loom can understand. Do you see?"

I did not, but I nodded anyway. Then he reached for my drawing again, holding out his hand, palm upward, in a silent request. When I gave it to him he opened it out and studied it. "You think in shapes, madam, but the loom only thinks in lines. You need to transcribe the design onto point paper and tell the loom row by row, square by square, precisely which thread is to go where. Then it would be possible to weave it."

It was the next step, taking my pattern from idea to design. It thrilled me to think of transferring my pattern to point paper, yet I was reluctant, almost fearful. I would be doing something of which Elias disapproved and I knew I would not tell him. Why should I? He had ridiculed my attempts to draw a pattern. But there was another reason for my apprehension. Thoughts of my pattern and weaving were now bound up with other things: linen stretched over muscle, and the sweet woodruff smell of that man as I had stood next to him at the loom.

Sara

I had been at 10 Spital Square a few weeks when I was sent out with a package for one of the master's journeymen. I didn't know where he lived, so I followed Moll's directions, turning right into White Lyon Yard, then cutting through Pearl Street to get there. I knew when I must be getting close. The milkmaids slopped the unsold buttermilk from their pails straight into the street. As the weather grew warmer, it would sour in the afternoon sun and by nightfall the air would be thick with its stench. No one with a nose could miss the entrance to Buttermilk Alley.

Who lived by this narrow alley? Who woke every morning to the clanking of pails on yokes and the milkmaids chattering and fussing like ducks on a pond? The master owned more than fifty looms in Spitalfields, tucked into the garrets of weavers' cottages, like the little row of houses next to Buttermilk Alley. Inside them, his journeymen weavers were busy turning his thread into silk cloth.

I approached the one at the most pungent end of the street, nearest the entrance to Buttermilk Alley. I knocked on the front door, smartly painted green, just as Moll had described it, but no one answered. Matching green shutters flanked a window to the left of the door but I couldn't see anyone inside. I stepped back and looked up at the house. On the second floor a wide lattice window stretched the width of the building. I could hear the dull thumping and clanking of those infernal looms, not just from this house but all along the row, starting and stopping so that the whole street seemed engaged in a mechanical conversation. I stood outside for a few moments, the package cumbersome in my hands, wondering how long to wait.

Then, in the distance, I heard the sound of the tenor bell at Christ Church and the chattering of the looms began to cease until the row of little houses was silent. I knocked sharply on the door before it all started up again. A man opened it, tall and stooping, almost as if the cottage were a doll's house filled with the wrong size dolls.

"I have a package from Mr. Thorel," I said, offering it, thinking he would take it, but instead he nodded and gestured for me to come inside.

We went into the parlor. It had a range with a fire already burning, a table and chairs—more dining room than parlor, perhaps, although as the house was only one room deep it was hard to know. Another man was sitting at the table, pouring ale into a tankard.

"There's a package from Thorel," the tall man said.

"What makes you think it's for me?" said the man at the table. He didn't look up, just started rolling his shoulders and moving his head from side to side as if they were stiff from his day's work.

"He gives me my thread up at the house."

The man at the table stilled and looked at us. "Of course, you're an *inside* weaver now, aren't you, Lambert? Up there in Thorel's garret, doing his bidding."

I felt I had walked into something charged and uneasy. The air seemed thick around me, as if I were standing among words unsaid. I stepped toward the table to leave the package and go.

"Open it," said the man at the table, before I could put it down. "Open it and let's see what's inside. If it's a spool of finest thread dyed the latest verditer shade, it will be for him. If it's a pile of plain thread for a lining, it will be for me."

I glanced at the other man, unsure what to do, until the package was taken from my hand. The seated man ripped open the paper and tipped the contents onto the table, about ten bobbins all tightly wound with glossy black thread.

"You were right, Lambert, it is for me." The man pushed the bobbins away from him. One rolled off the table and fell to the floor.

I turned to the man called Lambert. "Are you the journeyman weaving his master piece in the Thorels' garret?" I asked, trying to take the attention away from the man sitting glowering into his ale.

"Yes. I'm Bisby Lambert and this is John Barnstaple."

"His *master piece*," Barnstaple spat. "Do you really think they'll admit the likes of you into the Weavers' Company? You've sold out, Lambert. You're nothing but an inside weaver, toiling under the scrutiny of your master. I'd rather stay an outside weaver, with my freedom and pride, even if it means weaving handkerchiefs all day!"

I looked at Barnstaple properly then. He was unshaven, and a shadow of black defined his jaw. Dark hair fell around his face in thick, slightly curling hanks. He had the look of a misplaced pirate, wild and devil-may-care, as if the room were too small for him.

"I should go," I said, wishing that Barnstaple would shift his gaze toward me even for an instant, that my leaving would make some impression on him. But he was staring at Lambert, challenging him, with his coal-black eyes, to gainsay him.

Esther

I spread the point paper on the dining table. Elias would not miss this one sheet. It had faint lines hatched over it, vertically and horizontally, so it was completely covered with tiny squares. Next to it was my painting.

I had to somehow lift my watercolor from its paper and lay it over the lines, magnified four times over. I set about drawing free hand. The flowers looked well enough, but when I held it up it seemed lopsided, as if there were more harebells on one side than the other. I knew that the loom would be an uncompromising disciple. I rubbed out the sketch and tried again, searching for an elusive symmetry to the design among all the little boxes on the page.

Still it seemed uneven. There was no room here for artistic freedom: the drawing had to be more exact than nature itself. I rubbed so hard at the marks I had made that a hole appeared in the center of the paper. I exclaimed in frustration and started again beneath the mistake. This time I arranged the first part of the pattern correctly, but when it came to the repeat, only half would fit. Was this what Elias had meant? It was as if he stood beside me, mocking, *What is a dezine, Mrs. Thorel?* Plainly it was not enough to be able to paint. The point paper demanded order and symmetry, like a pedantic schoolmaster. When my third attempt ended with a leaf projecting four boxes to the left further than its counterpart, I snatched up the loathsome drawing and threw it into the fire, strip by torn strip. There was such satisfaction in watching it burn that I picked up my original watercolor and tossed that in too, as if punishing it for being so unhelpful. But once the brief, angry glow was over, I was left with nothing. No point paper, no watercolor, and no inclination to try again to design a silk pattern.

10

Sara

Madam had become lackluster and lethargic. I tried to find things that would interest her, but she pushed away the embroidery hoop when I handed it to her and merely sighed when I asked her if she was quite well, offering her some port-wine jelly. She seemed peevish, asking me constantly whether I had mended the loose stitching on her panniers and where I had put her bodkin, even though I hadn't touched it.

When I could hardly stand it, I suggested we go out to Spitalfields market together. At first, she was reluctant, complaining that there was nothing there of any interest nowadays, but I told her I needed to go. I had not been back since I had left Mrs. Swann and I could not hide in Spital Square forever. I hoped that my being with the quality would keep the likes of Mrs. Swann at bay, so I told Madam I had not the heart to go without her. She was pleased with that. Madam liked nothing better than to be needed.

Little had changed at the market. The same rotting meat and vegetables on the ground, the same strumpets and pickpockets round every corner.

But Madam did not see any of that. She was drawn to the stalls of flowers, stroking the delicate petals and smiling. How it must be to see only beauty in the world. I left her then, chatting to the nurseryman about when the first roses might be in, and turned toward the stalls of clothes, thinking I would ask Madam for a new apron.

That was when I saw her, glimpsed little more than the flash of the scarlet skirts of her slammerkin in the crowd. I tried to go after her, but she was gone, and I could only stand there, imagining I could smell her scent of orange flowers and jasmine.

I had spent the first months at Spital Square trying to forget the Wig and Feathers, but I could not forget Lucy Carey. Mrs. Swann had put me in Lucy's room when I first arrived. It fronted the street, and every evening Mrs. Swann would make Lucy dress in a slammerkin and stand at the window. She had a sweet voice and we would raise the sash a few inches so that her songs could float down to the street below. She knew all manner of ballads and saucy ditties and would sway and laugh while she sang as if she hardly knew, or cared, that anyone could see her.

She always stood with her back to the window and her face angled over her shoulder, as if she were about to walk away, but wouldn't be displeased were a passing gentleman to follow. Her hair—a wig, of course—was piled high on her head with a few fat ringlets underneath. She was as slight as a child, and if you glanced up from the street, you would think that was what she was. A tiny young thing, with a waist a man could circle with his hands as her voice dripped honey into his ear.

But I watched her from the other side. Lucy was forty if she was a day. The coquettish tilt of her chin hid the scars on her face. Mrs. Swann kept her going for as long as she could—years ago Lucy had been on *Harris' List of Covent Garden Ladies*—but once the skin had blistered all over her body the men would yelp when she undressed. It was as if they had unwrapped a parcel of meat to find it riddled with maggots. That was when Mrs. Swann began to douse her in perfume, as if they would be so taken with her sweet smell that they would notice nothing else.

But the sores on her skin were no more visible from the window than the patches on her gown, and Lucy swayed in the dusk each evening until she forgot the words of her songs. Then she began to stumble while she swayed as if she had been at the gin. One evening Mrs. Swann—who had been out on an errand—caught her leaning out of the window calling to the men on the street, clearly possessed of the notion that she was the queen of all England. Mrs. Swann marched up the stairs and threw open our door. She grasped Lucy's little white-gloved wrist, pulled her away from the window and slammed the shutters. Rightly so: nothing is less likely to arouse passion in a man than a syphilitic old whore.

But when I first arrived, the sight of Lucy Carey at our bedroom window had stopped men in the street and given them a mind to go whoring even if before they had none. And when they did they would be greeted by Mrs. Swann.

"Why, sir," she would say, as she took a gentleman's hat and greatcoat, "come into the warm and sit by our fire. 'Tis a cruel night to be out all alone." And if the gentleman was new to whoring and shuffled from one foot to the other, glancing awkwardly about him, Mrs. Swann would slip her arm through his, take him past the tavern and up the back stairs.

We all sat together in a room until the men came in. Mrs. Swann called us out one by one while Lucy stayed behind and tended the babies, feeding them gin to keep them quiet while their mothers worked. It was dawn by the time we were allowed to go to bed. In our room, the rising sun would frame the shutters with light and I would lie there watching Lucy as she sat at her dressing table, brushing her wispy hair as if it were still long and thick. Sometimes she would cock her head to one side and look quizzically at her own reflection, as if she questioned whom she saw there. Some nights I could not bear to watch and closed my eyes to the sight of what I might become. Then I could only smell her: bergamot, ambergris, orange flowers, and jasmine. Even now, I still think I hear her at night, singing of sailors in faraway places ...

"There you are, Sara!" Madam's voice was shrill, annoyed. "I've been looking for you everywhere."

"Sorry, madam, I thought I saw someone I knew."

Her face softened. "Yes, I am sure this place is full of ghosts for you. Come, let me show you something."

I followed her to one of the fruit stalls. She seemed very pleased with herself as she giggled and said, "There! Have you ever seen such a thing?"

The outside was ridged and scaly, like a mermaid's tail, and the top a prickly green fountain. "Why, madam," I said, picking it up, "it looks like something the ladies at court would wear in their enormous wigs!" I put it on top of my head like a hat and the stallholder scowled at me while Madam tittered into her gloved hand. Then I looked up at the railed gallery above us and saw him. Black hair loose around his shoulders, narrowed eyes on the brink of recognition. The most striking weaver in Spitalfields was staring down at me with a pineapple on my head.

Esther

I bought nothing at the market. Although the spring flowers were beautiful, I no longer wanted to paint for painting's sake. I needed there to be a purpose to it and that purpose was silk. I could not bear that the flowers I painted were trapped, useless, on the page.

I found myself listening for him. Within barely a half-hour after I had heard the Christ Church tenor bell, the noise would start. It became so familiar to me that on the days he didn't come it was the silence that struck me as strange. I hadn't known it was possible to feel the absence of someone you could not see.

Then one afternoon, after he had not come for almost a week, I heard him. I knew immediately that I would go up there. I had only to find a reason.

Christian charity. That was all the reason a good Huguenot wife needed to do anything.

"I brought you these."

He put down the shuttle and took the muslin cloth from me, still warm from the small cakes inside.

"My maid baked them this afternoon."

"Thank you, madam," he said, polite if a little surprised. He set them on the bench. Ives stared at them from his straw pallet.

"Take some," I told the boy. "They're best when they're fresh."

He looked at his master, but Bisby just smiled and nodded. Ives reached out a small hand and slid the cloth into his lap.

"You're making progress," I said to the weaver, walking round to the side of the loom. Ives shuffled his pallet out of the way, cheeks already fat with cake. Silk now stretched from the heddles to the gathering roller, the cream background shaded with cobalt blue.

He looked unconvinced. "Some progress, yes."

"But you work all day," I chided. "It will take time."

He nodded. "Sometimes I wonder why I am doing it at all."

"My husband says you are extraordinarily talented, Mr. Lambert. That is why."

"Mr. Thorel is too kind," he said.

"Really, he is not!" I laughed. "You should know that about him. He would not do this unless he believed in you."

"Do you know how many journeyman silk weavers become masters, madam?" He knew I did not, just watched me for a moment, his gaze earnest, his blue eyes searching my face.

"Almost none. Only the masters have the capital to establish themselves. Only the masters can afford the fee to the Weavers' Company. It's the sons of master weavers who become masters. The sons of journeyman weavers stay journeymen."

"Then all the more reason for you to do this, Mr. Lambert. My husband wants to help you and, of course, he wants to sell this beautiful silk when you are done." I indicated his work with my hand.

"And what about you, Mrs. Thorel?" he asked. "Have you transferred your beautiful design to point paper?"

"It is quite impossible," I sighed.

There was merriment in the look he gave me then. "So I must not give up on my master piece, but you may do so on your pattern designing?"

I said nothing, but looked at him in a way that told him I had taken his words in good part.

"Come," he said, gesturing for me to join him again. "You would not find it so hard if you understood the loom. Here is the mise-en-carte," he said, gesturing toward the point paper stretched across the loom. "Each square is colored to represent the pattern created by every movement of the warp threads. These are the simples." He ran his hand down some vertical drawstrings. When he pulled one a heddle lifted. "The simples are attached in groups to lashes in accordance with the pattern to be produced. When the drawboy pulls them in the proper order, it raises the correct heddles when I throw the weft. That is what you should have in mind when you draw your pattern. Every square that is black represents a simple to be raised. The weaver will always pass the white and take the black."

"Thank you, Mr. Lambert. That's all very clear now," I said.

His smile was warm and playful. "It's not as complicated as it sounds, Mrs. Thorel. All you have to do is enlarge the pattern and copy it onto a grid so that the weaver can see square by square—that is, thread by thread—how to proceed. Isn't that right, Ives? Ives?"

I turned to look at the boy. He was curled catlike on his pallet, nose to knees.

"He's asleep!" I said.

Bisby Lambert shook his head. "It's my fault. He's working all day and then as my drawboy here as well. No wonder he's exhausted."

I had some sympathy for the boy. All that talk of lashes and simples had had quite the same effect on me.

"And I'm afraid he's eaten all your cakes," said the weaver, picking up the discarded muslin from the floor.

"No matter," I said, smiling. "I can always bring you more."

Sara

Moll was in the wet kitchen, standing in front of the sink, sleeves rolled up to her elbows, scrubbing at the greasy pots with brick dust. She turned to me as I walked in, framed by the arch linking the two parts of the kitchen. "Come to help?" she called.

"No. I'm looking for food," I replied, opening the larder in the room next to hers.

"It's two hours till supper."

"It's not for me. I'm to collect some finished silk from the journeymen and I thought I'd take them something."

I heard Moll fill a bowl with water from the tank and start to rinse the pots. "Which journeymen might they be?" she said, over the clattering she was making.

I sighed, impatient. "John Barnstaple and the other one, Lambert, I think. Not that it's any of your concern."

"Oh, aye," she said. Her tone made me imagine her smirking face reflected in the shiny bottom of a just-rinsed pot. "Those two, is it? They can't bring the silk back themselves, then."

"I overheard the master saying he needed it now, so I offered to collect it. I'm just trying to help."

"Then why don't you take this and tip it into the privy?" She appeared in the archway and held out the bowl of water to me, murky with brick dust and slick with grease.

I ignored the little shrew. "So there's nothing I can take them?"

Moll rested the bowl on her hip. "What d'you think this is? A chophouse?"

⊱ · ⊰

I found some lamb patties in the larder and took them with me. I had indeed heard raised voices coming from the master's workshop, and at Barnstaple's name, I stopped outside the door, even though my arms were full of Madam's darned stockings. Some mercer was complaining that his order of plain weave velvet was long overdue. Once he had gone, I asked Elias Thorel if I could walk over to Buttermilk Alley for him and see if the order was ready. I wanted John Barnstaple to know who I really was: Mrs. Thorel's lady's maid, not some girl playing with fruit at the market.

"They can keep their food," said Barnstaple, glaring at the patties on the table.

"Barnstaple," Lambert spoke his name like a warning, "there's no need for that. Thank them for us," he said, turning to me. I didn't have the heart to tell them that Elias Thorel would sooner have wrung Barnstaple's neck than give him food.

"The order?" I said.

"He can have it when it's ready." Barnstaple scowled.

"But he needs it now," I said. "The mercer is waiting."

"If he wants it now he can pay a proper price for it."

"Does Thorel not pay you for the silk you weave?"

"Oh, he pays, all right," said Barnstaple, setting aside his scruples about the food and reaching for a patty. "Just less than he did before. He's reduced the piece rate for the silk and now he's expecting me to put myself out weaving it quickly!"

"Why did he reduce the price?"

68

"Because the mercers are buying their silk from France. Because people don't want to pay for silk anymore." Barnstaple sounded exasperated, as if explaining to a child. "If the master can't sell it, he won't pay us to weave it. Why pay for Spitalfields silk when you can cut your cloth from calico?"

I didn't have an answer, but he didn't want one. His words seemed to inflame him. They brought color to his cheeks and urgency to his voice. I found myself staring at his mouth, watching it shape the words. He sat up straight and leaned toward me. "Do you know there are master weavers who have put down their looms entirely? Their journeymen have nothing to eat."

I shook my head, feeling I should say something, but too fixed on his face to speak.

"But," he said, carefully crafting the word, "they will not be allowed to get away with it." Then he pulled his eyes away from mine and grasped a jug of ale on the table. For a moment I felt almost abandoned and searched his face, hoping he would look upon me again. He must have thought I was concerned for my own sake, because then he smirked and said, "Don't worry, they'll always need someone to empty their chamber pots for them."

I smarted, glad that the half-light masked the effect of his words.

"It's hardly the maid's fault," said Lambert.

His words brought me to my senses. I stopped staring at John Barnstaple as if he were some kind of prophet and tilted my chin. "I'm Sara Kemp," I said, "Mrs. Thorel's new *lady's* maid."

Barnstaple looked me up and down. "Tell them to send the *scullery* maid next time. She's prettier than you."

I felt like I crumpled in front of him, folding in on myself like a napkin at the dinner table, crushed and tossed away.

"Ignore him," said Lambert. "He's in a bad mood and he's had too much to drink."

Barnstaple laughed and poured more ale. "Still," he said, as much to himself as anyone else, "we're not likely to see Moll round here very soon. The master will barely let her out of his sight."

"What do you mean by that?" I asked.

"You'll see," said Barnstaple, tipping his tankard toward me in a mock salute. He downed the ale and banged the pot onto the table. "Come back next week," he said. "I'll have Thorel's silk then, God damn the man."

✌ · ✍

Later, back in the kitchens at Spital Square, I looked at Moll afresh. Until then, I had barely noticed more than the rough skin on her heels as they grazed mine in our bed and that her too-big apron was tied twice around her tiny frame. I had thought Moll was a girl grown too tall for her body, colt-legged and clumsy about the house. But that evening I stood silent in the doorway and watched her as she sat at the kitchen table, bent over a wooden board piled high with sweet herbs. She hummed softly as she worked her knife over the marjoram and thyme, stopping occasionally to brush the chopped fragments from her long, pale fingers. A thick plait the color of butter hung over one shoulder, and her lips were like the curved inside of a shell, smooth and delicately pink.

A thought occurred to me then: this girl is too beautiful for her own good. What mistress in her right mind would want such a peach ripening under her roof? Of course, some might call Madam a beauty, but we are all in our own season, and if Madam was summer, then Moll was a new spring just bursting into color.

Esther

"But why, madam?"

"Why? That is like asking why would one eat, or sleep at night. Our souls need the same nourishment as our bodies, Sara. We take that from prayer and attending church."

"But I never went to church when I was with Mrs. Swann."

"That I can well imagine. Now, pull harder, please."

Sara leaned back and tugged on the lacing of my stays. I held my breath so she could close the gap an extra inch. I had to teach her almost everything. Although she had claimed ample experience of a lady's toilette, it was clear she barely knew how to thread a bodkin with silk ribbon and lace my stays from the bottom to the top. How she laced her own, I could not fathom and was never inclined to ask. I just showed her how to knot the ribbon properly, round the last pass through the eyelets, and tuck the loose end neatly behind the white kidskin edge.

"But it doesn't seem right, after the life I have led."

"Sara …" I put my hands on my waist and squeezed to help press the edges of the corset together "… that life is behind you now. It is important that you go to church and are seen to do so. We would not want people wondering why you are not there. You are part of a pious household now."

"Is that tight enough?"

"One more pull, please." I had to look my best for church. I fiddled with the front of the stays, adjusting them down a little, then lifting my bust over the wool-filled cushions fitted to the inside edge of the corset. "Pick me out a gown, Sara."

She tied the silk ribbons, then walked over to my wardrobe. I sat down at my dressing table in just my corset and shift so I could powder my face before putting on my dress. In the mirror, I saw Sara appear behind me and hold up a red damask gown with a pattern of green scrolls. I let out such a sigh that I sent up a flurry of powder from the pot. It stung my eyes and made me sneeze.

"Not that one," I snapped, batting at the powder to clear it. "It's church we are going to, not the theater!" I put down the powder and went to the wardrobe myself, running my hand over the many gowns that hung inside. "This one will do." I pulled out a gray velvet with a modest edge of white lace.

Sara slipped the sleeves onto my arms, then stood in front of me to arrange the lace across the front. "It seems strange," she said, pointedly looking at my breasts spilling out over the top of the corset, "to make such an effort for God's benefit." I brushed her hand away and arranged the trim myself to punish her for her impertinence.

Pastor Gabeau leaned on the pulpit at L'Église Neuve. Behind him the modest chancel provided a gloomy backdrop to his exhortations. After reading the French liturgy, he began his sermon. His theme was familiar, and the words came to me in snatches, breaking through my thoughts: "… the growing aversion of the young for the language of their fathers, from whom they seem almost ashamed to be descended …"

Elias, straight-backed and stern beside me, stared ahead as if at the pastor, but more likely his attention was on the best pews in front of him, occupied by the foremost Huguenot families. Pews he used to occupy before we married, but now finds full, no one prepared to move up for Elias Thorel and his English bride. Such a small thing, a petty slight. Even four years later, I kept asking myself whether it was me who kept him tethered to the outskirts of his community.

Behind us sat the journeymen, worshipping at the same church, equal before God, if not before the loom. Was he among them? I wondered whether Bisby Lambert could see me as he looked across the congregation toward the pastor. Did I distract him from the sermon? Did he find himself dragging his attention from the curve of my neck to the safety of Gabeau's moral tones? Of course not: he would not worship in the Huguenot chapel.

Sara was prim as a schoolgirl on the bench next to me, hands folded in her lap, her eyes fixed on Pastor Gabeau as his arms waved and his mouth worked to emphasize his point. It struck me that no one could look at her and see her for what she had been: it was as if she now wore virtue along with neat collars and a white apron. Her face was in profile, tilted up toward the pastor, and it was not without envy that I noticed her neat nose and chin. Her skin was pleasingly pale, and thick, dark lashes fanned over her cheeks. I jabbed her side and those lashes flicked up to reveal hazel eyes, made newly bright and interested. Perhaps I should not have made her come. What had it to do with her, after all, if the Huguenots no longer spoke French?

Elias had recently begun to insist that the whole household came to church. Moll sat on his other side: a master silk weaver and a scullery maid. That was one of the things I most admired about Elias: his concern for those beneath us. As we had walked in, I had noticed how solicitous of her he had been, holding the door open and smiling at her as she passed. That a respected and wealthy man could show such consideration for a maidservant was admirable indeed.

12

Sara

The master was not extravagant by nature, but he did employ a French cook. The Finet family had been linked to the Thorels for more than a hundred years. They had told me that Monsieur Finet's grandfather grew up in the same household as the master's grandfather in France. When the troubles began, they escaped Lyon together in the back of a cart, under a horse's weight of fine silk bound for England. How strange that silk was their salvation, even then. They say that when the cloth was finally lifted off them, Thorel had lain as pale as a hung pig in the back of the cart and Finet had revived him with his own breath.

Two generations later Monsieur Finet was as French as my left foot. Yet he liked to hold on to the customs of his grandfather's birthplace. He insisted we call him "Monsieur" and had his clothes cut in the French manner. If his great girth were anything to go by, you would think him the finest cook in the parish, but that was not the case. I once wondered aloud to Madam why the household employed a cook who barely knew goose fat from lard. But she told me that the master would sooner give up his looms than turn out Monsieur Finet. So we were stuck with him, our cook *à la mode*.

One afternoon in late spring I went into the kitchens. It had been a glorious day, sunny with a breeze that brought the blossom drifting down from the trees, like snow. Monsieur Finet had not been able to withstand the gentle birdsong and soporific sunshine and was dozing in his chair by the hearth. His stew was turning sticky on the range, so I took a spoon from the dresser and gave it a stir. Finet opened his eyes and watched me without comment. We had come to an uneasy truce since I arrived at Spital Square. He tolerated me, like he did the tomcat lying curled at his feet. I took *The Art of Cookery* down from the shelf, looking for ideas to save Monsieur Finet's stew.

"A half-gill of sack, that's all it needs," he said.

I snapped the book shut and turned to him. "Indeed, and by the smell of you, that's the last thing *you* need."

Monsieur Finet chuckled. The bottle of sack stood empty on the kitchen table. Clearly, it was not just the sunshine that had gone to his head. As I moved around the kitchen, tidying as I went, I could feel his eyes following me.

"Where is it you said you used to work?" he asked me presently.

My hand stopped in the middle of sweeping crumbs from the worktop. "In a tavern," I said, and brushed the crumbs into a bucket. I stood up straight and turned to face Monsieur Finet, wiping my hands on my apron as I did so.

"I see," he said, sitting up. "And which tavern was that?"

"You would not know it," I said. "It was in the next parish."

"What did you do there?"

I sighed with mock exasperation and began stacking the clean plates. I did it loudly, clattering one on top of another. Monsieur Finet winced every time as the pile grew higher. "I told you, *Monsieur*. I helped in the kitchens."

Finet nodded slowly. "It's just Moll said you were a housemaid. And not a very good one, by all accounts."

"Housemaid, kitchen maid, what's the difference?"

"Big difference," said Finet. "Anyone who's worked in a household knows that."

I left the plates. My stories were becoming as muddled as the peelings of carrots and potatoes piled next to Finet's stew. I turned round. Finet was still watching me from his chair. "I was a housemaid. Then I found work in a tavern helping the cook. It seems I am better at cooking than I am at cleaning."

"I see," said Finet. "What luck. Plenty would be happy to go from housemaid to cook. Like going from housemaid to lady's maid, isn't it?"

I ignored him. He was probably too addled to remember the conversation. I slid the plates onto the shelf of the dresser and put water on the stove to boil.

"How well do you know Moll?" I asked, as he sank down into his chair.

He shrugged. "Well enough. Why do you ask?"

"No reason." I fidgeted with the dishcloth and smoothed it out along the warm handle of the range. "It's just something one of the journeymen said."

"I'd pay them no heed. They're only happy when they're causing trouble."

"It was about the master and Moll," I persisted. "Something about him not letting her out of his sight." I let the thought drop into his head, leaving it a moment to swirl into his mind with the sack. "And sometimes, when I wake at night, she's not there."

"Don't meddle, woman," tutted Finet. "It's nothing to do with either of us."

"But it is something to do with Mrs. Thorel, surely. I am her lady's maid. I have her best interests at heart."

"The only thing you have at heart is your own nosiness."

The kettle let out an indignant puff of steam. I picked it up and poured the boiling water into Monsieur Finet's congealing stew. That is what this household needs, I thought, as I scraped a spoon round the crusty sides of the pot: stirring up a bit.

Esther

I knelt on the low velvet stool by my bed and steepled my hands together, resting my elbows on the silk counterpane. We had much to be grateful for. Our material blessings were nothing compared to the opportunity to praise God in deed as well as voice by taking in Sara. I had truly saved a soul for him. I was in the middle of praying for the lady next door who had fallen ill with a pox, when Sara came in. She had a pinched look on her face, but that was not unusual. I was coming to understand that Sara experienced life much as other people experienced sucking a lemon.

"Is something the matter?" I asked her.

Sara gave a sigh and busied herself laying out a clean nightgown for me. Something about the affected way she did so made me think she wanted my attention, so I got up from my prayer stool and asked her again what troubled her.

"You are too good to me, madam," she said.

I clicked my tongue. It was getting late and I was tired. Surely that was not what she had to say. She fiddled with the lace of the nightgown for a moment, then said, "It pains me to have to tell you this, it really does."

"Tell me what, Sara?" I said, rather tersely. She stopped fiddling and looked up at me.

"It is the master, madam. And Moll."

"What about them?" I didn't have the patience for this cat-and-mouse conversation.

She took a deep breath, as if steeling herself against what she was about to say. "Madam, sometimes Moll does not sleep in her bed. I have looked all over for her, but I cannot find her anywhere."

I frowned for a moment, trying to work out what she meant. Then I smiled. "When Moll was small she used to sleep in the cubbyhole behind the range, just to be warm. I'm sure that's where she must be." I tugged impatiently at the lacing of my stays, keen for Sara to turn her attention to something more useful. She took the hint and stood behind me, easing the corset away from my waist. I sighed with the freedom, and rubbed my hands over my face.

There was her soft voice in my ear again. "But she is not there, madam. I have checked everywhere. Everywhere except your room, of course. And the master's."

I spun round to face her. "Well, she is not in my room!"

Sara looked at the floor. "Of course not, madam."

Trying to follow her train of thought was like chasing smoke. There was nothing fathomable about what she was saying. Yet still her words had created unease in me. I did not want to say it, but in the end I felt I had to: "You are not suggesting that she is in Mr. Thorel's room? Really, Sara, you do not know him at all."

I'll own that Elias was not the most attentive of husbands, but this was because his head was full of his silk. What Sara did not realize was that he was a man unlike most men. He wouldn't even notice a girl like Moll, unless he happened upon her in one of his ledgers. I sighed impatiently and shooed Sara out of my way. Really, another mistress would have clipped her ear for the impertinence. I changed into my nightgown alone and climbed into bed.

Sleep did not come. I lay in bed staring at the canopy above me. A single candle burned on the bedside table, tricking my tired eyes into seeing things that weren't there. Illusion and reality, I couldn't tell them apart anymore. Where was Moll at night? Either what Sara had suggested was a phantom, or my marriage was. They could not both be real.

This was nonsense. I did not doubt Sara's good intentions—the girl must have felt she owed me a debt of more than money after all I had done for her—but it was ridiculous to lose sleep over the fanciful imagination of a servant.

I sat up and swung my legs over the side of the bed. I would go and speak to Elias myself. Even if all I found was my husband snoring in his bed, then at least I could sleep myself. I pulled my dressing gown around me, picked up the candle, and opened the door of my room. For a moment I stood in the unclaimed space between my room and Elias', almost nervous to proceed. I never visited Elias in his chamber. It was only he who came to mine. The thudding of my heart suddenly seemed loud enough to wake the sleeping household. I took a deep breath and turned toward Elias' door. My hand had just closed over the handle when a laugh rang out from inside. High-pitched and bell-like, as innocent-sounding as a child's. My hand froze. Then there was a rumbling in response, low and warm. A voice you could wrap yourself in and feel safe. If you were her. Then silence again, building like a wall around them.

I stood there, still holding the door handle, while my life reshuffled around me, like a deck of cards. I could not go in. There was nothing in there that I wanted to see, nothing that I wanted to intrude upon my life. Opening that door would have been like opening Pandora's box. Something awful would flood out and it would be impossible ever to put it back. Instead, I turned and walked toward my room, unsteady, feeling my way as if somewhere so familiar had suddenly become altered and alien. Once inside I leaned against the door until it gave a reassuring click, signaling my separation from Moll and her tinkling laugh, and from my husband. A man I no longer knew.

In the morning, I took the chocolate that Sara brought me. When she asked me how I was, I replied that I was well. I sipped at my chocolate while she silently moved around my room. The warm liquid brought color to my face. I could feel it, spreading pinkly across my cheeks, like shame. I set down the cup and told her to take out one of my favorite damask gowns—a blue so muted that it was almost gray, overlaid with white fans—and dressed with great care, making sure that my hair curled perfectly beneath my cap. Then I went down to breakfast and greeted my husband cheerfully. He looked up briefly from his paper and nodded. He did not comment on my dress or my hair that morning, any more than he did on any other. I took the napkin and laid it over my lap. While we waited for breakfast, I announced that the weather was fine and that summer must finally be here. Elias grunted from behind the wall of print, so engrossed in what was going on in the world that he was unable to summon any interest for what was right in front of him.

When Moll brought my eggs, I smiled and thanked her. In fact, I did everything I usually did. But inside I felt hollow, as if I had been emptied of all that had defined me. There was no more substance to me now than there was in any of my gowns, and when I stood up, I almost thought I would crumple onto the floor. So I took our daily routine and made a structure of it, fitting myself around it so that it supported me, like the whalebones of my corset or the wires that gave shape to my hair.

Sara

"The Arnauds are coming to dinner."

Madam was pacing round the kitchen, picking up jars and bottles, peering into them, then putting them back on the shelf as if what she was looking for might be hidden inside. Then she turned to Monsieur Finet. "What shall we give them to eat?" He was sitting at the kitchen table sharpening his cleaver, echoing Madam's shrill voice with the metallic ring of knife on stone.

"What about a game pie, madame?"

"*Game pie?*" She emphasized each word as if he had suggested something disgusting. "We cannot have game pie again. They must have had *game pie* the past three times they have come! Don't you understand how important Mr. Arnaud is?"

Finet flared his nostrils and inspected the edge of his blade as if contemplating whether to use it on Madam. We all knew how important Mr. Arnaud was. Madam had been at great pains to tell me that he was the most influential mercer in Spitalfields. Without Mr. Arnaud how would the master sell his silk? To hear her talk, you would have thought that Mr. Arnaud was the sun that shone on the Thorel household.

"Then per'aps a saddle of mutton, madame."

Madam rolled her eyes. "Something *different*, Monsieur Finet. We have mutton all the time."

Finet banged the knife onto the kitchen table and even Madam started.

"May I suggest salmon?" I said quickly. "Served with a fennel sauce and lemon pickle?"

They both turned to stare at me, Finet annoyed, Madam relieved.

"Yes." She nodded. "That would be perfect. And can you dust the London china?"

"Yes, madam."

"And lay the table with the best damask cloth."

"Yes, madam."

"And make sure my pale green gown with the pink flowers is aired. I should like to wear it this afternoon."

"Of course, madam."

She had been insufferable of late. It made me wonder whether she had taken more notice of what I had said about Moll than I had thought. I was half expecting her to stride up to Moll at any minute, catch her by the ear and turn her out onto the doorstep, but instead she had thrown herself into managing her household. It was as if Esther Thorel was sugarcoating her life. She was building a veneer of such perfection around herself that no one could look at her or her home and find anything lacking. Of course, by then I was not on the outside. I could see her life for what it really was, behind the face powder, whalebones, and shiny London china.

Our household followed a strict routine and dinner was to be served at the fashionable hour of four o'clock. I made pea soup to be served before the salmon, and Monsieur Finet did little more than get under my feet, then take the credit. Mr. and Mrs. Arnaud arrived promptly at half past three. Moll let them in while I was in the kitchens with Monsieur Finet, pouring the soup into a tureen and sprinkling it with parsley.

After a few minutes of slicing bread and filling the butter dish, I made my way up the stairs to the dining room carrying the tureen by its handles. Moll trotted behind me with the bread and butter. They were already seated when I came in. Over the heads of the gentlemen, I could see Madam and Mrs. Arnaud chattering with their heads together. Mrs. Arnaud was not a comely woman. She was of an age when the best any woman could hope for was to be called *handsome*, and she herself was far from that. Her nose hooked downward, while her chin jutted up as if they were determined to meet in the middle.

I put the soup on the table and Mrs. Arnaud caught the scent. She stopped her chatter with Madam and turned to inspect it.

"Pea soup," she exclaimed. "Mr. Arnaud's favorite!" She beamed across the table at her husband. He was turned toward Mr. Thorel and did not look round. Mrs. Arnaud's gaze was left directionless so she turned it on her empty soup bowl, watching as I filled it. Once I had served her, I moved to Mr. Arnaud. I must have been thinking about how it was his favorite as I filled the ladle to the brim, then brought it over to his bowl, conscious all the time of the best damask tablecloth. As I poured it in, my eyes fell on Mr. Arnaud, or rather the lower part of him. His waistcoat. A pale cream silk, detailed with mulberry trees, stretched gamely across a barrel belly. And for a moment I must have just stood there staring, because Madam suddenly gave a forced laugh and said, "Will Mr. Arnaud not get another spoonful?"

I flushed and stammered, "Of course, madam," before dipping the ladle into the tureen again. I kept my eyes fixed on the table, the bowls, the spoons, anything but his face, while I served the master and Madam. Then, when they were all busy spooning soup into their mouths, I allowed my eyes to rise up from the straining waistcoat, past the jowls spreading over his collar as he bent toward his food, and up to his face. When he sat back and licked his lips, patting at them with his napkin, I knew that those lips had dragged themselves across my skin. Those fingers gripping the napkin had dug into my wrists and thighs. He must have sensed me watching him because he stopped his patting and looked at me. I felt as naked under his gaze as I had been that day at the Wig and Feathers. I could do nothing but wait for everything to fit together in his mind in a moment of complete recognition. He narrowed his eyes at me and put down his napkin. "Get me some salt," he said.

I need not have worried. He did not recognize me any more than he would have noticed the same hackney coachman twice. The people who served his needs were as unremarkable to him as the shoes he put on his feet. He saw no more humanity in me than he did in the salt cellar he took from my hand without another word.

Esther

The sound of Moll's happiness had flitted like a moth across the hallway and landed on my heart. As much as I had tried to carry on as if nothing had happened, I was not myself and even Mrs. Arnaud noticed.

"My dear," she said, when we were settled in the parlor and the men continued to discuss their business downstairs, "are you quite well?"

I could not tell her, of course. Ours was a friendship of circumstance, not affection.

"I am, thank you, Mrs. Arnaud, but I have much to think about at the moment."

"Indeed." She looked at me quite kindly and nodded. "It's just that I wondered whether all is as it should be …" she paused then and glanced away from me "… at home."

I blushed and looked down at my hands. "Sometimes," I ventured, "I feel invisible. As if I am no more to him than the table he sits at, or the ornaments on the shelves."

"Come, my dear," she said, placing her hand over my own and squeezing it, "you are young and pretty. This cannot be so. All men are preoccupied, but none more so than those whose business is silk. Do not take it to heart."

It was an odd sensation, her hand over mine. She had never touched me before and I felt strangely comforted, as if she had connected me to her because our lives were the same, both in the shadow of a mistress more beautiful and demanding than any other.

"It is not just the silk."

"Ah." Mrs. Arnaud took back her hand as if the intimacy was suddenly too much. "If he is … distracted, then you must find something to busy yourself with. Is it not time you had a child?"

"But we have not been blessed."

Mrs. Arnaud smiled. "A child will come, when God feels you are ready."

"But what if it does not? I already feel that I have failed him. He has no heir—perhaps that is why …" We sat in silence, my words slowly turning stale. "We should return to the men," I said presently.

She caught my arm as I went to stand up. "You cannot change him, so you must learn to live with it. It will be like a piece of grit in your shoe, painful and annoying, but you must carry on regardless. Do you understand?"

"Is that what you do?" I asked her, surprised at my own directness.

"It is easier now I am older," she said, quite matter-of-fact. "I choose to busy myself with other things." She let go of me then and gave my arm an awkward pat. "Find something to do which makes you truly happy, my dear. That is all I can suggest."

I already knew what would make me happy. The next day I waited until Elias went out to Mr. Arnaud's house in Artillery Lane, then stepped into his workshop. There were piles of books and papers and ledgers, covering every stage of the silk-weaving process, from the sticky little worms to the startling vermilion shades of the dyes. There must be something here about preparing the *mise-en-carte*, I thought, as I pulled book after book down from the shelf. The watercolor painting and the point-paper design were simply two parts of the same process, one artistic, the other technical. If artistry was talent and could not be learned, then technical drawing was craft and certainly could be.

Seven years an apprentice, and twelve books to show for it, three written in French. I had to love Elias for his attention to detail. There was not one element of his profession that he had not studied and mastered.

I took the book on point-paper preparation to the counter. Then I found a silk design, the one with the Chinese temples, already paired with its *mise-en-carte*, waiting to be sent out to a journeyman, with the silk threads that would make it real.

I skimmed through the book, stopping occasionally to see how its directions had been put into practice in the example in front of me. The pattern was reduced to shades of black and gray, plotted over the lines. Letters of the alphabet labeled each grid. Each shade had been assigned a color beneath the pattern: *jaune, lilas clair, lilas foncé.* I spent all afternoon there, willing Elias not to return and shooing Sara away when her head appeared round the door and she exclaimed, "There you are, madam!" By the afternoon, I was beginning to understand. When I looked again at the temple pattern, the watercolor seemed mute and fragile while the point paper was like the advocate that would speak for it to the loom. I just had to reduce my designs to their most elemental level, then rebuild them, color by color, across those tiny boxes.

14

Sara

I returned to Buttermilk Alley just before the tenor bell sounded. I waited, but the noise from the second floor didn't stop. He must be busy, I thought, imagining John Barnstaple grudgingly finishing Thorel's silk order. I was wondering whether there was any point in knocking when the door opened and Bisby Lambert came out with a young boy.

"I've come to collect Thorel's order," I told them. "Like Barnstaple told me to."

Lambert nodded. "He's upstairs," he said, holding open the door for me before they went on their way. Off to Spital Square, I supposed, to clank above Madam while she tutted about the noise, trying to read her latest novel.

I walked up the stairs to the garret where Barnstaple was working at his loom, placed directly under the wide lattice windows. Because the cottage was only one room deep, there were large windows on each side of the top floor. Opposite Barnstaple's there was a second loom, larger and with more beams and pulleys, standing still and silent, like the angular skeleton of some strange creature. Straw pallets lay on the floor, one beside the bigger loom and one under the slope of the catslide roof, next to a simple washstand and mirror. Otherwise the room was empty, save for bobbins and quills scattered about the shelves and silk waste collecting in drifts on the floor. A place to work and sleep. Sleep and work.

Barnstaple stopped pushing on the pedals under the loom with his feet and hung up the shuttle. "It's done," he said, sullen, as if he begrudged even his own achievement.

"Mr. Thorel will be pleased." I watched him with a slight smile as he walked round to the end of the loom and began cutting the threads tethering the silk to it and knotting them together.

"What's this one for?" I asked, inspecting the other loom while Barnstaple continued to cut and knot.

"Flowered silk," he said. "That's Lambert's drawloom. He weaves the tricky figured silk. I weave the simple stuff. Like this," he said, finally freeing his silk from the loom.

"What is it?"

"A plain weave lustring. It'll end up as the lining to some woman's muff, or at least that's how I like to imagine it."

I gave him a sharp glance. He was grinning, a filthy look on his face. It was the first time I had seen him smile. I wondered whether I didn't prefer the dark, brooding rebel to this coarse man. "Is that where you sleep?" I asked, nodding toward the pallet under the roof.

"It is. I get up, piss in the pot, then weave all day until I go to sleep again. Six days a week, every week, just to line the pockets of a man like Thorel."

Of course the weavers slept by their looms. It amused me to imagine that weaver in Spital Square curling up on his pallet in Madam's garret. How would she feel if she thought that a journeyman—muscles taut from working the looms, skin sharp with sweat—was lying only a few feet above her? Would it turn her delicate stomach or would she find it rather thrilling?

"Where does Lambert sleep?"

"Downstairs. We'd kill each other otherwise. It's bad enough that I have to look at him all day." He glanced toward Lambert's drawloom.

"Does Thorel not weave?"

Barnstaple scoffed. "He's barely touched a shuttle since he finished his apprenticeship. It's not that he doesn't know how to weave—he knows as much as Lambert even—it's just too much like hard work for him. He commissions the patterns, buys the silk and puts it out to his weavers. There's fifty or more of us, working his looms throughout Spitalfields. When we're done, we give him the finished silk."

"Except Lambert's allowed into Spital Square."

Barnstaple's face clouded. "Lambert thinks he's got it in him to be a master. More fool him. He'll work his guts out, only for Thorel to take the silk from him for nothing. Worshipful Company of Weavers indeed."

He dropped the silk onto the bench and walked over to me. "But you're not really interested in weaving, are you?"

I said nothing, conscious of the silence. No milkmaids calling out their wares in Buttermilk Alley, no weavers clanking out a living, thread by gossamer thread, in the row of cottages. Just this man and me, alone in an attic room.

"Why d'you keep coming here?" He stepped closer to me. I could feel him all the way down the length of my body, even though he barely touched me, such was the energy in him. Wound like a coiled spring, the moment before release.

"To get the master's silk," I said flatly.

"No." He shook his head. "That's not what you really want."

"How do you know what I want?"

"I can tell. You're not like other girls squealing blue murder if you so much as put a hand on them." He reached for the back of my neck and drew me toward him. "Are you?" he whispered against my lips.

It was the first time a man had touched me since Mrs. Swann's. It was at once completely familiar yet startlingly different, like the same tune played on an upturned bucket, then a harpsichord. But still I pushed him away, just because I could, even though the urgent press of him against me was as thrilling as the opium had been that first evening at Mrs. Swann's.

Now it was up to me to decide.

Esther

I rose early and left the house to escape from my gilded cage. The streets were quiet. Only the nurseryman was up, standing with his cart at the corner of Spital Square and White Lyon Yard. He knew me well and nodded a greeting as I approached. I never left buying flowers to servants: I wanted the pleasure of choosing them myself and of walking away carrying a small handful of the season with me. But he had not seen me in a while. Flowers in the house made me want to paint, and I had drawn nothing since the day I burned the point paper.

I paused alongside his cart. It was the beginning of June, and it was laden with the blooms of early summer. Elias had dismissed my first attempt at a silk pattern and told me to go back to my sewing. I had been put in my place, wife and mistress of the household, a role I had been tethered to almost all my life by a silken cord of privilege and ease. But that tinkling laugh had cut through it, as easily as snipping an embroidery thread. I would still be the wife and manage the house, but a little part of me had been set free.

Elias was wrong. There was nothing more beautiful than what was laid out before me on that cart—irises and carnations, bees squabbling over white and purple lilacs. I could not look at all of this and fail to imagine it captured somehow on silk. Not in some stiff, stylized way, but in its natural form, so realistic that you could almost reach out and pluck the flower from the fabric.

I turned to the nurseryman. "I should like to buy some flowers," I said.

He grinned at me, his first customer of the morning. I couldn't decide whether to take the summer flowers or make a bough pot for the empty fireplace. In the end, I asked him to cut me some flowers, but he added a few sprigs of green. The nurseryman didn't seem to mind the thorns—his hands were as twisted and gnarled as the branches.

"The season's a-changing, ma'am," he said, as he handed the bouquet to me.

"Yes," I said. "It looks to be a hot summer."

"Hot summer, cold winter," he said simply. And he was right: a winter was coming that would freeze the very breath in our lungs. I wish I could remember his name, but perhaps I never asked it. You won't find him there now. He did not survive the winter that was to come.

I was arranging the flowers in a vase when Moll came in. I had got up so early that she had not had a chance to clean the hearth. She made as if to leave when she saw me, but I gestured for her to come in. She looked at the floor as she passed me, as was her habit. I had always thought it was out of shyness, or respect for my position compared to hers, but now I saw things differently. She could not meet my gaze any more than the hangman looks into the eyes of the condemned. I watched her as she worked. I could not help it. If I had been asked before then what color her eyes were, I would not have been able to say, but now I studied every inch of her. She had a neat, heart-shaped face tapering to a pointed chin. The kind of chin you could imagine taking between thumb and forefinger and tilting upward.

I set my jaw and turned determinedly away from her. Instead of tormenting myself with every sweet plane of her face, I concentrated on my flowers and the watercolor they would become. *Silk? No, you cannot do that.* It was only because I had believed Elias' words that the point paper had defeated me. Now I knew him so much better. He was not the man I had thought he was, and I no longer took his word for granted. And now there was another voice in my head: *You have a gift, Mrs. Thorel.*

Once Moll had gone I laid out my paper and watercolors and threw open the shutters so that the light fell straight onto the vase, picking out every curve of leaf and stem. The nurseryman had given me carnations and I began to sketch their showy sun of petals, but they seemed too fussy somehow. Then my eye was drawn to a single dog rose caught among them almost as if it should not have been there; a little Cinderella finding itself at the ball. It was the color of a blush on a creamy cheek. There was something captivating about its open face and downy yellow center, and the perfect simplicity of its shape, like the flower a child might draw. I found it easy to paint because it was pure and uncomplicated—quite unlike everything else in my life—and I lost myself in the delicate heart shape at the end of each petal and the way the pink turned to white before the yellow began. I ignored Sara's pleas to come down to breakfast and by midmorning I had finished. Meandering across the width of the paper, spare sprays of flowers entwined with their leaves. As a watercolor it was good, but as a silk it needed more. I had to balance the subtle repeat of the flowers with something stronger, so I accented each cluster with a berry motif, drawn from memory. I chose blackberries for their intense color; a reminder of the autumn to come, even as the summer is still in bloom. When I took a step back, I could see it: the perfect symmetry down the entire length of the design, serpentine, Hogarth's own Line of Beauty. I knew instinctively that this was something the loom could understand. A simple design that I could plot on those numerous squares, line by line and row by row.

My new pattern needed a name. I couldn't think of anything more apt than those of the plants so I wrote "Blackberry and Wild Rose" across the top, along with the date, 2nd June 1768. There was a drawer in my dressing table with a lock. I took the tiny key from the locket round my neck and opened it, placing the watercolor, neatly folded, inside. It would be obvious to anyone that this was no ordinary painting and there were some questions that I did not want to have to answer.

Sara was creaking around the hallway outside. When she came in, she colored as she saw me close and lock my drawer, as if it were a personal affront for me to lock anything away. By then Sara knew almost everything there was to know about me. The scent of my favorite pomade and the color of my stockings. She sorted through my dirty shifts and stitched my petticoats. Was I to keep nothing to myself?

15

Sara

God blessed me with neither great brains nor great beauty, but I am no dolt. Did she think she was the only one with secrets? She fumbled with her little keys and drawers in the same way that she shielded her breasts with her hands when I undressed her. But why should I avert my eyes from the curve of her flesh when I am allowed to see the contents of her chamber pot?

Seeing Mr. Arnaud again had made me realize that I could never escape the Wig and Feathers. Its roots spread from the end of the little lane next to Spitalfields market throughout the parish, tunneling everywhere, cracking the very ground I walked on. This life of churchgoing and piety was not mine. It had been forced upon me, traded in return for my good behavior. I dusted and darned, I scrubbed and sewed, but I would never do any more than that. Virtue had a price, which had turned out to be relentless hard work and tedium. It made me think: If your lot in life really is to lie on a bed of straw, then why should you lie there alone?

The next time Monsieur Finet had asked Moll to take a message to the journeymen in Buttermilk Alley, she pulled such a face you'd have thought he had asked her to empty the slops. So I offered to take it. By the time I had finished catering to Madam's every whim and could leave, it was late evening. Buttermilk Alley was deserted but the sour tang lingered. Raised voices were coming from inside the weavers' cottage and it took a while for anyone to answer. When the door finally opened, it was not John Barnstaple or Bisby Lambert who stood before me.

"I have a message from Mr. Thorel for the journeymen." The man twisted round to look at John Barnstaple, surrounded by men. He saw me through the doorway and nodded to the man, who stepped to one side and allowed me to pass. Inside, Bisby Lambert and Barnstaple were sitting at the ends of the table, while other journeymen squeezed onto benches on either side, or leaned against the walls. That little room was so full I could barely get into it. They must have been discussing something important, as they didn't look up when I hung my shawl on the hook by the door. I made myself useful, filling their empty ale pots from a jug. It was no place for a woman, but if I kept quiet and served some purpose they tolerated me well enough.

John Barnstaple banged his fist upon the table, making me jump and the froth slop over the top of his ale pot. "By God, they will be the death of us. We cannot afford for them to put down even one more loom."

The other journeymen nodded and murmured.

The man who had let me in had been leaning against the wall. At Barnstaple's words he stood upright and said: "We have already had four of our six looms put down. With no income, the weavers cannot eat. Their families are starving."

Barnstaple held up his hands as if to stem the strength of the man's feeling. "You are right, Duff. They cannot be allowed to get away with what they are doing. Look what happened to young Ives." He gestured to the boy sitting next to him. He seemed barely more than a child, with high cheekbones and luminous skin, still smooth as a girl's. Barnstaple hung an arm over Ives' shoulders. "Tell them what happened, Ives."

Barnstaple's attention made Ives puff with pride. "I started work at five years old. Worked for the same master, I did, for nearly eight years. I picked his silk clean, filled his quills and drew up the figures.

I thought I was going to be a proper journeyman, really make something of myself. Didn't know that he had taken on ten other boys just the same. He never was goin' to give me an apprenticeship. We was all just cheap labor to him."

The journeymen started murmuring again. One of them tipped some ale into a spare pot and pushed it across the table toward the boy. Barnstaple gave Ives' shoulders a quick shake, then took back his arm and rubbed his hands together. "So we are agreed, then? We will demand sixpence per loom from each master."

My eyes became drawn to Lambert. He sat straight in his chair, holding his head still, while all about him the other men dipped theirs in assent.

Barnstaple noticed it too. "And what of you, Lambert? Are you not with us?"

"I am with you," he replied, his voice even, "but I have no quarrel with my master. Thorel has not put down any of his looms. Even Ives has a job now, as my drawboy, working Thorel's figured silk."

"Of course, the great *master piece*. How is that coming along?" Some of the men chuckled. "Thorel will not put down his best drawloom, I grant you," continued Barnstaple. "It's not the weavers of the flowered brocades who are in trouble, it's the plain silk weavers. Men like all of us!"

"We are all in trouble," said Lambert. "The mercers are buying figured silks smuggled in from France. Silk is Thorel's livelihood too." He shifted slightly to address the rest of the weavers. "What if he refuses to pay? What if all the master weavers refuse to pay? If the mercers are not buying their silk because they can get the same thing from France, they have no money themselves to pay you. Have you thought of that?"

Duff leaned forward and set his thick jaw into a determined jut. "Then we will damn well make them."

Lambert stared at Barnstaple from across the table. The other men quietened. I found it remarkable how these men looked to Barnstaple to know what to do.

Barnstaple said, "If they do not pay, they will find out how powerful we are. We are just one combination, but there are many more in Spitalfields, and all are as angry as we are. Who can say what a poor and hungry man might do?"

"I want no violence," said Lambert.

"Nor I," said Barnstaple, "but if it comes to that, then so be it." Their exchange muted the atmosphere in the room. Duff raised his eyes to mine as if challenging me to speak out. Did he worry that my loyalties would be split between the journeymen and the household I worked for?

"What are you still doing here, anyway?" Duff said. "I thought you had a message from Thorel."

"I have."

"Well, what is it?"

I handed the paper to Barnstaple, who ripped it open and read it quickly. "He says that the mercer has canceled his order for the watered tabby and I'm to return the thread to Spital Square tomorrow."

"See?" said Duff, his eyes becoming bright and round as pennies. "This is just the start."

After a while the weavers dispersed to their own lodgings until only Lambert, Barnstaple, and Ives were left.

"You shouldn't have involved the child," said Lambert.

"What?" Barnstaple sounded tired and annoyed.

"Ives, he has no place in this."

"I'm not a child," said Ives, indignant.

Lambert ignored him. "You used him to stir up the feeling of the men," he said to Barnstaple. "Leave him out of it from now on."

"I'll do, or not do, whatever I damn well please."

"He's my nephew and I am telling you to leave him out of it."

"Indeed he is your nephew," said Barnstaple, "but he seems to do what *I* say." Then he turned to Ives. "Who can blame you, eh, boy? You just need a man to look up to, don't you?"

"Who would that be?" said Lambert. "You? Sitting upstairs weaving ribbons like a girl?"

Barnstaple stood up with such force his chair toppled over. Lambert rose too, and, for a moment, I feared they would come to blows.

"It's late," I said quickly. "We should all get some rest." They stared at each other until Barnstaple picked up his chair and set it upright so hard I thought it might break apart.

Lambert glared at him, then said, "I'm taking Ives home," and left without bidding us good-night.

Barnstaple glowered at me across the table. "Isn't it time you got back to the Thorels?" he said, picking up a piece of bread from the table and chewing it.

I held his gaze. His hair, black as a bat, hung over his eyes, wayward and disobedient, suggesting the temperament of the man. I shook my head slowly. His eyes were jet in the candlelight, unfathomable. "I would rather stay here," I said.

Barnstaple swallowed the bread, then picked up his ale and swilled another mouthful, his eyes never leaving me. "Would you indeed?" he said. "You didn't feel that way the last time you came here."

"I want to know you," I said. "I find you interesting. The men, they listen to everything you say. It's like you're fearless."

"Fearless or reckless?"

I smiled. "Why don't you tell me?"

Barnstaple reached across the table for the jug of ale and filled his pot. "Do you know what my father was?" he asked.

I didn't answer. Something about his openness and the quiet night surrounding us created a fragile intimacy that might shatter if I spoke.

"He was a night-soil man. He spent his life shoveling other people's filth until one night he was so exhausted he fell into the cesspit he was emptying. No one came to help him. Can you imagine that? Your own father lying in a cesspit because no one cared enough to get their hands dirty." Barnstaple took a swig of his ale. "He was dead by morning."

There was the tiniest crack in his bravado. When he looked at me he seemed almost boyish. I would have reached out to touch his face if I hadn't known that my hand would be batted away.

"I learned something then," he said. "No one's going to listen to a night-soil man or a journeyman. We have no voice alone. That's why I bring all the men here and tell them what I do. When we stand together they will *have* to listen to us." It felt heady indeed to look upon a man with real desire.

At Mrs. Swann's I had learned to see men through different eyes, as the cook views the giblets pulled from a turkey, or the tanner turns his face from the stench of lime on leather.

I walked over and leaned against the table in front of him. When he went to lift the ale to his mouth again, I closed my hand over his and gently took the pot from him.

Esther

Clutching my long roll of point paper to my chest, as if I were going into battle, I climbed the stairs to the trapdoor. They were just finishing as I stepped inside the garret. Ives' boyish shoulders sagged when he saw me and he dropped his bag to the floor, unable to hide his scowl.

"Ives," said Lambert, "you can still go home."

The boy didn't wait for anyone to change their mind and disappeared through the trapdoor, his bag bouncing down the steps behind him.

"He's just tired," said Lambert.

"It's a long day for him. I don't want to keep you. I came only to show you this." I held up the point paper to him. "If you don't mind?"

"Of course," he said. "Why don't you put it here?" He indicated the stretch of flat threads across the loom. I laid the roll of paper on top and smoothed out the *mise-en-carte* for *Blackberry and Wild Rose*. I felt nervous, somehow, showing it to him. It seemed as personal as if he had brushed aside the lace at my neckline and was gazing on my skin.

He nodded, studying the curve of flower and fruit across the little squares, reduced to shades of gray for the loom. "You haven't chosen the colors yet?" he asked.

"I thought that I could see what thread you have here."

"Shall we do that now?"

I felt such relief and gratitude for his kindness. He hadn't mocked my work, or dismissed my attempts to draw up a pattern. I nodded and we walked over to the shelf of silk spools. He contemplated them for a moment, then reached up and took down three.

He had chosen a dusky pink, a mid-green, and a purple so dark you might think it black, until you twisted it in the light and saw its mulberry tones. "What about these?" he asked, his eyes searching my face to gauge my reaction. Then he walked over to the empty loom and placed the spools on the heddles, as I had myself weeks before. I joined him at the loom and contemplated the colors for a moment. The pink was too brash for a dog rose, so I took the spool back to the shelf. There were so many colors … How could I choose one that worked in the silk but remained true to the subtle beauty of the wild rose? Then I saw it, a yellow as pale as buttermilk. I brought it back to the loom and placed it next to the others. It contrasted with the intense plum and made the green look sharp and bright.

Lambert nodded his approval. "I would keep the ground pale," he commented, "almost white." He was as straightforward as if he were talking to a mercer, or my husband. He did not talk to me as if I were a foolish girl.

"Will you weave it for me?" My voice came out almost as a whisper.

"Madam?"

"Mr. Lambert, it is my dearest wish to weave this silk. I should be so grateful if you would weave it for me. I will pay you, of course." I spoke fast, the words chasing each other out of my mouth.

He looked quite taken aback. All our talk of colors and threads, the small cakes and linnet seeds, all reduced to nothing in the face of the baffled stare he gave me.

"I cannot weave this silk, ma'am. I already work for the master all day and in my spare time I am here, weaving my master piece. How could I weave this as well?"

"I understand." His response was painfully obvious, and my hope had been foolish.

"I'm sure the master will find someone to weave it for you," he said, his face wrinkled with concern.

"No, he will not." I turned abruptly, walking away from the small intimacy I had revealed. When I reached the other loom, I rolled up the *mise-en-carte* roughly, not caring if the paper creased. It would never be used after all.

"Please," he was beside me then, his voice gentle but insistent, "you cannot give up."

I turned toward him, blinking away frustrated tears. "This," I tightened my hands around the point paper, denting the hollow tube, "is all I have ever wanted to do. You will understand that, Mr. Lambert. There is nothing wrong with being a journeyman, but you want to be a master weaver. That is why you are here. There is nothing wrong with being mistress of this household, but I want to design silk. And that is why I am here."

He pulled at his lower lip with his teeth, sighing through the small gap. "I wish I could help you." He sounded genuinely regretful.

"I know, and you have been so kind already. It was wrong of me to ask." I turned to leave, ready to walk away from everything I had thought I might do.

"He would see it anyway."

Something about his voice made me stop. The tone, the slight acknowledgment. It marked a shift into a different place, the very beginning of an understanding.

I nodded, not turning.

"He might come here to check on my progress."

Elias had even followed me up here. Just his mastery over the house was enough to stop me weaving my pattern. I turned back toward Lambert. "How often does he come up here?"

He shrugged. "He's very busy so not often. But if he did he would see the silk on the other loom. We could not hide it from him."

"I could bring something," I said, "to cover it."

Lambert let out a slow breath. "I will mount the loom for you," he said. "I will set up the treads and the pattern mechanism. What you do with it after that is up to you."

Sara

My mother made almond cakes when I was a child, sweet and sticky inside, crisp and sugar-dusted on top. In the summer she would leave them to cool on the sill with the window ajar. I would catch the smell as I played in the garden. When I thought she wasn't looking, I would reach inside to snatch one and run off with it, passing it from one hand to the other until it was cool enough to eat. I should have left them alone, but I couldn't help myself.

And that was how I felt about him.

Barnstaple rolled over with a sigh and reached behind his head, wedging the pillow under his neck. The coverlet was twisted and crumpled around our legs and his chest was bare. I moved onto my side so that I could lie closer to him. His skin was damp under my fingers as I played with the tight curls of black hair on his chest. He shifted slightly on his straw pallet, moving away from me, breaking the sticky seal of our skin.

"It's so hot in here," I said, looking around the garret. The muggy summer night pressed in on the lattice windows, sealed shut, offering the promise of light but no air. Barnstaple grunted, his breathing still quick. I knew better than to try to talk to him, so I let him rest until I began to see the dawn nudge up over the rooftops of the weavers' cottages.

"I should get back soon," I said. I could already hear Lambert downstairs, clanking a pot onto the hearth, whistling to himself. Making as much noise as possible, I supposed, to rouse us before he came up to the garret to start work.

Barnstaple opened his eyes and squinted at the window as if faintly surprised by the intrusion of day into his little attic. He pushed himself up to sitting, his head almost touching the sloping roof, and ran his hands through his hair, scraping it away from his face. "You should," he said. "The Thorels will be wanting their money's worth out of us both."

"They're not that bad," I chided.

He gave me a look that said otherwise. "You've not heard Thorel's canceled another order then?" I stayed silent. I could see the muscles of his jaw work under his skin. "Of course," he went on, "it's not Lambert who suffers. He's still there all hours. It's me who's had my work cut by half."

"Why do you not get the same work?"

"Because Lambert's a golden boy and he can do no wrong. He puts up with whatever they dish out and they love him for it. Me, I don't take that nonsense from them, so it's my hours that are cut. Makes me spit, it does."

"Hush." I sat up, too, and reached out to stroke the side of his face as if he was a child. A bluish vein stood proud of his forehead and I felt his rage twitch beneath my fingers. "Why don't you work for other masters?"

He clicked his tongue and batted my hand away. "It's the same all over Spitalfields! Greedy masters stopping honest men earning their living to protect their profits. Either that or they have reduced the piece rate for the silk so much that only an Irishman would weave it."

I circled my arms round his neck, pressing my face into his hair and my lips against his ear. I could almost taste his anger in the salty tang of his sweat. "Then let's not rush back to them," I murmured, but he shrugged me from him and stood up, as uncompromising as the relentless creep of dawn.

৵ · ৫

Madam's face pinched. "Only half a crown?"

I had returned to the house with fresh bread, butter, eggs, and cheese so that if anyone had noticed I was gone I could say that I had been to the market for breakfast provisions. The change from the housekeeping money Madam gave me every week was next to the basket of food. Madam poked at it with her finger as if it were a beetle with the audacity to be walking across her kitchen table.

"That's the change he gave me, madam." I tried to keep the exasperation from my voice, but I felt leaden with tiredness and the dull ache of separation from a lover.

"Well, it seems expensive for what you've bought," she said, lifting out the loaf and peering underneath it as if there must be more in the basket than I had said there was. "Next time go to the baker on Quaker Street. It's at least tuppence cheaper there and he puts no alum in it."

Then she picked up her half-crown and dropped it into the pocket of her silk dressing gown before she turned to go back upstairs to change for breakfast. I took the eggs out of the basket and set them on the table so hard that one cracked. How could she talk of saving pennies when Barnstaple barely had enough work to put food on his table?

"Careful, Sara!" came her shrill voice from the doorway. "You can put that egg in a bowl and use it in a cake later. Frugality is a virtue, you know."

Esther

"Will this do?"

We were alone in the garret again, Ives already sent on his way, standing by the second loom, now threaded with the pale warp threads and hung with shuttles attached to the buttermilk yellow weft. I had not waited long before I went back up there. I told myself that it was because I couldn't

103

risk Elias seeing the loom before it was covered, but really it was because I couldn't stay away.

He took the bundle of material from me and shook out its full length, holding it up against the loom. "Yes," he said, considering it, "it's perfect. In any event, it's a good idea to cover the loom to protect it from the dust and the sunlight."

I suppressed a smile, not wanting him to know that I was amused by the thought that he unknowingly held aloft my most voluminous petticoat, cut and opened out into a plain cloth.

He made as if to throw the petticoat over the loom, but I stopped him. "Weave just a little," I said. "Please."

The light was dwindling, the world fading around us. The assembling darkness was like a wall shielding the garret from the prosaic goings-on outside. Decisions seemed straightforward within those sloping walls.

"I want to see you do it," my voice pushed against his reluctance, "just for a moment. Just to see it happen."

He nodded, an almost imperceptible dip of his head.

I lit a candle and placed it on a shelf near the loom. When he sat down, something about the candlelight and the way he settled himself on the weaving bench made me think of a pianist about to play. I almost held my breath with anticipation, as if the boy Mozart was about to bring my pattern to life.

"I cannot do this alone," he said. "You will have to be my drawboy."

Of course. Ives. I looked down at the unappealing straw pallet.

He smiled at me. "You need not sit on that. There's a stool over there."

I found it in the corner and brought it over to the loom. I was glad I was wearing my most modest gown, so that I could smooth my skirts underneath me before I sat down.

"When I weave," began Lambert, "I select from the point paper which simples are to have lashes applied to them at every change." His voice was quietly authoritative. Outside this room, I was the mistress, but in here I did his bidding. "Before we begin we need to set up the lashes and the simples."

He showed me how to do it, then I passed a lash around every simple he pointed out, knotted the lashes together and connected them to a cord.

"You are the drawboy," he said finally. "It is your job to sit beside the loom and pull the correct lashes that are laced to simples. These in turn produce the figured design of the cloth as I put through the weft. Do you understand?"

This time I almost did. As I tentatively pulled on a lash I could see that it drew down some of the cords making up the simple. When certain strands of the warp were raised, and the rest lay flat, a space was created through which he could pass the shuttle attached to the weft. I nodded. "I do understand."

"Just pull, hold, and release them as I direct, that's all." He was grinning. I felt at ease with him, not nervous or afraid of doing it wrong, just excited to see even a few threads come together to mark the beginning of *Blackberry and Wild Rose*.

The loom began to move under his hands, like a huge puppet, as he worked the treadles, calling to me to pull the lashes and draw the simples. As I did so, he threw the shuttle so that it slipped through the warp threads. For some time I was lost in the strange cadence of the contraption. There were moments, when I was just holding the same lash through successive passes of the shuttle, when I could look at him, the concentration knitting his brow and the flex of the muscles in his arms as he worked. I wished I could stop the sink of the sun in the sky.

By the time the candle had burned down to a waxy stump, the thinnest sliver of iridescent silk clung to the heddles. "I can't believe it," I breathed. I was finally looking at the very beginning of a silk made to a pattern I had designed. My own creation. "How long will it take to finish it?"

Lambert laughed and rose from the weaving bench. "There is one more thing you need to weave silk, Mrs. Thorel," he said.

"What's that?" I sounded exasperated.

He came and stood beside me, looking down at me with a serious expression. "Patience," he said. He held my gaze for a second, then broke into another wide grin. "In fact, that is the most important part."

I felt a connection to him then, a familiarity, as we laughed together, that I could not remember ever feeling before. "But really," I said, "how long does it take? It seems my own hair would grow faster than this."

"If I worked a full day, I could weave about a yard."

For the first time it occurred to me that there was a limit to the time he would spend in our house. He worked on his master piece for perhaps two hours each afternoon he came. Even if he only came once a week he could weave a yard of silk in a month. How many yards did it have to be?

Then he would be gone.

17

Sara

Shifts	*six items*
	(one stained at the back)
Stockings	*ten pairs*
	(three darned, two more needing stitching)
Petticoats	*four items*
	(one ripped at hem)
Stays	*three items*
Cost	*one shilling*

I kept a detailed inventory of my mistress' apparel. I knew every crease in the linens and every curve of her stays. When any item went out to the washerwoman, I noted it in my inventory, along with any stains I expected to be removed and any darning I would do on its return. With the cost, of course. Every ha'penny was accounted for in the Thorel household.

I came to know each of her gowns and when she liked to wear them. She favored the demure blues and pale grays on Sundays, but on a Saturday

I would lay out a selection of pale pinks and yellows. They were aired in the summer and stored in lavender and sandalwood when winter came. Madam loved each of them, as if they were household pets.

Why then, when I went through my lady's wardrobe that morning, were there only three petticoats?

I had gone round her room in my usual fashion, refilling the water jugs and cleaning the glasses that bore the print of her lips. Then I tidied the pots and jars and replaced their lids. All this took place out of her sight, of course. It would not do for her to know how filthy she was. There was powder everywhere. She thought only about what went on her face and in her hair. The rest fell in a cloud around her, unnoticed unless she tutted and brushed it from her sleeve. I opened the windows to let in some air and banged the cushion of her dressing table stool out of the window. The dust and powder caught on the breeze in flurries.

In the street below, the watercress seller sauntered across the cobblestones with her basket and her bosom overflowing, whistling to the boys. She caught the eye of the brick-dust seller, who stared at her as he passed. For a moment I looked at his mule, plodding along behind him laden with sacks. Of late, I had felt as tired and burdened as that animal. I left the window open to air the room and drew the bed curtains. Inside it was fusty with sleep and turned my stomach. The pillows on both sides were dented and rumpled, which could mean only one thing. I threw back the coverlet and clicked my tongue. More sheets to change, more laundry for the washerwoman.

And that was what reminded me. There was a petticoat in the linen cupboard with a hem that needed mending. Except that when I looked, there wasn't.

How a lady and her petticoat could come to be parted, I didn't know.

⁂

I remember the night before my mother had told me to go. She came up to the attic that we shared. Her face was flushed and her usually neat hair was falling out from underneath her cap. Tears had made tracks down her face, cutting through the coal dust left on her skin from where she had tried to brush them away with hands that had stoked the kitchen fires. When I reached for her, she pushed me away and did not allow me to comfort her. That night we lay in our little bed like two strangers, rather than with me curled against her, listening to her breathing as I fell asleep.

It was not until the next morning that she gave me the parcel and pressed the purse into my hand, but it was that night that she truly left me. I did not know what I had done wrong. Even when she told me that there was no place for me in the household and I would have to go to London to make my own way, it was as if the master were telling me, not my own mother. She clipped out the words as if they held no real significance, even as my little world—me and her as long as I could remember—was ripped apart. I asked her why she was doing this all the way down to the Old London Road, but all she would say was that I would have a better life in London, she was certain of it. I just had to trust her and ask no more questions.

We stood in silence by the side of the road and waited for the cart to appear as it came through the woods at the edge of our master's land. I sensed her stiffen at the sight of it as if she sought strength from her rigid limbs. I remember my distress as the horses slowed their heavy tread and she pushed me up into the cart. I tried to cling to her, but the driver whipped up the horses, and she slipped through my hands as the cart jolted forward.

Over the years I had tried not to think of her. I allowed the wound to close, rather than worry and pick at it with memories. The only times I had thought of her were when I opened her book and started to make the recipes inside. When I smelled the fragrance of cakes swelling in the oven, memories of her flooded through me, like my own blood. And I thought of her now, when I had seen the moon wax and wane three times since the summer began and no blood had stained my shift.

Widow Anstis lived in a little wood-and-pitch house in the fields of Whitechapel. If she had had a fancy shop and measured out her potions into fine cobalt glass, she would have been called an apothecary. As it was, she was called far worse, but it was not the Middle Ages and a woman could be left to her herbs in relative peace. She made the best pomades this side of Tottenham Court—that was why all the Spitalfields ladies went to her—but her wisdom went far beyond vanity, for those who cared to know. And Mrs. Swann did want to know. She would take her girls to Mrs. Anstis by the cartload, forcing potions down our necks every month that tasted of borage and dandelion leaves.

Mrs. Anstis explained that humors ebb and flow inside us, like tides. Women live in thrall to the moon, and the right draught at the right time can change the balance of our humors. We walked through her herb garden many times. In the summer, the scent of rosemary rose from the ground as our skirts brushed over the woody stems. Every so often she would bend to pick chamomile and put it in her poultice bag. When the draught was ready, she would line us up, like children at the poorhouse, and spoon out a dose to us all. I drank mine quickly, trying not to flinch at its bitter taste, then took the peppermint leaves she held out to me.

I had not seen her since I left Mrs. Swann's. Was this the result? A wretched creature inside me that no amount of stewed leaves could ever get out?

Every Sunday morning after church we were allowed some free time, so I asked John Barnstaple to meet me in the tea gardens at Vauxhall. There was a large white pavilion in the center, which was covered with climbing roses in the summer, but that day it was October and the flowers had already turned to orange hips and the leaves were falling. There was hardly anyone else about. It was cold and a fine, misty rain dampened my face.

I was annoyed to see him approaching the pavilion with another man. We had so little time together that I didn't want to share him with anyone else. Besides, I had something important to tell him.

They were deep in conversation and merely nodded at me as they sat down on the bench that curved round the inside of the pavilion. Now that he was closer I recognized the man from Buttermilk Alley. It was Roger Duff.

"We need to do more," said Duff. "Sixpence per loom is nothing."

"The problem," replied Barnstaple, "is the demand for cheap imported cotton. We need to persuade people not to buy it and not to wear it."

"But it is already banned," I said. I didn't want to state the obvious, but I found being ignored a little tedious. They looked at me as if one of the ornamental urns decorating the pavilion had spoken.

"Banned it may be," said Barnstaple, "but there are still plenty of shops selling Indian calico."

Duff leaned forward, resting his elbows on his knees. "Other combinations are taking more of a stand," he said. "Someone told me that a woman had the calico dress ripped from her back by a couple of weavers from a combination called the Rebellion Sloop." His voice was urgent, as if he secretly enjoyed the image his words created, but Barnstaple's face clouded.

"The Conquering and Bold Defiance does not assault defenseless women in the street," he said gravely.

"Then what would you have us do? Go with Bisby Lambert to lobby Parliament?" There was a mocking edge to Duff's voice, and I glanced warily at Barnstaple. His mood was like a tossed farthing: it could land either way.

Then he guffawed and even Duff looked relieved. "We are not yet reduced to that," he said, clapping Duff on the back.

When Duff had left, Barnstaple bought us each a cup of sweet tea and we sat warming our hands on them at a table in the tea gardens.

"What times we live in," I ventured, blowing at the tea so that the steam clouded in the cold air. "I admire you. Your children will be born into a better place because of what you are doing."

"I would not want to bring a child into this world," he said, staring around him, as if the gray skies and the cold metal chairs of the tea gardens were the best the world had to offer.

"But you would have much to teach a son. You could show him how to stand up for himself, how to demand proper wages for his work."

"At this rate there will be no work left for any son of mine."

"But what of Ives?" I persisted. "You are like a father to him—more than his own uncle, even. Does he not make you wish for a son of your own?"

Barnstaple set down his tea with a clatter. "What is the point of all this?" he asked. "I do not wish for a son any more than I wish for a millstone around my neck. Have you understood nothing? I cannot make enough of a living for myself, let alone a child."

I nodded mutely and stared down at the tiny ripples the breeze made on the surface of my tea. I would not get the answer I wanted from him any more than I would find it in the tea leaves at the bottom of my cup.

Esther

If Sunday mornings were about duty and obligation, Sunday afternoons were about freedom. I often had the house to myself. Once we had attended church and had lunch, the servants were free to do as they pleased. That Sunday, Sara had gone for a walk in the tea gardens at Vauxhall and Elias had taken his horse out to ride in the fields beyond Hare Street. I tried to sit with my sewing, but the knowledge that a loom upstairs was mounted with thread for my own pattern was like a siren call and I could not resist going up there.

I sat in front of the loom. My palms felt sticky as I fiddled with the shuttle, trying to summon the courage to begin. How hard could it be? I had everything set up and Bisby Lambert had already shown me what to do. I knew I should have a drawboy, but surely I could do a little bit on my own. Just until the first pattern change, even if I had to keep getting up and lifting the lashes myself. It would take longer, but it would not be impossible.

I couldn't remember exactly which treadle to press, but I felt sure it would all fall into place as soon as I could start. I pulled on the heddles and tried to pass the shuttle, but it flew out of my hand and tangled limply in the warp. I tutted and untangled it, trying to throw it again. When it seemed to work, I grabbed at a pulley and yanked it. The loom seemed to awaken like a sleeping beast and parts I didn't even know could move started sliding and grating together. I felt out of control, immediately regretting that I had ever thought I could weave the silk myself. It was as if I had begun to push a boulder down a hill, and now that it had gained momentum, I couldn't stop it rolling. I reached out with my foot for a treadle, pressing it repeatedly, trying to still the determined loom. Then I felt a tugging at the hem of my skirts, gradually increasing in pressure until I realized that my gown had become caught in the moving parts. I let go of everything I was touching as if the loom were on fire.

There was a strange quiet in the attic. It was midafternoon and the house was empty. I sat at the bench, tethered to the loom, inseparable now from the instrument I had sought to control. The linnets trilled and chirped in their cage, as if discussing my predicament. I tugged at my skirt, but it was so caught in the mechanism that there was no give at all.

"Sara!" My voice dropped to the floor of the garret like a spent firework.

She was not back yet. In truth, I didn't want her to come. How would I begin to explain? A pair of scissors lay on the shelves among the spools of silk. Only three yards away, but it might as well have been a mile as I could not so much as stand up. I cried out in fury and frustration and started banging on the loom, as if it were a dog that held me in its jaws. The linnets took flight in surprise and fluttered against the bars of their cage, as futile in their endeavors as I was in mine.

When the garret trapdoor lifted I was bent double, trying again to twist my skirts free. I wasn't even aware of him until he was standing next to me. I let go of my skirts and sat up. Bisby Lambert didn't look at me, just silently crouched to inspect the awkward union of my dress and the loom. The material had snarled in the mechanism and two parts were wedged together. He leaned across me and pulled at it. For a moment, his side—from his shoulder to his waist—was pressed against my legs. Even through my petticoats I could feel the muscles of his back flex as he worked. I looked away to lessen my embarrassment, staring at the linnets jostling on their perch, quietly watchful.

"What are you doing here?" I asked him, trying not to glance down.

"I need to work on Sundays, ma'am. I have not made as much progress on my master piece as I had hoped."

I was glad, in that moment at least, that he was bent down among my skirts. I did not want to look at him, knowing that I was likely the reason he had achieved so little.

He let out a breath of exertion, then the whole mechanism seemed to swing back and I was free. I gathered my skirts in delight and, for a brief moment, they came up and revealed my stockinged ankles just as he was sitting back on his haunches. It was as fleeting as the snap of a twig, but his glance made me feel as if I had stepped into hot water.

He stayed crouched at my feet. "Does the weaving really mean so much to you, madam?"

"*Yes*," I said, and all my frustration and longing to bring my pattern to life seemed to gush out on the wave of that one word.

He nodded and stood up. "Then I will help you," he said.

We fell into a rhythm. For every two days he came with Ives to work on his master piece, he came one day alone to weave with me. I sat on the stool next to the loom pulling the lashes and drawing the simples as he directed. There was something inevitable about the time we spent together, the direction of our lives already mapped out with the same precision that a pattern is drafted onto point paper. I was observing a transition, the strands of silk thread disappearing from the bobbins and becoming so woven together that they would be impossible to pick apart. And with every pass of the shuttle his life and mine intertwined. For as long as I continued to pull the lashes in the correct sequence, the pattern would be drawn up, line by line, on the warp. The result was predetermined.

It is a woman's duty to bear children, no matter if it kills her. And I have seen that happen often enough, not least to my own sister, who panted and screamed her way to God for the sake of a half-formed infant who outlived her by less than an hour. As they put her into the ground, along with the child who had killed her, my mother turned to me and said, "This is what it means to be a woman."

Sometimes I watched the children playing in the street from my parlor window. They would bounce their hoops over the cobblestones like cartwheels, and run, shrieking and laughing, after them with their sticks. It was not that I didn't want a child of my own—I did, desperately—it was that I found it hard to long for the very thing that might take me from this world. It was not something that Elias would ever understand. Despite his domestic distractions, he knew his duty in the bedchamber and fulfilled it with the same sense of purpose he did everything else. There had been a baby once, but as soon as it had made its presence known, it had disappeared in a trail of blood down my shift. God forgive me, but before the crushing sadness, there had been relief. Every day I have remained childless since, I have wondered whether I was being punished for that brief moment of release. And not just by God. I felt my husband punished me every day for not being the woman he had thought I was, for not being Sophia Courtauld, perfect wife and mother, beloved of his community, for being the wrong choice. He had paid too high a price for me and seen no return.

Infatuation turned to resentment is a bitter thing. It sours the wine and turns the bed cold. But I did not complain.

"Looking for love in marriage," my mother used to tell me, "is like looking for currants in a bun. Nice enough if they're there." And yet Elias was a man who could create beauty from next to nothing. No one could feel the sensual slip of one of his silks over their skin and doubt that. Sometimes I wondered what my life might have been like if Elias had ever focused the same exquisite attention on me.

After a while, I couldn't recall what it was to truly love, any more than a caged bird can remember its freedom. Until he reminded me. In those hours in the garret I realized what it was to feel a man's presence so strongly that I could barely look at him. I came to know how just the press of him against my leg could wipe all else from my mind.

18

Sara

The scent of lavender pomade in the garret. That was how I knew she'd been there. Madam had taken to appearing and disappearing, like a phantom. Even when she was around, she was half-hearted about everything. Not so much about reading her psalms—she was always half-hearted about that—but with her needlework. Usually she could sit for hours in front of the window with her head bent over some sewing, but she had become distracted, her lips pursed in a thin line, plucking at the stitches as if they had annoyed her on purpose.

It hadn't occurred to me to check the attic, but I sensed her from the moment I stepped though the trapdoor. I know what a weaving garret smells like. It smells of silk and weavers and both are rich, musky odors, like damp wool or an earthy forest floor. But this one was sweet with gentility, the same flowery elegance that I found so cloying downstairs. For a moment I stood there in the silence. It was so peaceful, with the light fading from the long lights and the shadows creeping, like mice, from under the looms. What brought her up here, I wondered, where the only living things were the weavers and the songbirds?

116

⚘ · ⚘

Mr. and Mrs. Arnaud proved frequent visitors at Spital Square. Every time I saw him I worried that he would finally recognize me, but over the months I realized that the eyes peering out from that fleshy face saw only the Madeira wine or the pork stuffed with apple and sage. I was able to serve him his food and drink, and stand right in front of him, hoping that one day he might choke on it.

Mr. Arnaud was as dour as his wife was amiable. It made him an easy dinner guest—his needs were met by a meat pie and a glass of port—but Mrs. Arnaud was much harder work. She came for the conversation. I had thought that Madam's ability to chatter about the latest textiles was without match, but even she was glassy-eyed by the time the soup was served.

"But have you seen them, Mrs. Thorel?" said Mrs. Arnaud. "They are so plain!"

Madam laid down her soup spoon for a moment. "But is that so bad, Mrs. Arnaud? I mean, silk design has been much the same for these hundred years past. Perhaps it is time for a change."

Mr. Arnaud scoffed into his soup, spattering it over the best damask. "You see, wife, Mrs. Thorel does not live in the past as you do. She is a young woman after all."

Mr. Arnaud glanced at Madam over his spoon, and I saw her through his eyes: her face flush-pink against the white lace of her collar, her eyes large and wide-spaced like a child's. Next to Madam, Mrs. Arnaud was a faded bloom, the kind of flower that should be plucked from the vase before the petals fall.

I looked at the master to see whether he had noticed Mr. Arnaud staring at his wife, but he was busy with his soup.

"Of course," said Madam, patting her lips with the cloth, "I love the old baroque styles as much as anyone, but perhaps there is room for both, the more elaborate designs for formal attire and the simple silks for other occasions."

"Other occasions? Why, Mrs. Thorel, you'll have us all wearing calico next!"

They were childless, these two, as was Madam. But there was something hopeful about Mrs. Thorel. She was not yet thirty, after all, while Mrs. Arnaud was already wrinkling like a walnut. Mrs. Arnaud's fertility was a book that was closing, the last pages turning, and Mr. Arnaud lacked the time or the inclination to pull down the ribbon to save the place. Poor Mrs. Arnaud talked brightly of the children she would have in the same way that we planned for the last days of autumn, even though we knew that the cold was coming.

It was while I was pinning Madam's hair the next morning that I first felt the baby twist, like a newt, inside my belly. I gave a little gasp and put my hand to it, but all I felt was the bones of my stays, as if the infant already knew what kind of world lay outside and had sought refuge behind them.

Madam looked at me strangely and I mumbled something about the kippers we had had for breakfast. But I knew it was the slippery flip of new life, the first unmistakable confirmation of everything I had suspected. I glanced at Madam again in the mirror: she was undoing the hair I had just pinned and curling it again higher on her head, unconcerned about anything other than her own appearance. I had no fear of her noticing yet. I was there for my usefulness, not my beauty, and she would no more look closely at me than she would gaze upon her chamber pot.

Esther

Sara was airing my summer gowns before packing them away for the winter. Inside the house it was still warm, but a cool breeze laced with woodsmoke blew through my open window. My chamber was covered with a blanket of silk. On my bed was a damask gown with an ornate pattern. It used to belong to my sister, Anne, and my mother had given it to me after Anne died. I liked neither the pattern nor the memories it held. I lifted it from the bed and turned to Sara, who was kneeling by my blanket chest, lifting out my woolen petticoats.

"Sara, you may have this now."

She stood up quickly, her arms full of undergarments. Dried sprigs of last year's lavender fell to the floor. "Madam, are you sure? It's a very fine gown."

And it was. The silk was a shaded damask background with a geometric pattern. You could imagine how it would have looked in the firelight, each of the twelve hundred threads per inch catching the light slightly differently. A Spitalfields silk is an investment, not something to be thrown away. It should be passed down through generations, cut and remade from gown to waistcoat, through every garment in between.

"Of course I'm sure," I told her. In truth, although the silk was fine, the style was far too old-fashioned for me to wear again. "Come, let's see how it looks."

Sara placed the woolens on the bed in the space left by the gown. I took her arm and led her to my dressing mirror. I stood behind her and held the bodice up to her chin. I was a few inches taller than her, so I could see over her shoulder how the subtle reds and greens complemented her hazel eyes.

"There, it looks well on you."

Sara flushed and looked at the floor. I had hoped to see her smile. I hung the garment over one of my arms and turned her toward me with the other.

"Why don't you try it on properly?"

"Try it on? Why, madam, I couldn't possibly."

"I should like to see how it becomes you," I said crisply. "Now turn around."

Sara, reluctant, took the bodice from me and turned so that I could begin to loosen the lacing of her own clothes. Then I shrugged the sleeves from her shoulders and pulled them off. When she turned back to me, she had folded her arms across her chest, as if I were a rake intent on seducing her rather than her mistress.

"Come," I said, gently opening her arms, "you see me in such a state every day."

The skin under her clothes was impossibly white. Her soft breasts spilled over the top of her stays, like fresh milk tipping out of the pail.

I slipped the bodice onto her arms and smoothed it. Her cloth cap looked odd next to such a fine silk so I pulled it from her head. As I did so, her hair fell from its knot and spread over her shoulders. I had hardly noticed it before, but it was the color of the horse chestnuts just beginning to fall from the trees outside and as glossy as a well-groomed mare.

"Indeed, Sara, you are far from plain," I said, as I stepped around her skirts to begin lacing up the back. "Once I have fitted the bodice, I am sure I will finally see you smile."

I was chattering to compensate for her own silence. But as I came to the bottom of the lacing, my voice faded away. The material would not meet, no matter that I tugged and pulled on the lacing, which was strange because the top fitted well. I walked round to stand in front of her and looked at her more closely than I had ever done before, but her arms had crept back to her waist and hovered there as if she had an attack of the gripes.

"Well," I said, much more curtly now, "it is yours if you wish to have it. You can make something new out of the material. If you do not care for it, then you may sell it. There is a good trade in old silks at Spitalfields market. You may well be glad of a few extra shillings." I said the last words rather pointedly, but she did not take the bait. Instead, she hurriedly took off the gown. I watched her undress, slipping the silk from her pale limbs, then hiding herself again in the forgiving folds of a servant's dress. She took up the basket of freshly dried herbs from my dressing table and silently began to lay out my summer gowns with sprigs of lavender.

Sara's last task of the evening was to dampen down the fire. That night she helped me to change out of my clothes, untied my hair and combed it through while I sat at my dressing table in my shift and dressing gown. Afterward, as I knelt on the low velvet stool by my bed, I heard the clank and scrape of irons in the grate. She left me without saying good-night, backing noiselessly out of the door so as not to disturb my prayers.

When I climbed into bed a few minutes later, it was like lying on the marble shelf in the pantry. The cold had crept up on us that autumn. It strengthened like bindweed in the garden and choked the warmth out of the nights. I chided myself for not asking Sara to put the hot coals from the fire into a warming pan for my bed. Still, it was not yet late, so I slipped out of bed and pulled on my dressing gown.

I had expected to see her on the landing—extinguishing the lights lining the staircase one by one as she made her way up to bed—but the candles still flickered dully against the walls and the hallway was empty. I took a chamber stick and held it out in front of me, following its glow up the stairs toward her room. I knocked on her door, then called to her, but there was no answer. I opened the door slowly, hoping its reluctant creak would rouse her before I had to. When the door had swung wide, I held the candle aloft and whispered her name, but my words were swallowed by a darkness that offered nothing in return. I patted over her bed, feeling for her body under the coverlet, even though I knew she was not there.

I made my way back down the stairs, intending to search for her in the kitchens, more interested now in her whereabouts than my warming pan. But as I reached my landing the stairs leading down to the floors below began to creak and the light from a candle rose up from the stairwell.

"There you are," I said a little tartly, stepping toward the light.

It was not Sara who emerged, but Elias. "That is a fine greeting for a husband," he said, with a smile, setting down his candle and taking my hand. I looked at him expectantly. There must be a reason for his good humor, especially at this hour.

"Arnaud has commissioned another fine brocaded silk," he announced. "It is good work in these difficult times."

"I am glad, husband," I said.

"Indeed," he murmured, as he took the chamber stick from my other hand and blew out the flame. In the gloom smoke curled up from the spent wick and stung my nostrils. He gripped my hand tightly. "Shall we go to bed, wife?"

I tried to nod, but his lips were already on mine, bringing with them the lingering sweetness of Madeira wine.

Sara

"I came looking for you last night."

I took a moment to finish my stitch, tying and cutting off the thread, before I looked up at her and said, "I'm sorry, madam. The night was cold and I slept in the kitchen downstairs."

She continued to study me, her needle dipping and rising under her practiced fingers. "I see," she said presently.

The circumstances of our meeting were a constant presence in the room, like the ticking of the clock or the crackle and spit of the fire. Madam had bought my virtue for three pounds, eight shillings, and sixpence, as if she was purchasing new ribbons for her hair. As far as she was concerned, it was no longer mine to give away. But what right had she to judge me? She had taken on the piety of her husband's people as easily as she had slipped into the fine silks they made. She had adopted their manners, their industriousness and their thrifty ways, but she was neither French nor Huguenot. She had said no more about her mother after the day I had first arrived and I had not questioned her further. I had never quite understood what she had been trying to tell me until I overheard Finet telling Moll that the master had set

123

many tongues wagging when he married a girl who wasn't French. I tried not to listen to servants' gossip, of course, but their chatter filled the kitchen, like the heat from the range, and I could no more take their words out of my ears than I could keep the warmth from my bones. Everyone knew that Madam was the daughter of a wealthy surgeon. He had a shop on Mincing Lane and some say he attended the King himself, lancing his boils and cutting off his bunions, but no one knew a thing about her mother. At least, not until the pair of them were run out of town for being a murderer and a whore. So, it seemed we were not so different, Madam's mother and I. When I think on it, I wonder whether it was not me she saw that day behind the Wig and Feathers but her own mother, standing in her petticoats having her ears boxed.

Esther

Early the next morning, I found Moll in the parlor. She stood uneasily before me, shifting from one foot to the other, with a brush in one hand, a pan in the other. Ashes from the hearth scattered the floorboards where she had jumped up suddenly when I entered. Her expression was almost comic: half annoyed that I had ambushed her, half bashful to be in my presence.

She dipped a quick curtsy and tried to hide the brush and pan behind her skirts.

"I won't keep you long," I said. Nor did I intend to. Looking at the girl gave me no pleasure. She was like a painting hanging on the wall that I had never particularly liked and wanted to get rid of. Pretty enough to some, but mawkish to me. But if a painting is taken down when it has been there a while, you are left with its grubby outline for all to see, and sooner or later something equally tawdry will take its place.

"Did Sara sleep with you last night?"

Moll looked vague, chewing at her pretty pink lips and letting her blue eyes wander round the room. "I don't know, ma'am."

"What do you mean, you don't know? Surely she did or she didn't."

"Perhaps she came to bed after I was asleep."

"So she was not there when you went to bed?"

Moll gave a little shrug. The girl was infuriating.

"Moll, I want to know what Sara is doing at night when she is not in her room. If she leaves, I want you to follow her and tell me where she goes."

Moll's eyes widened but her words, if there were any, were stuck somewhere in her throat.

"There is a shilling for you, if you do it."

Moll gave a tentative nod.

"You may come to my room when you have something to tell me."

She nodded again, this time more confidently, and I left her to her ashes.

🙦 · 🙤

I did not have to wait long before she came. There was a quiet knock on my dressing room door that I knew could not be Sara as she was running an errand for me.

Moll was blushing. The only time she would ever be in this room would be to light the fire or clean the hearth and almost never with me present. What a shame she did not appear to have the same qualms about my husband's room.

She peered at me from behind the straw-colored curls coming loose from her cap and said, "You were right, ma'am. Sara is leaving the house at night."

I nodded to encourage her. "Where is she going?"

Moll didn't speak. I couldn't tell whether this was true reluctance or a show to make me think that my shilling had been well spent.

Then she looked up at me and said, "The weavers' cottages by Buttermilk Alley, ma'am."

"What is she doing there?"

Moll shrugged as if that information might cost me more. Elias owned many weavers' cottages around Spitalfields, which he rented to the journeymen with the looms they contained. "Do you know which weavers live there?" I asked her. She nodded. "John Barnstaple, ma'am," she said, "and Bisby Lambert."

125

I tried not to react to her words. I didn't want her to see my shock when she said his name. I just pressed the coin into her palm and watched her slip round the door. I sank down onto my stool. This was my own doing. I had brought it upon myself, taking in a girl from the street.

Judge not, that ye be not judged. This was what I had done for her, and in return she had taken me for a fool. And with one of our own journeymen.

⁂

The evenings were fast drawing in. Each passing day stole the light from our windows and robbed us of precious time. Silk is its own master and cannot be coaxed from the loom before it is ready. I yearned for it to be finished at the same time as I dreaded the final pass of the shuttle.

Bisby Lambert was bent over the loom while I clung to one of the lashes. The garret was cold. There was no fireplace; only the house warmed us from below. Sitting hunched on my stool, hardly moving in the cold, I began to feel like I was turning to ice.

With every draw of the simples, I waited for the right opportunity to ask him about Sara.

"You know my lady's maid, Sara Kemp, I believe?"

He looked up, surprised. There was no right moment: I had just come out with it.

"She runs errands to Buttermilk Alley sometimes," he replied, neutrally.

"Yes, but she does more than just that, doesn't she?"

"Pass twenty and take two," he said.

I tutted, then slackened the drawn simples and pulled the second set of lashes. "I mean that her purpose at Buttermilk Alley is not running errands. She is coming to see someone there."

"Pass two, take eight."

My breath came out in an exasperated puff, which clouded in the garret's cold air. "Even at night," I said deliberately. "She is even there at night time."

"Pass eight, take seven."

126

I had lost all feeling in my immobile hands and the lash slipped from my fingers.

"I said take seven!"

"I can't!" I said. "My fingers are numb!"

He stopped the loom, releasing the treadles and setting down the shuttle. Then he was kneeling beside me. My pale hands were pressed together, a single balled fist in my lap. He circled them with his own and lifted them to his lips. His hands were wide and warm over mine, enclosing them completely. He inhaled then breathed into the space between our fingers. Over the top of our hands he lifted his eyes to mine. "You cannot think that your maid is coming to see me?"

The pressure of his hands was secure and reassuring. I wanted to stay sitting in that cold garret forever, just so he would never let go.

I found then that I could barely speak. I had not really thought that it was him Sara was visiting, but I had been surprised by how much I wanted it not to be true, by how much I needed to hear him say it wasn't. I gave a slight nod.

"Good." He gave my hands a quick squeeze, then dropped them back into my lap. "Take lash seven, please."

I couldn't get out of my mind the moment he had held my hands in his and reassured me about Sara. I thought about it constantly, mining the memory for any nuggets of emotion it might reveal. He had touched me, brought my hands to his lips and breathed his hot breath against my skin. It was an unspeakable intimacy and yet ... What journeyman would not deny that he was courting the maid of the household he worked for? Had he never taken Ives' small hands in his and rubbed the life back into them?

Sara

Gin.

I had never tried it before that night, even at Mrs. Swann's. Most of London seemed to be laid out on the streets dead-drunk on it, and the sight of Mrs. Swann's daughters reeling and giggling before they'd had breakfast was enough to make me decide never to touch it. But it was as easy to purchase as bread and just as cheap. Everyone was buying it, from the washerwomen to the footmen. Men received it as part of their wages. Women gave it to their babies. It was everywhere.

I sat on my bed and took my first sip, grimacing at the floral taste. Drinking one of Madam's perfumes could not have been more unpleasant. I made myself drink more and more until my head spun and my mind altered. I imagined the baby flushed away along a river of gin, disappearing in its frothy churn. Then I was running down the riverbank alongside him, watching as he tumbled and fought for air. I could not let him drown, so I knelt by the river and tried to fish him out. But when I grabbed hold of him, he turned into a huge flapping fish with great jaws that snapped down on my arm and dragged me into the swirling river of gin. Then I hung there with him, in the strange tranquility of the riverbed, neither trapped nor free. Neither breathing nor drowning.

My stomach heaved, but I kept drinking until I could see the bottom of the bottle appear when I tipped it up. I let it fall to the floor next to my bed and the remaining liquid seeped into the floorboards. Then I slept the kind of sleep that rendered me a dead weight until the next morning. When I awoke I checked the bed all around me to see whether it had left my body during the night. But it was still there, a resistant bump, like a crease in a garment I could not iron out, no matter how hard I tried.

John Barnstaple lay back on the pallet and let out a long breath, his eyes brown-black in the candlelight. When he looked at me again he glanced at my belly as if he needed proof of my condition.

I lay alongside him, close enough to place my hand on his jaw and tilt his face toward me. The most striking weaver in Spitalfields. I still thought him so. His skin was rough and scratched my fingers as they slid across it. Finally, I had had to tell him and now he would not even look at me.

"There are ways," he said presently, "to remedy this."

"Remedy it?" I wasn't sure what he meant. "You mean marriage?"

He blew air into his cheeks and looked up at the ceiling.

"Marriage! That is not what I was thinking."

He got up and pulled on his shirt. Over at the washstand he splashed water on his face and stared at himself in the cracked mirror, as if his own image might advise him what to do. "Go to see someone. There are ways."

A flush of shame colored my face. Although I fought against them, I could feel tears welling in my eyes.

"I have already drunk as much gin as I can manage," I said. "It didn't work."

He laughed. "If gin did the job then the population of London would be half what it is."

"But why should we not think of marriage?" I persisted. It was the most obvious of solutions to this kind of difficulty. I'll own I almost felt a fraud, suggesting that he marry a whore, but I had kept that from him and I was a different person now. Just like Mrs. Thorel's mother, the tavern singer turned wife of a surgeon.

He peered closer to the looking glass and started picking at his teeth. "Why all the talk of marriage? You weren't thinking of it when you first jumped into my bed."

I was glad of his interest in his teeth, so he did not see me flinch at his words.

"There is a child to think of now," I said, keeping my voice even.

He shrugged at himself, then turned toward me again. "What about the Thorels? What would they say? You wouldn't be able to keep your room and Lord knows there's precious little space for you both here." He cast a glance around the garret. A loom and a straw pallet: no place for a baby.

"What do you care for the Thorels? They do not pay you a fair wage as it is."

"No, but they pay for the bed you're lying on."

"It's hardly a bed," I said, sitting up. "We could get new lodgings together." But he was already pulling on his breeches and tucking in his shirt as if he had somewhere more important to be, as if anything were more important than me and my baby. I felt the first bitter sting of resentment as I watched him go on with his life as if nothing had changed. "You will have to pay to support me."

He paused for a moment as he was putting on his waistcoat and stared hard at me. "What makes you think that?"

"You have to. The parish won't pay for me when the father of the child should."

He turned sour then, no longer even trying to dress his words with kindness. "How can they know I'm the father? How can *I* even know I'm the father?"

"I will swear an oath to it," I said, defiant.

He tutted. "Calm yourself, woman, there is no need for that." He looked as if he was about to go, but then walked back over to the pallet, as if I were an afterthought, and knelt beside me. He took my hand and said, "We still have time before the baby comes."

Esther

Pastor Gabeau leaned on the pulpit of L'Église Neuve. The Sunday congregation was a sea of muted browns and black before me, heads dipping and murmuring in prayer.

"And we must guard against the dangers of drink," intoned Gabeau. "Take heed of what you see on the streets and shun the paths that lead to destruction." The thought of Elias' peace-loving kinsfolk lying drunk in the street was almost laughable. The Huguenots were more likely to enjoy flowers and the music of songbirds. I was not so sure, though, about Sara. Only the other day I had found her in her room in the morning, trying to put her shoes on the wrong feet. The smell in the air pricked my nostrils and Sara was as green about the gills as a person could be.

I glanced at Elias. He was doing a good impression of paying attention to the sermon. His head was bent forward at a respectful angle and he held his prayer book in his lap, rubbing occasionally at the silver clasp with his thumb. But I knew that his mind would be full of the escalating price of the finest raw silk from Italy, not the dangers of sin. In truth, my mind was not on the sermon either. It was the sin closer to home that concerned me most. I was convinced that Sara was with child. I had managed to keep Sara's past hidden from Elias over the months, but what would I do when she was betrayed by her own belly?

In the next pew, I spotted Mr. and Mrs. Arnaud. Mrs. Arnaud caught my eye and we nodded in acknowledgment. I watched her for a moment, sitting perfectly still and upright next to her husband. She was the very model of the sobriety and hard work for which the Huguenot people are known. What would she think about my pregnant maid? She was like a barometer, gauging my success as a wife and the mistress of a Huguenot household; the bellwether of our community.

When the sermon was over, Elias made sure that the press and flow of the crowd pushed us toward the Arnauds. Soon he was a few steps ahead of me, shaking hands with Mr. Arnaud, finding a way to draw the conversation toward business, making sure this trip to church was not a wasted opportunity. Mrs. Arnaud was surrounded by a group of lace-collared, white-capped ladies, all waiting for her direction, which poorhouse to visit next and how many shirts to stitch beforehand. I felt completely alone among this righteous flock.

Then Pastor Gabeau was alongside me, matching his slow stride to mine, hands clasped behind his back. He could see Elias and Mr. Arnaud deep in conversation by the pulpit, so he drew me toward the door, where we stood—half in the early winter sunlight, half in the cavernous gloom of the church—while Pastor Gabeau said his goodbyes and accepted thanks.

"You have seemed preoccupied these past weeks, Mrs. Thorel," he commented, still smiling and nodding, as the last of the congregation retreated.

I found it easier without his gaze upon me; I did not want to be subjected to the scrutiny of the Church and be found lacking.

"May I help?" he said, in response to my silence. He stood out on the steps while I was still inside, light meeting darkness, good versus evil.

"I have a friend …" I hesitated, knowing that the pastor would see through this half-hearted deception, but he just smiled and gave me an encouraging nod.

"Well, she suspects that her maid might be …" I did not know how to say the words to a minister.

Gabeau drew a breath, part resigned sigh, part summoning his resolve. "I have seen all of humanity walk through these doors, Mrs. Thorel. I doubt there is any aspect of the human condition that would surprise me."

"Indeed not, Pastor. It is just that my friend does not know what to do with her. What is the right thing to do?"

"If there is a child, then it is for the father to do the right thing," said Gabeau, sternly. "But if he cannot," he continued, when I did not respond, "or will not, then we can help."

I looked up at him and must have appeared so surprised and grateful that he said, "Your friend is not the first mistress of a household to find herself in such a situation, Mrs. Thorel. In fact, here is the lady you should speak to."

Pastor Gabeau held out his arm to Mrs. Arnaud as she approached. They exchanged the smiles of trusted friends, warm and genuine. I stepped out of the chill of the nave and joined them in the pale sunshine.

"Mrs. Arnaud has a friend on the Committee of Enquiry of the Foundling Hospital, I believe."

"Yes," said Mrs. Arnaud.

"Mrs. Thorel has a friend whose maid is with child. Is there any advice we can offer her?"

Mrs. Arnaud looked kindly and concerned. There was no trace of the judgment and condemnation I had feared. "I am sorry to hear that. It is always a difficult situation, but your friend can send her to a lying-in hospital when her time is near. Then, the very best thing for the baby would be to place it in the Foundling Hospital. I can help, if your friend is prepared to support the girl with the petition to the Foundling Hospital?"

"Oh, she is," I said eagerly.

"Good," said Pastor Gabeau. "The best way to love God is in our benevolent deeds, not just our worship."

21

Sara

Moll was avoiding me. I could tell by the way she slipped past me in the hallway, and my voice rang out into empty stairwells whenever I called her. I took to creeping around outside closed doors until one day I heard her talking to Monsieur Finet in the kitchens. I opened the door noiselessly so as not to give her the chance to disappear.

They stopped talking when I walked in. Moll made a great show of busying herself with her broom. When she tried to step around me to get to the door, I grabbed her skinny arm and held it tight. She yelped like a puppy.

Monsieur Finet got to his feet. "Leave the girl be. She's just trying to get on."

How typical of him to take her side before even a word had been spoken. I suspected he could not see the truth past her doll-like features and slender waist. I gripped her harder. "Why did you tell Madam about Buttermilk Alley?"

"Tell her what about Buttermilk Alley?" she said, her smooth brow creasing.

"That I have been going there. You've been following me. I saw you one night—you don't know it, but I did. And now Madam is watching every move I make. You have told her, I know you have. Who else could it have been?"

"I never," she said, and started to twist her arm.

Monsieur Finet took another step toward us. "I don't care what's been going on, let her go."

"Who else was it, then? You, Monsieur Finet?"

Finet laughed. "What interest have I in the comings and goings of women? If you have been leaving the house, you must accept the consequences. It's not the girl's fault." He took hold of my wrist in one hand and Moll's arm in the other and pulled them apart. Moll rewarded Finet with such a smile you'd have thought he'd saved her from a burning house.

She must have thought she had escaped when she shot up the stairs to sweep the hearths with more enthusiasm than I had ever seen from her before, but I was watchful from then on. She saw me reflected in every pot she polished and every grate she shone.

Esther

As we drew further into winter the darkness came earlier each day. There was less and less time left after the tenor bell sounded for Bisby Lambert to come to Spital Square and weave. That should have meant I saw him less, but it didn't. His master piece lay unfinished in its loom, while my own silk gained length with every week that passed.

I set down the lashes and stretched my arms. It was cripplingly repetitive being a drawboy. "I am seeing lashes when I close my eyes," I said. "I dream of them!"

He had halted the loom when I let go of the lash. Before he spoke, he moved to the edge of the bench so he could see me without looking through the vertical lines of the warp. "I understand. It's harder work than it seems."

He was caught between the candlelight coming from inside the attic and the last of the daylight filtering through the windows. His face was planes of light and shade while the shadows gathered around him. As he sat at the loom, perfectly still, it was as if he posed for Hogarth. In front of him, the loom defined him and his place in the world. And what kind of picture did I make, with my silk gown settling around my feet and my soft white hands folded on my lap? I did little all day, then complained about two hours spent sitting beside a loom. If he was Industry then surely I was Idleness.

"I want to feel what you feel," I said. "Let me try to weave." He watched me as I stood up and walked around him to the weaver's bench. I gathered my skirts and made sure to fold them beneath me before I slipped into the space between the bench and the heddles, so that I was sitting next to him. He stared at me for a moment, then got up and stood behind me. I could feel his presence all the way down my back. Then he leaned over and spoke, his mouth so close to my ear that I could feel the warmth of his breath. "May I?" he said.

He reached over and took hold of the lace of my sleeve, which was hanging down from my elbow. "You do not want this to get caught," he said. "Not after last time." His fingers grazed my skin as he tucked the lace under my sleeve. I should have pulled away and told him I would do it, but I didn't. Then he shifted slightly and leaned over the other side. He must have been emboldened by my acquiescence because this time he was not so careful to avoid touching me. He drew the lace slowly back from my forearm, exposing my skin. Then he reached for the shuttle and handed it to me.

"Start the loom," he said. I rested my foot on the treadle and he laid his hand over the top of my leg, pressing down gently, showing me the right pressure to put the machine into motion. He checked the correct simples were raised, then told me to pass the shuttle. As the loom began its rhythmic dance, it suddenly seemed more wayward and powerful than it ever had from my stool at the side of the pattern mechanism. It was like trying to hold a ten-pound fish straight out of the water and the shuttle flew from my hand.

"Not as easy as it looks, Mrs. Thorel?" he suggested, looking pleased with himself.

I gazed up at him, but I didn't return his smile. "None of this is easy," I said.

He turned away from me then, busying himself with securing the lashes.

"You need to finish your master piece," I said. "I have been selfish taking up all your time. I just—"

Acknowledging something makes it real. It ends the pretense that there is nothing wrong with what you are doing. I still couldn't give that up—I couldn't finish the sentence.

"I don't care about my master piece," he said fiercely, turning back to me. "What are you saying? That you want to stop coming here?"

"I cannot stop," I said simply. "If you want this to end you will have to be the one to end it."

He seemed to find himself then, close down the person who had spoken to me so ardently, the man who had trailed his fingers over my skin and pushed the lace up my arm. "The silk will end this for us," he said, as if he were talking to a fellow journeyman. "We cannot just keep weaving. The gathering roller will only hold six yards and we have almost that already. I will finish this silk for you. Then it will be over."

ﻉ · ﻉ

Sara was turning down my bed when I walked in. She made a brief curtsy and said something under her breath, which sounded like, "There you are, madam."

I felt no need to explain why she had not found me in my room when she came to stoke the fire that now burned brightly in the hearth. Her whereabouts were the concern, not mine. I watched as she leaned over my bed and smoothed the sheets in an arc with her hand. Her belly pressed against it as she did so, preventing her from reaching the other side.

"Here, let me help you." I stood opposite her and stretched out my hand until it almost met hers. I swept upward, gathering the ripples of cloth and smoothing them over the side. When we both stood, we were facing each other across the bed.

She tried to turn away, but I said, "No, wait," so that she stopped, halfway toward the door.

"I know that you have been leaving the house at night."

She stood for a moment, then rotated back toward me. There was a slight jut to her chin as she looked at me.

"You go to Buttermilk Alley, where the journeymen live. Who is it you see?"

And still she just looked at me. I had expected denial and hoped for an apology, but her silence infuriated me. As if I did not deserve so much as an explanation after all I had done for her! A passage from the Bible came unbidden to my mind.

The Book of Ezekiel, chapter twenty-three, verse nineteen.

I marched around the bed and grabbed her upper arms. Although I blush to own it, I wanted to slap her, just to see if that would loosen the words from her mouth. I was surprised by my own anger. She had insulted our household with her disobedience and her immorality.

Yet she multiplied her whoredoms, in calling to remembrance the days of her youth wherein she had played the harlot …

I gave her a shake. "You must tell me, Sara." How dare she stay silent? How dare she walk out of my house at night as if it were her right to do just as she pleased? "Sara, you are with child. I can see it. We have to do something or you will end up in the workhouse."

I wanted to frighten her. I had every intention of helping her, but in that moment, I wanted her to feel the terror of life in the poorhouse to punish her for her brazen willfulness. And for standing there smugly fertile in front of me, when I was all but barren myself. Almost five years married and no child to show for it and this girl was ripening like a plum right under my nose.

Sara

With child. What a strange expression. Of course, I was with child. I could not have dug that creature out from inside me if I tried. It was with me every moment of every day, like a strange malady that never passed. As I became more lethargic, it seemed only to get stronger, pushing out my belly as if demanding to be acknowledged.

And now it had been. I could still feel the sharp dig of her thumbs into my arms as she held me, her questions confusing me, making me unsure where to start. The less I said, the more those thumbs pressed into my flesh. Then she became calmer, sitting next to me on the bed as if we were equals, holding her face in a look of studied patience.

"Are you?" she asked.

I looked up at her miserably and nodded.

"Oh, Sara." She shook her head and sighed, as if I had told her that I had ripped her favorite gown.

"Who is the father?" She feigned indifference, but there was an edge to her voice that told otherwise.

"I cannot tell you that, madam. You know I cannot."

She sprang up from the bed and stood over me. She was so tall that I had to look up at her, like a child being scolded.

"But you must! Is it one of our own journeymen? Who is it? Tell me!" She was most particular about knowing which journeyman it might be. I wouldn't have thought it would matter much to her. "Or are you meeting someone else entirely at Buttermilk Alley?" Her imagination was really taking hold now. "No matter," she said, almost to herself, "they should all be dismissed for their part in this." Then she paused, glaring at me. "And so should you be."

I stared hard at her, but her look was defiant. Did she want to see me hang? If she turned me out I would have nowhere to go. Mrs. Swann was like a hog rooting for truffles. She had her nose in every corner of this parish and the next. Without the protection of a household like the Thorels', she would find me and I would be up before the magistrate as quick as I could untie my bonnet.

Madam was pacing the floor. Her skirts swished as she changed direction abruptly when she reached the end of the room. She looked strangely threatening, with her face in shadow and the light of the window behind her. "You cannot keep the child. You must know that." She said it as if it were a fact, plain and unquestionable, like announcing that we would have mutton for supper. I had tried not to think of the fate of the creature that pressed against my flesh with its tiny limbs, of the moment I would sink gasping to the floor as God forced the sin from my body.

"You must give the child away." She took a few steps toward me and, as she became less silhouetted by the window, I saw the determined set of her mouth. "It will save the child from a life in the workhouse and you from your shame."

My belly clenched as she spoke, and the infant squirmed inside me in protest. I had accepted months ago that I was owned, like the pots and pans in the kitchen and the combs she fixed in her hair. But the thought that she had decided I should give away my child before it had taken its first breath flooded my veins with rage.

She must have sensed this as she came and knelt before me, taking my hands in hers. "You know it is the right thing to do. The child will have a better life."

Better than with me? Is that what she was thinking as she squeezed my hands in hers and looked up at me with her gray-green eyes. She was gentle then, like she was handling a fractious horse. I forced a smile as if I accepted what she said, but I did not. I felt her words like physical violence, as if she had reached inside me and wrenched the child out herself.

"But what if we were to be married?" I said. "We could give the child a good home."

"Married! If you were going to get married, surely you would be by now. Will he pay to support you and the child?"

"We have talked of it. I need to give him time."

She snorted and stood up. "I wish time was all you had given him," she said.

I could not bear to listen to her mock me. Why did she pretend to be above me when she had almost certainly taken a lover herself? She had enough of her own secrets that she should not be telling me what I could, and could not, do. "If you make me give away the child, everyone will know who I am and what I did before I came here."

Madam stood, staring up at the coving. Then she turned back toward me and said, "How would they know?"

"Because I shall tell them."

"Then you will destroy us both and your child as well. There is only one thing worse than a bastard, and that is the bastard of a whore."

Then she swept past me in a waft of lavender and privilege, flouncing out of the room to her cards or her sewing. I got up and continued making her bed, shaking air into her feather pillows and arranging them to her liking. As I was leaving, I caught sight of a bottle of pomade on her dressing table lying on its side. As I turned it upright my eyes rested on the drawer and the tiny lock, sitting keyless at its center. I tugged on the gold handle but it did not open. What lay hidden there in that dark drawer? A memento? Letters too scandalous to see the light of day? Before, I had hardly cared, but from that moment, I wanted to know everything she was trying to hide.

Esther

Elias closed the ledger with a thud. He rested his head in his hands, pushed his fingers up under his wig and scratched at his temples. I had been picking my moment to approach him and, until a minute ago, he had seemed good-humored enough. But now his jaw worked silently, and he stared down at the desk as if he expected answers magically to appear there.

Elias was spending too much time indoors. Perhaps he was as frustrated with the same four walls around him as with anything in that ledger.

"Husband, I wanted to talk to you about Twelfth Night."

He pushed away the ledger and leaned back in his chair. This was as much of an invitation to speak as I could expect.

"I thought we could invite the Ogiers, Mr. and Mrs. Arnaud, of course, and perhaps the Vautiers."

Elias rested his head against his chair and stared up at the ceiling for a moment. When he looked at me again, he had cultivated an expression of incomprehension. "The Ogiers, the Vautiers? Do you suggest that I should spend my Twelfth Night with someone just because we share a pew at church? Just because their wives accompany you to the workhouse with bowls of soup and neatly stitched shirts?"

I colored in spite of myself. I had chosen people whom I had thought he would be happy with, other master weavers, God-fearing Huguenots. Now he mocked me.

"And where, wife, will the money come from this twelvemonth?" He gestured toward the ledger. "Do you understand how hard it is to sell silk nowadays?" He let out a breath of exasperation and batted away the suggestion with his hand. "Of course, you don't. You are but a woman."

He picked up the ledger and tucked it under his arm. As he rose, he said, "We shall invite the Arnauds and no one else, and you will do all you can to use that pretty face of yours to get another order out of him."

He smiled then, as if it were all but a jest. I smiled too and nodded agreement to his wishes, but inside I thought of my silk: something precious and beautiful, emerging from nothing. Something mine.

༄ · ༄

The nurseryman had been right. By December the winter he had predicted set in. The frozen streets of Spitalfields became oddly silent, save for occasional children on makeshift sledges spinning, squealing, on the ice. Only the market was defiant, keeping the cold at bay with burning braziers scattered with orange peel and the hot breath of the livestock.

Stalls that had displayed flowers months before were now full of branches of bay, laurel, and rosemary. Holly and ivy, tied together with string, hung in bunches from the gallery. Sara and I linked arms, a gesture of necessity, not affection. The ground was slippery and unaccommodating to heeled shoes and low hems. When we approached the stalls, a man emerged from under the gallery, clapping his arms around himself in an exaggerated attempt to warm up. He smiled. "I can't remember a winter like it," he said to Sara, as he looked her up and down. She feigned indifference and busied herself inspecting branches for insects and wilting leaves.

My elder sister, Anne, had been born early in 1740 during a winter so cold that the Thames had frozen over, joining the two halves of London with an icy seam. She seemed never to feel the cold and I sometimes wondered whether that was why, just like babies born still enclosed in their sacs can never drown, protected somehow from the dangers the rest of us face. She would have been twenty-nine that winter.

Among the branches, wax dolls studded with glass dangled from string, turning slowly in the chill air, sparkling figures dancing endlessly through the twelvemonth, tiny apparitions of the people yet to be born and the people who are gone.

The decorations we bought filled the house. Each doorway was arched with laurel, paper flowers filled vases circled with strings of beads, and the mantelpieces were draped with holly. I did not usually go to such lengths to decorate the house, but that year the festive scene belied the tension in my home.

23

Sara

Madam thought herself a good deal cleverer than she was. I didn't bother with her pots of trinkets and jewelery: she would not hide anything there. Instead, I studied her person and the way she moved. While we dressed the mantelpiece—with great bushes that would surely start dropping their leaves all over the hearth the minute a fire was lit, and glass beads just asking to be broken with the first swipe of Moll's dusting brush— she fiddled with the locket around her neck. It was made of enameled gold and given to her, she told me, by the master on their wedding day. I thought it too large for her delicate neck and didn't care for it, but it could certainly hold a small key and that was surely where it was. She ran the locket idly back and forth along the chain as she surveyed our morning's work.

"It looks well, does it not?" she asked me. I nodded and forced a smile. I knew it would not be long before I unclasped that locket from her pretty throat.

Mrs. Thorel bathed more than anyone else I knew. I dare say she even enjoyed it. Near every week I had Moll light a fire under the coppers to heat the water. The morning after we decorated the house she was sitting in her dressing room, still wearing her nightgown, while a lively fire burned in the grate. I had asked Moll to make sure the water was boiling because of the bitter weather and it still steamed in the bowl on the floor at her feet. While it cooled I laid out a clean shift for her to wear and a petticoat to go over it. Then I put a pannier on the chair and asked her what she might like to wear. She chose the flowered tabby in cream silk. I remember because it was my favorite of all her gowns. While she pulled her fingers through her hair to loosen the plaits, I picked out lace sleeves for the gown and ribbons for her hair.

I always started at the top and worked down. I dipped the washcloth in the water and squeezed out the excess. I opened the cloth fully and draped it over her face, pressing the warm material down around her eyes and nose. Then I gently wiped her face and up around her hair, which darkened with the damp like the tarnishing of a copper pot. As I worked downward, I dropped the cloth back into the basin and slipped my hands around her neck. The clasp was fiddly and, for a moment, I thought she would lose patience and tell me to leave it be. But then it came open and I put the locket to one side. She leaned her head back and I gently parted the neck of her nightgown. She reminded me of an animal at the butcher, head bent back for the slaughter. I swept the cloth right down from behind her ear to the very top of her breasts then under her arms. When I had finished, I sprinkled lavender water into the basin and drew it up to her chair so that she could immerse her feet in it. She sat there wriggling her toes in the water while I tidied up behind her. Later, as I dressed her, I asked what combs she might like to put in her hair. Such was her interest in her appearance that she clean forgot I had failed to clasp the locket back round her neck.

She breakfasted from a tray in her room, then left to her sewing in the parlor. Once she had gone, I opened the locket. The inside of the top half was inlaid with a tiny scene of trees and flowers. The other side was mother-of-pearl and resting on it was a tiny gold key.

I went quickly to her dressing table drawer, wondering what I would find there. Letters and love notes, I felt sure. When I came to think on it, Madam had been taking "rests" in the afternoon of late, disappearing into her room with a headache or other malady and telling me she must not be disturbed. But how could I just leave her? What maid would not bring her mistress something to fortify her? I had stopped on the stairs once and turned to go back to ask her if I could bring her a piece of fruit or some soup, but I had seen only the sweep of her skirts as she disappeared up into the garret, drawn to that strange sound.

The drawer unlocked with a satisfying click and I pulled it open. There were certainly papers inside, but they were plain and neatly folded on top of a leather-bound book. I took out the top one and unfolded it. The paper was covered lengthwise and vertically with faint lines, and drawn over them were flowers. And every paper the same! Just drawing after drawing of plants and flowers in snakelike patterns across the lines. I almost ripped one up in disgust. Why was this worth locking away? Even the ledger contained nothing but lists of flowers, *Blackberry and Wild Rose, Holly and Cherry Blossom*. Was this the extent of her secret life? A few jottings on fancy paper?

Esther

"Husband?" I raised my voice as I tried to attract his attention. Elias was sitting across the table from Mr. Arnaud and they were in animated discussion. I will not say that they were arguing as I was so desperate for them not to be, on this day of all days. We had prepared for Twelfth Night for weeks and I wanted everyone to enjoy the festivities.

I waved Sara away with her jug of wine. Plainly Elias did not want his glass filled, if he did not care to acknowledge either me or her.

"The problem," he said, "is that some mercers are not above buying foreign silks imported by the East India Company. Do you know of anyone who would do that?"

Arnaud shifted in his chair. His girth had increased considerably of late and the heavy meal had done him no favors. "Of course not," he said levelly. "But it is not just the Chinese silks, or even the French ones. What about the Indian calicoes? They fill the hulls of the East India ships. Just pay the subscription and be done with it."

Elias set his jaw. "It's protection money and no more. I will not pay."

"Why not consider it a tax?"

"A tax? Of sixpence per loom? I own more than fifty!"

Arnaud shrugged. "You have reduced the piece rate, have you not? You can see why the weavers protest."

Elias' face flushed with indignation. "I have reduced the piece rate because the price that the mercers will pay for the silk has dropped." Elias gestured toward Arnaud with his glass still in his hand and wine slopped over the rim. "You care only for buying silk at the cheapest price, but we master weavers are trying to preserve the artistry of our craft. It cannot be rushed or cheapened." Sara grimaced and eyed the stain spreading through the damask tablecloth from where she still stood, jug in hand.

Arnaud clicked his tongue. "If you do not pay, you must be prepared for the consequences. These are not educated men. They think with their fists and I, for one, would not wish to pit myself against a mob for the sake of a few pounds."

How little he knew Elias. My husband would pit himself against the King for the sake of a ha'penny if he felt a principle were at stake.

There was no need for me and Mrs. Arnaud to sit watching our husbands turn Twelfth Night into a cock fight, so I led her up to the parlor. I sent Sara to bring us some hot water while I got out the tea caddy and unlocked it. When Sara returned, I saw Mrs. Arnaud watching her as she arranged the cups and set out lemon cakes. Once she had gone, Mrs. Arnaud turned to me and said, "How is your friend with the maid?"

I blushed. "But you know it is I."

"I had some idea," she replied, glancing toward the door as if the space Sara had just left had offered up my little secret. "Have you thought what you will do?"

I poured the hot water over the tea I had added to the pot and watched the leaves spin in the little currents while the water darkened. "I would like you to help me, if you would, Mrs. Arnaud. If we could place the child in the Foundling Hospital, it would be best ... for everyone."

"It's not easy," said Mrs. Arnaud, cautiously. "Girls in your maid's situation seem to be two-a-penny nowadays, unfortunately."

"But you said you know someone on the committee?"

"I do. Perhaps I should make the petition on your maid's behalf."

"Could you, Mrs. Arnaud?"

She nodded kindly and I poured her some tea. "What must we do?"

"Well," she said, dropping sugar into her cup, "we have to show the present necessity of the mother—that is, that the father has deserted her. Then, if the committee feels that taking the child will restore the mother in virtue, and an honest livelihood, they will accept it. Are you willing to guarantee she will still have a job after arrangements have been made for the baby?"

I thought for a moment. Sara was not the easiest of lady's maids but, despite our squabbles, I had grown used to her, even fond of her, like a shoe that had given me blisters but was now comfortable.

"I would, Mrs. Arnaud," I said, meaning it.

"Then her chances are good, and there will be the minimum of disruption for you. It is so hard to find good maids, isn't it?"

I agreed and offered her a cake. She bit into one and pronounced them very good indeed. "So," she said, finishing her mouthful, "provided your maid is of previous good character, it should be straightforward."

A piece of lemon cake stuck in the back of my throat. I coughed and patted at my chest until Mrs. Arnaud looked quite concerned.

"Previous good character?" I ventured.

Mrs. Arnaud chuckled. "Nothing for you to worry about, surely. Just that the girl is basically moral and decent. The committee needs to know that this was a temporary fall from grace. They do not help lewd women, Mrs. Thorel."

"What happens to the lewd women?"

Mrs. Arnaud looked grim. "They are not so fortunate."

Sara

While Madam whispered with Mrs. Arnaud—heads bent together as if I would not notice their hushed chatter—Mr. Arnaud did not care to keep his voice down. He belched out his opinions while the master eyed him silently, an icy breeze to Mr. Arnaud's blustery gale. But Mr. Arnaud seemed not to notice me. Clearly it had never occurred to him that our paths might have crossed in another setting altogether. Complete disregard: that is both the best and the worst part of servitude.

Once the ladies had rejoined the men, Madam asked me to bring in the Twelfth cake. Monsieur Finet had to carry it and even he struggled with its weight. Moll followed him, eyes cast down as was her habit, playing the modest serving girl, as if she were unused to being in such company and did not know where to look. I had endured this tawdry pantomime at Mrs. Swann's. I already knew how to fix a smile on my face as if I were grateful for the opportunity to stand shoulder to shoulder with Mr. and Mrs. Thorel, as equals for this one night.

Still, the cake made a magnificent centerpiece for the table, which was its purpose after all. I held my breath as Madam broke apart one of the sugar crowns on top and sliced through the filigree icing. She handed us all a slice and we forked it into our mouths, pretending that we were all quite comfortable to be eating together like this. As I ate, I noted each of the flavors I had suggested Monsieur Finet put in, the candied lemon and sultanas, laced with cinnamon, mace, and nutmeg. If nothing else went right this year, at least the cake was good.

"Ha!" said Mr. Arnaud, spitting his mouthful of cake back onto his plate and poking at it with his fat finger. "There it is!" He held up a small bean while Madam put down her plate to smile and clap politely. "Well done, Mr. Arnaud. You are the King of Misrule. Now, who shall be your Queen?" She looked round at us all, chewing like cows on our cake. Monsieur Finet and I had pushed the dried bean and the pea into the baked cake before we decorated it, just beneath one of the crowns, so that Madam knew exactly where to cut: then her guests would be sure of finding at least one of them in their slices. Otherwise—such was the huge quantity of cake we had to get through—it could well be March before it turned up.

And there it was, the pea sitting half visible in the rest of my cake. "It's me!" I cried, with slight enthusiasm. Madam was delighted. I knew she would love it if one of the servants was the King or Queen of Misrule. It gave her a chance to show off how little she really cared for class. We are all equal before God, after all.

Madam began to deal out the character cards facedown on the table. As if we needed cards to tell us who was Mrs. Prittle-Prattle. Madam mistook my quiet smirk for genuine enjoyment and beamed happily at me. While everyone busied themselves drawing cards and laughing at the prospect of being Toby Tipple for the night, she draped an arm across my shoulders and drew me to one side. She leaned her flushed face toward me and spoke, soft and urgent. "I just want to help you," she said. I could smell the wine on her breath and I wondered whether the arm still resting on me was for my benefit or hers.

"Come," she went on brightly, "you are the Queen of Misrule tonight. We shall all do your bidding. Tell me what you would like to do."

She was like a child, waiting for me to tell her what game we should play next. Over by the table even the master managed a smile when Mr. Arnaud drew Justice Double-Fee as his card. I dipped my shoulder, freeing myself from her touch. "I should like to keep my baby," I said in a harsh whisper.

Madam's face pinched. She glanced at Mrs. Arnaud with a little look of consternation that confirmed everything for me. While the master was selling silk, Madam had been busy peddling babies. She opened her mouth as if to speak, but before she could say anything I walked back to the table and clapped my hands.

"Why, Mrs. Thorel has yet to draw her card," I announced, indicating that she should take one of the few that were left. She glanced at the card she had chosen and pulled a tight smile, as if the night's merrymaking was already wearing thin.

I plucked the card from her fingers. "Ah, Mrs. Duplicity!" I said, suddenly finding I was enjoying myself. "So, madam, you must not tell the truth for the whole night. More than that, whenever anyone asks you anything you must spin them a tall tale, the most elaborate you can think of. Everyone, when Mrs. Thorel speaks, not one of us shall be able to trust a word she says!" I clasped my hands together and looked at her as if I found the very idea hilarious. Her mouth smiled back at me, but her eyes gave me a stony glare.

Esther

I had tried to keep separate my life in the garret, as if the sloping walls were enough to contain what was going on there. But it was seeping out into the rest of the house. Sara knew, I was sure of it. I had the sense of a book closing, time running out. The silk would not end this. Sara would do it instead.

It is painful to think that there will be a last time, even if that time marks a new beginning, an altered existence, our lives shifting from one form to another.

I had to see him. I needed to see the silk we had almost finished, not snatches of it hidden in folds as if it were something shameful, but stretched out to its full length. Touching it, knowing that it existed, proved somehow that what we had was real.

Bisby Lambert unwound the silk slowly, stepping backward until the other end pulled taut from the heddles, still owned by the loom. It hung in the air like a frozen stream, gently lambent in the half-light as if it were as sentient as the man who held it. The intense plum and the creamy yellow had been formed into perfect little images that traversed the width of the silk, over and over in a relentless repeat as if they were leading somewhere, until they ended abruptly at the naked warp. Cut off at their most exquisite.

"It's more beautiful than I could have hoped it would be," I said. The wind spat freezing rain against the windows, real life, brutal and unpleasant, hammering at our door. "Thank you."

"You made this happen, not me," he said. "You designed the house. What did I do but lay one brick upon another?"

"No, you are the talented one. Extraordinarily talented. Even my husband says that about you. You *will* be a master one day, I know it."

He began to roll the silk. "Do you really think that?" His voice was flat. The dusk had extinguished the blue from his eyes making him look unfamiliar. Even the silk was drained of its color as night fell. It was as if, here in the garret, we were just impressions of ourselves.

"You know I do. If that's what you really want."

"I'll never be able to have what I really want." His voice had a strange, cracked quality.

"Why not? You are a better weaver than—"

"I am not talking about weaving."

There it was: finally spoken. A candle lit, a door opened.

He came toward me then, leaving our silk behind him, stepping beyond what had brought us together. He left a space between us, a gap for me to bridge. I don't remember moving. Instead, the world shrank, everything in our lives concentrated into that one moment.

I cannot stop.

Our foreheads touching, his skin damp, despite the sleet driving against the window.

If you want this to end, you will have to be the one to end it.

His mouth alongside mine. The almost-taste of him, his sweat a salt-promise as I dragged my lips across his skin.

Then the cruel rasp of his breath as he pulled away, reason and sense dragged into his lungs and pumped though him. Our bodies shifting like lodestones, poles repelling.

The shame shocked me. Certainly his rejection, but more how much I had wanted him. How completely I had been prepared to set aside everything just for that one moment with him. It didn't matter that he pulled away. In that instant of connection, I had been reminded of what it was to love. Or perhaps I had never truly known.

Sara

I had not set foot in a tavern since I had left the Wig and Feathers, but one night in February I found myself approaching the Eight Bells alehouse in Spitalfields. It was unnaturally quiet for a tavern, being past the time that even the most sociable of drinkers might be found sitting at a table with a pot of ale in hand. John Barnstaple had told to me to come down to the cellar, and as I walked down the outside steps, I had a fancy that Nathanial would be waiting below and I would hear the *clip-clip* of Mrs. Swann's heels on the flagstones as she came to see who it was. Her eyes would saucer when she saw me: *There you are, you wretched, wretched girl! Call for the constable, Nathanial, and be quick about it!*

It was pitch black—as if no one had given a thought to setting a taper to a candle—but I could sense someone standing sentinel outside the door and make out the dull glint of a musket as my eyes adjusted to the dark. He tensed at my approach and the musket came up to point toward me.

"John Barnstaple bade me come," I said.

He lowered his musket and opened the door. Inside there was scarcely more light but I could see the shapes of barrels and crates of bottles lining the walls. At the far end there was a table, and a man was seated behind it. Others sat at either side of him, leaning their arms on the table and whispering into his ear. The cellar was lit in such a way that I could see none of the men's faces. They were just shapes and murmured voices. But I knew John Barnstaple by the set of his shoulders and the way he raked his hand through his hair. I knew him from his smell when I stood behind him, his salty sharp scent mingling with the warm nutty smell of the silk he worked with all day.

The men fell silent when I approached them, some gawping at me as if a woman were as unexpected as an elephant. "Miss Kemp works in the Thorel household," said Barnstaple, his voice low. "She will take the demand to Elias Thorel."

"Is it ready?" I asked him. The darkness and the muskets were not what I had been expecting. The blank, anonymous faces of the weavers scared me, and I wanted to get out of the cellar as soon as I could.

"What time is it?" asked Barnstaple.

"Time enough," said one of the men. "He's had his chance."

Barnstaple picked up a quill and dipped it into the ink pot. One of the men lit an extra candle and the paper in front of him became illuminated in a circle of light among the shadows. "What would you have me write then, Duff?"

Duff planted his fists on the table and spoke, his voice rough as carriage wheels over gravel. "Tell him we waited here until the agreed hour. Tell him that he has failed to pay the subscription required by our committee."

Barnstaple started to write, the scratching of his quill stopping and starting in time with Duff's gruff voice.

"Tell him he has one more week to pay his subscription and that if he does not …"

Barnstaple's quill paused over the paper, a bead of ink gathering at its tip. It hung there—a tiny threat suspended over the page—while he looked from one man to another. One stepped forward. "Perhaps we do not need to say more. It is enough to tell him that he needs to pay by the end of the week. He will come to his senses."

"King George will come to his senses before he does," said one of the others. A snigger rippled among them.

"We'll tell him," said Barnstaple, coldly, "that this is his last chance." I glanced around, wondering whether Bisby Lambert was about to step out of the shadows, but he didn't. I was glad he wasn't there. Standing between them, I would have felt as if I were in the middle of a thoroughfare with two carriages hurtling toward me from opposite directions.

The drop of ink from Barnstaple's quill fell onto the letter and bloomed, like spilled blood, over the paper. Barnstaple growled in annoyance and crumpled it, taking another. "We need say no more than this," he said. I read over his shoulder as he wrote.

Mr. Thorel,

You are desired to send the full donation of all your looms to the Eight Bells on Red Lion Street. To be levied, 6 pence per loom. This, from the Conquering and Bold Defiance

What had possessed me to come here? I had known that bad blood flowed between the masters and their weavers, but I had not expected this simmering resentment. I was risking so much. When Madam had found out that I had been going to Buttermilk Alley, she had yanked the keys to 10 Spital Square from around my waist and hidden them from me. I was no longer trusted to come and go from the house. A penny—which I had pressed into Moll's palm that evening—had ensured the door would be left off the latch when I got back, but no one could conjure me from my empty room if Madam happened to need an extra blanket. But even as these thoughts came into my mind, I knew the simple answer: I still hoped Barnstaple would do the right thing by me and his child.

"Will he pay, d'you think?" said a voice opposite me. When I looked up to see who had spoken, I saw that he was little more than a boy, his chin jutting and proud, his eyes gleaming with appetite for a fight. I had seen him before: it was Ives, the boy from that night at Buttermilk Alley. I knew him to be Lambert's nephew. What would Lambert say if he knew

Ives was in a tavern cellar in the middle of the night, plotting against Lambert's own master?

"He will, if he knows what's good for him." Barnstaple folded the letter, then picked up the candle and dripped a few drops of wax onto the overlapping edge. He had no seal so he pressed a shilling onto the wax, as if to remind Elias Thorel of what was expected of him.

When I got back, I took the note to the master's withdrawing room. His wig was next to his desk, placed correctly on its stand. In the light from my single candle the shadows played tricks on me and I could almost feel the smooth, faceless wood of the stand watching me as I put the weavers' final demand on top of his pile of ledgers.

Esther

I watched Sara's belly as if I were scanning the earth for signs of spring. But Sara was a slight girl and her infant looked to be no different. I gave her a draping shawl and she took to it like an old woman, wrapping herself in it, shielding herself from the household's curious gaze. She kept to my rooms mostly, and if Elias needed anything, Moll was sent. An arrangement that occasioned no complaint from anyone.

But, still, the birth could not be far away, and she had to agree what would be done with the child.

"Sara," I said to her, as she sat beside me, sewing, "do you know when your confinement will come?"

She said nothing, keeping her head bent to her stitches.

"It must be soon, surely no more than a month or two," I went on. "I'm worried that the weather is so bad that travel will be difficult. Perhaps you should go to the lying-in hospital sooner, rather than later."

She nodded slightly, then carried on with her stitches.

"You are very lucky," I continued. "Mrs. Arnaud has agreed to help us make a petition to the Foundling Hospital. Your baby will be well looked after there. He will be educated and learn a trade. Shoemaker or glover, perhaps."

She gave her thread such a sharp little tug that the material puckered. "My baby is not a foundling."

"It is a child whose mother cannot look after it. That is much the same thing."

She did not respond.

"Really, Sara, do you know how difficult it is to get a place there? Mrs. Arnaud says—"

"I do not want the Arnauds to have anything to do with my child."

Her vehemence surprised me. "Whatever do you mean? They are one of the most respected couples in our community. If it were not for Mrs. Arnaud's connections with the committee, you would not have the chance of a place that you do."

"Respected?" she almost spat.

"Listen, Sara," I tried to keep my voice measured, "I have promised Mrs. Arnaud that you will still have a position here if the Foundling Hospital takes your baby. Your child's place depends on it. Please don't make me go back on my word."

"You don't understand, madam."

"Then tell me."

"I met Mr. Arnaud before I came here."

"Really?" It wasn't that I didn't believe her, more that I thought she must be mistaken. I couldn't imagine how the paths of a girl like Sara and the most influential mercer in Spitalfields could possibly cross.

"At the Wig and Feathers."

I shook my head. "No, Sara, don't tell stories—"

"Stories?"

"They are trying to help us. We mustn't do anything to jeopardize that."

"Must we not?" Her voice was deliberately high-handed, mocking my own. "What if I told you that Arnaud is a disgusting old man who almost killed me because he likes to bake his bread in a cold oven?"

"I don't even know what you are talking about!"

She glared darkly at her sewing. "No, of course you don't. Why would you?"

"Sara, whatever it is that you feel, you must set it aside. D'you hear me? They *cannot* find out about you."

She didn't look up, but I saw her needle pause as it pricked up through the unbleached linen, heading a trail of spidery stitches. "What do you mean?" Her voice was airy with false innocence.

"The authorities cannot find out about your life at Mrs. Swann's."

She drew the thread slowly though the material. "And what if they do?" She was almost cavalier, as if it would be my problem, not hers.

"You don't want to know," I said simply.

I saw her blanch and, for a snatched moment, I enjoyed her discomfort. Then I heard a shout of rage from Elias' withdrawing room, the like of which I had never heard before.

26

Sara

I had already imagined Elias Thorel's reaction when he sat down at his desk and saw the note. The set of his jaw and the narrowing of his eyes. His finger sliding through the wax seal and the impatient search through the letter. And when he had read it, would he clench his fist and thump the desk so that the pile of ledgers jumped and slid? I imagined Madam coming in at just the wrong moment, chattering about reupholstering the chairs, until he cursed her trivial concerns and snapped at her to leave.

But it did not happen like that. Instead, he howled like a dog from his withdrawing room and Madam flew in there with her embroidery still in her hand. Even Moll was startled, craning her neck from the stairs to see what was going on.

"Who put this here?" he shouted at her. "Was it Lambert?" He sounded hurt, confused. Guilt crept across my skin in hot little prickles. I heard Madam denying it, saying that such a trusted journeyman would never do such a thing. "No matter," he said. I imagined the defiant shake of his head. "I'll see them all hang before I submit to this." There was a rustle of paper, as if he balled up the letter in his fist. Perhaps he brandished it under her nose as if she had written it herself. Then came the sounds of her trying to pacify him, soft murmurings as if she were speaking to a child, but he continued to rant until his rage burned itself out and he became like a fire in the grate, merely glowering unless disturbed, in which case he would start to crackle and spit again.

The strength of his anger took me by surprise. The unease I had felt in the tavern grew stronger, until it fluttered like a trapped moth in my chest. I could not imagine reconciliation between the men in the tavern with their muskets, and Elias fuming in his withdrawing room. And what of Madam and her little drawings? They had seemed mere trifles to me, just another way that a woman who has too little to do might amuse herself. But perhaps they were more than that.

Esther

At the broad part of Oxford Street there was a creaking sign—a pair of scissors painted bright gold—above a door that opened onto a courtyard. Mrs. Astley's French Warehouse was in the far corner, its plate-glass windows distorting the colors of the silks behind so that the shop front resembled a patchwork quilt. Many of Elias' silks were sold there—bolts of lustrings, satins, velvets, and damasks—lined up on shelves among the work of other master weavers.

When I opened the door, Mrs. Astley was rolling out a bolt over her wooden worktop and cutting it to the yard. The shop was unusually quiet. Often it was full of *le bon ton* fussing over her new wares. When she saw me, she put down her scissors and came over, tucking her hair up under her cap and smoothing her skirts as she stepped across the stone floor. She greeted me pleasantly, but she did not know me: it was Mr. Arnaud who sold our silks across London.

"A perfume for you, perhaps, madam?" she said, smiling. I caught the scent of violet, musk, and jasmine as Mrs. Astley waved her hand in front of a shelf of the latest French perfumes.

"Actually, Mrs. Astley, I am here to see your silks."

She nodded encouragingly. There was far more money to be made from a silk than a perfume. But I was not there to buy. I wanted to sell the silks I designed and to do that I needed to know whether fashion was favoring shades of pink or green or something else entirely.

She left me to browse and went back to her cutting, only glancing up at me occasionally, no doubt wondering when to time her sale. There were more than ten different silks on offer, all with designs much larger and less realistic than my own. It occurred to me that mine was something new and quite unlike any other silk you could buy.

Mrs. Astley appeared beside me. "Have you seen something you like?"

"They are all lovely," I said, "but none *quite* what I am looking for."

Mrs. Astley's gaze grew flinty. "I understand, madam. Come with me." She touched her hand to my arm and guided me to the back of the shop, ignoring my gentle protests. She ushered me through a door so low that I had to bend to avoid hitting my head on the frame. I went down a few steps and then I was standing inside a small room. The only light came from a long window high on the far wall. We were below street level and I could see the busy footfall of Oxford Street passing by the window and hear the jolt and clatter of the carriages. It was some kind of store room and the walls were lined floor to ceiling with shelves of wines, cordials, and jars of capers.

"Now then," said Mrs. Astley, taking a key from around her waist and unlocking a cabinet in the corner, "I think I have just what you are looking for."

She took out a pile of folded cloth and brought it to a table in the center of the room. She unfolded each square and began to lay them out. Soon the space was covered by sections of cloth with bold floral designs.

"Feel one," suggested Mrs. Astley, holding out the piece nearest to me. I took it in my hand. It was soft to the touch, but the weave was firm and neatly done. Up close I could see that the design had been printed, rather than woven into the fabric.

"Indian calico," said Mrs. Astley, her voice a loud whisper. So there it was: the pretty contraband fabric that was causing us so much difficulty.

"Where did you get this?"

"Best you don't ask me, madam," said Mrs. Astley. Then she took the piece from my hand and shook it out so that I could see it properly. "It's so light and delicate, isn't it?" she said, swishing it in front of me. "You could make a gown in time for this summer. Imagine how cool and comfortable it will be. And a fraction of the price of silk," she added pointedly, fixing me with that same flinty stare.

I bought some. Just a yard, printed with a bright pattern of a flower I could not identify. I thought it was important to have a sample for the sake of comparison. I could always make something with it later and take it to the poorhouse.

Mrs. Astley packaged it neatly for me and I left holding the parcel as I had not brought a basket with me. I was halfway across the courtyard when I sensed someone come up behind me. Then another man stepped out in front of me as if from nowhere. He had a tricorne pulled so low over his eyes that I could not make out his face, but it was clear from his clothes and shoes that he was a working man.

"Made a purchase, have you, madam?"

"What concern is it of yours?" I asked him, more annoyed than worried.

"It's every bit our concern if it's calico," said the other man, rounding on me and standing next to his companion. He had the same style of hat tilted over his eyes, and as I was trying to see his face, the other man snatched the parcel from my hands and ripped the paper apart.

"Ha!" he said, thrusting it back at me. I clutched it in surprise, my eyes searching the empty courtyard for someone who could help me. Then I felt something spatter over me.

"Calico, madam!" the men hissed in unison. I looked down and saw that the calico was soaked in a black liquid and my bodice was spattered with blotches of the same stuff. I tried to cry out, but somehow terror muted me and I stood there half gasping, half sobbing while the men laughed and ran off.

Sara

"It's just ink, Sara," said Madam, batting away my hand as I dabbed at her bodice with a cloth.

"What an awful thing to happen," I said. "Where did they come from?"

"I don't know." She seemed tired and exasperated. Her eyes were rimmed with red and she still looked tearful. Even her pale cheeks were peppered with tiny black dots. "I think they were waiting for me. They must know that Mrs. Astley sells calico and watched me through the glass. I'm sure there's only one reason customers go into that back room. What a fool I've been!"

I said nothing, but I knew enough of the Spitalfields weavers to think that she was probably right. I went to her wardrobe and chose a clean gown for her to wear. I would have washed her face and helped her to dress, but she didn't seem to want anyone near her, so I went downstairs to ask Monsieur Finet about dinner.

Then, almost as soon as the tenor bell had sounded, Madam came downstairs and claimed to have a headache. She announced she was

164

going to lie down and did not wish to be disturbed. I left her for a few minutes—she'd had quite a shock—but then I thought that a cup of sweet tea might be just the thing she needed to calm her nerves. I opened her bedroom door slowly, in case she was already resting, but the only thing asleep on her bed was the cat. I set the teacup down on her bedside table.

I knew where she was. Madam was a meddler who didn't know what was good for her. Just see what a mess she was in already! Any other woman would have been content as the mistress of a house like 10 Spital Square and married to one of the finest master weavers in all Spitalfields. But not her, I thought, as I climbed the stairs to the attic on the very tips of my toes. She always had to be more than she was. Just like her mother.

I sat on the top step beneath the trapdoor while I caught my breath. I could hear them inside. His low voice punctuated by her own chiming through. She sounded agitated. Whatever they were discussing, it would be worth listening to. I lifted the door just a crack. They were standing by the loom and the stained calico lay crumpled on the weaving bench. She seemed to be telling him what had happened as I saw her gesture suddenly to her bodice as if to say, *It went all over me.*

Then he took a step toward her and she was as close to him as I have ever seen a woman stand with a man who was neither her husband nor paying for the privilege. His jaw was set with rage but to look at his eyes, you'd have thought he might cry. He raised his hand as if he wanted to reach out for her, but he must have thought better of it as it hovered awkwardly until he brought it down again. "I'm so sorry," he said.

"Why? You didn't do it."

"I feel responsible. They are out of control."

She nodded grimly and turned her face slightly away from him. "I had not known," she said tentatively, "what they were capable of." Then she turned her face back toward him and said, "We cannot do this anymore. It's too dangerous. If the weavers found out ... if *Mr. Thorel* found out, I can't imagine—"

"No," he said, shaking his head, "don't say that. No one will find out. I promised you I would help you weave this silk and I will do it."

"It is not myself I am frightened for. If they would do something like this to me, think what they might do to you."

"I can handle the weavers." He was surprisingly abrupt, but she seemed not to care.

"I am scared of what might happen," she said. There was something about the pointed way she said it and in the way they looked at each other that told me some unspoken conversation was going on that no one could eavesdrop.

"The silk is almost finished anyway," she said, her voice gentle.

"It is not finished. I promised you I would see it through to the end, and I will."

"But I won't come here again," she said, so reluctantly you'd have thought each word had cost her a guinea.

His face twisted.

"Bisby, please."

Bisby? My goodness, what on earth has been going on? She reached out toward him, but Lambert shrank from her. Then he snatched up the ink-spattered calico and threw it hard against the wall. Ever so gently, I lowered the trapdoor.

⁕ · ⁕

So that was what all those pretty drawings were about. Why could Madam not stick to the matters that concerned her? The dinners, the embroidery, the gowns, and the books of psalms. Why did my mistress consider herself among that order of women who wanted to create art, not just wear it? Many might find that laudable, but not Elias Thorel. There was no mistress of silk in this house, only a master. And even if he could accept his wife's passion for silk, what husband could accept her spending time in an attic room with another man and no one but the mice and linnets to bear witness?

Esther

I went straight from the attic to my room and lay down on the bed. The cat opened a sleepy eye and watched me as I buried my face in the pillow.

I had no need to feign illness: I was as wretched as I could ever have pretended to be. I would not see him again. For months, each day, I had longed for those snatched hours in the garret and now they had been taken from me. I was left with my life as it had been before: Elias and Moll, endless sewing and a troublesome lady's maid.

I rolled onto my side and stared at the door. That was when I saw it. A full cup of tea I had not asked for on the bedside table.

"Madam."

A singsong voice. I opened my eyes.

"Mrs. Arnaud is here to see you," announced Sara. "Are you well enough to receive her?" She looked pointedly at the tea, untouched and stone-cold beside me. I nodded and sat up, smoothing my clothes and tidying my jabot.

When I got downstairs, Mrs. Arnaud was unfolding a tiny shift. It was made of white silk, turned slightly brown with age, and edged with pale lace. "It was one of mine when I was a baby," she explained, after we had greeted each other. "I thought it might do for the maid's child. Just something to send with her to the lying-in hospital. I presume she does not have much."

I was surprised by my deepening affection for this sincere and kind woman.

"Shall we tell her together?" she asked.

I nodded, and Mrs. Arnaud placed the shift over the arm of the sofa where it hung like a little ghost baby, reminding us of what we would have to do. We talked idly of other matters until the door opened and Sara came in. When she placed the tray of sweetmeats she was carrying on the table and saw the little garment, her expression became hawkish. I was grateful that Mrs. Arnaud was sitting, so composed, beside me.

"Miss Kemp," she began, "do please sit down." She gestured to the sofa opposite us, but Sara shook her head.

"We have some good news." Mrs. Arnaud's voice was kind but unapologetic. "The Foundling Hospital has agreed to take your baby after your lying-in. You will be able to return to work after a few weeks and know that your child will have the best possible future."

"How can it be best for a baby to be taken from its mother?" Sara's chin jutted out, mutinous yet wobbly, like a child's.

I rose from the sofa and went toward her. "It is for the best," I said, placing my hands gently on her upper arms. "It is hard now, but one day you will understand that."

She shrugged me from her. "I'll not do it," she said.

I was trying to be patient because I was well aware of the tragedy that awaited her, but she seemed to have no idea what Mrs. Arnaud and I had done for her and how fortunate she was. "Sara, believe us when we tell you that there is no other option."

"Believe you? Why should I? All you want is for someone to keep dressing your hair and darning your stockings!"

I pursed my lips. How could she do this in front of Mrs. Arnaud of all people?

"That is not true." I tried to be like Mrs. Arnaud and speak firmly. "We want only the best for you both."

Sara's gaze became steely. "No, you don't. You're just jealous!"

"What are you talking about?"

"There's not a child between the two of you, is there?" She was glancing from me to Mrs. Arnaud and back again, with a wild, spiteful look. "You want me to give up my baby because neither of you can bear the thought that I should have a child when you cannot!"

Mrs. Arnaud shook her head sadly. "Mrs. Thorel, this is really more than I can be expected to endure. I will have to leave you to deal with her." She gathered her things, rose from the sofa and walked out, letting the door close behind her with a dignified little click.

When I knew she had quite gone, I looked at Sara and slapped her so hard across the face that the sound rang through the room as if someone had dropped the fire irons onto the stone hearth.

28

Sara

I stood in front of Elias Thorel with Madam's slap still branded across my face. He seemed surprised to see me and looked beyond me toward the door, to see who else of more importance might be behind me. When his eyes finally settled on me, I pulled my shawl more tightly round me. The bitter weather had allowed me to spend the past few months shuffling around, stooped and covered, without raising eyebrows at my condition.

"I'm sorry to disturb you, sir," I said, curtsying as best as I could.

"Well," he said, "what do you want?"

I had found him in his withdrawing room, not the workshop. It was getting late and he was tired, settling into his high-backed chair and lacing his fingers together. His wig was on its stand and without his customary silk jacket, he looked as ordinary as I had ever seen him, like any other man at his desk in shirt sleeves and waistcoat. His commonplace appearance made me feel bold: he was not a master, he was just a man.

"It's Madam, sir."

"What about Mrs. Thorel?" There was an edge to his voice, impatience gnawing at the words already. But I knew he would want to hear what I had to say, and it was hardly my fault for telling him.

"I have noticed things, sir. She seems to be hiding papers in the drawer of her dressing table. I say hiding, because as soon as I come into her room, she locks them away."

Elias Thorel looked unconvinced. "She is your mistress. She can lock away what she chooses." He pulled his hands apart then and leaned forward.

He was telling me he wanted to get on, shifting closer to the books lying open on his desk and the quill with its ink turning dry at the nib. I did not have long. "Then there is the journeyman, sir."

A flicked-up gaze and narrowed eyes. I had caught him.

"Which journeyman?"

"Bisby Lambert. I have seen them together. Not that I am prying, sir, not at all. I was merely looking for her because she had said she was feeling unwell. I had thought to bring her some tea to make her feel better, but she was not in her room. So I went looking for her."

He frowned and circled his hand in the air as if to speed me on. "Well, where did you find her?"

I should have remembered that he is the most efficient of men and been more economical with my words. "In the garret."

"The garret?"

I might just as well have said the Wig and Feathers. There was no reason a respectable married lady would be found in either.

"What was she doing in there?"

I had his interest now. He was leaning forward, his forearms resting on the desk, smudging his careful columns of figures. "I'm sure I don't know. I can only tell you what I saw. They were talking, sir, but not normal talking, like she might talk to me. They were talking as if they were …" I chose the word carefully, "… intimates."

He looked grim. "And what of these papers? Are they letters?"

I would have loved to be able to tell him they were. A neat pile of scribbled sweet nothings, perhaps, tied together with a blue ribbon and smelling faintly of perfume. "I don't know, sir."

"Where did you say she keeps these papers?"

"In her dressing table drawer, and she is certainly at great pains to keep them hidden."

Elias Thorel held up his hand, silencing me with the gesture. He did not want to hear more. No matter, I had said enough.

Esther

Elias blazed a trail to my room. I ran after him, tripping over my skirts as I stumbled up the stairs, begging him to slow down and talk to me. I had no idea what Sara had said to him. I only saw him slam out of the withdrawing room, leaving her standing by his desk, eyes wide as if she had just held a flame to tinder.

When he got to my room, he went straight to my dressing table. He pulled on the tiny handle of the drawer, but it held fast. Then he took one of my metal combs and forced it into the gap between the drawer and the frame and pulled it upward until the wood splintered and the lock gave way.

He reached inside and pulled out a fistful of my drawings.

"What are these?" he said, brandishing them in my face.

"Just drawings." I clutched at the papers, but he held them just out of my reach.

"Drawings of what?" He began to look through them, still holding them high above me. I felt faint. My breath came in short gasps and the room began to spin. I sensed my world shifting with every drawing he looked at. Then he stopped and stood completely still. In that instant of pause I knew what he was listening for and I willed it not to come, prayed that he would not still be here. But there it was, his diligence and industry resonating through our house.

Elias flung the designs onto my bed and walked out.

I grabbed handfuls of my skirts and tried to keep up with him as he climbed the stairs to the garret. He lifted the trapdoor and pushed it open so that it fell back onto the attic floor with a bang. The pulse of the loom halted. Elias climbed into the garret and I followed, stepping into the flood of light that had become so familiar to me.

Even in winter the huge windows made the garret seem almost ethereal, otherworldly and separate from our humdrum lives below. But nothing about this place was to stay separate. When Elias flung open the trapdoor he connected this existence to my real life, tainting both.

Bisby got up from the weaving bench to face his master. He could see me behind Elias so he was watchful, on edge. But Elias rounded on him with a smile and an air of forced geniality.

"How is our master piece coming along, Lambert?" he asked. Though his voice was amiable, it still made Ives put down his lashes and hug his knees to his chest. "Well?" Elias insisted. "Have you finished?"

"No, sir."

"No? Why not?"

Elias approached his loom and inspected the gathering roller with a practiced eye. "There cannot be more than a few yards here. Not much, considering how long you've been working on it."

Bisby looked at me, a glanced betrayal.

"Oh, how rude of me," said Elias. "This is my wife." A heartbeat's pause, before the charade ended. "But, of course, you know that, don't you?"

Bisby was silent, offering neither truth nor lies.

Elias stepped over to Ives. "Stand up, boy." Ives jumped up, sending his pallet skidding out from underneath him.

"Please," I began, "leave the boy—"

"Have you seen my wife up here before?" asked Elias, ignoring me.

Wide saucered eyes, a trembling lip. Then a nod, the faintest treachery.

"Go on," said Elias, his voice gentle as a nursemaid's. "What does she do up here?"

"She brings us cakes, sir. And seeds for the birds." Ives looked up at the linnets as if their existence were proof enough.

Elias stared at the songbirds and let out a breath of exasperation. "Of course she does. That sounds just like my wife!" Then his eyes dropped to the other loom. He strode over to it and pulled off my petticoat, revealing a stretch of white brocade from the warp threads to the take-up beam. Meandering across it was the repeating pattern of buttermilk dog roses and the deep plum of the blackberries, a reminder of the autumn when Bisby and I had started making it. Elias stared at it, captivated not by its beauty but by its betrayal.

"What is this?" He had turned and was looking straight at Bisby. With every moment that he hesitated, Elias took another step toward him.

"It's mine," I said. "I designed the pattern and Mr. Lambert helped me to set it onto point paper."

Elias stopped in the center of the garret and nodded slowly. "And has he been weaving it for you?"

"Yes." Finally Bisby spoke, clear and emphatic. "I have."

"Finished, is it?"

"Almost, yes."

"So you have completed a silk for my wife, while your own master piece lies unfinished in the loom next to it?"

"Sir, I—"

But Elias did not want to listen. "I trusted you, Lambert. I invited you into my home and I allowed you to use my grandfather's loom to weave your own master piece. I wanted to help you become a master." His voice was increasingly incredulous until, right at the end, it cracked and my husband was laid bare in front of his wife, his journeyman, and a drawboy. "I tried to help you and you have made a fool of me."

"Mr. Thorel, I have not. I have done nothing."

"Done nothing? Weaving silk with my wife, in my own house, without my knowledge? While the silk I asked you to weave gathers dust? That is not nothing!"

It was silent in the attic for a moment, save for the rustling and scratching of the linnets. "Get out," said Elias, more resigned than angry. Ives shot toward the trapdoor, as if he could not wait to get away, while Bisby turned, then bent to pick up the shuttle and store it carefully.

"Was it you?" said Elias, watching him.

"Sir?"

"Was it you who put that note in my room?" Elias' voice wavered slightly, as if his words were fragile enough to be destroyed by Bisby's answer.

"I don't know anything about a note."

"The *demand*," clarified Elias, "from the weavers' combination. Sixpence per loom."

"I have no part in any of that," said Bisby.

Elias nodded. "An hour ago I would have believed you."

My husband and I were left alone in the darkening garret.

"Elias?" My voice searched for him, probed into the darkness for his reassurance.

"You have humiliated me," he said flatly.

"No," I breathed. "I wanted only to be part of what you do."

"What *I* do? But I have no part in this. You've done it all with him."

"Because you wouldn't help me."

"So it's my fault?"

"No, I'm just trying to explain."

"Explain what?"

"Why I ..." I let go of my breath as if I had no use for it.

"I'll be the laughingstock of all Spitalfields. You do know that, don't you? They will say that I cannot weave a decent silk so my wife has to do it for me."

"He will not say anything. He is an honorable man." Elias stepped toward me, resolving out of the darkness.

"Is he? But you know my journeyman so well."

I shook my head, a futile gesture.

"What have you been doing here with that man?" He caught hold of the top of my arm. In the moments I stayed silent, his grip tightened, squeezing the answer out of me.

"I told you, I intended only to design and weave a silk."

His thumb dug into my arm. "What happened that you did not intend?"

I shook myself free of him. "Stop it, Elias. I have done nothing wrong." Almost the truth. And truth enough compared to what he had done with our own housemaid. "Why don't you tell me what you have done with Moll?"

"Moll? The scullery maid? What has she to do with this?"

"You complain that I have spent time with Bisby Lambert, when you have had Moll in your bed!"

"What?"

"I heard you." I was unable to stop now, all the thoughts that had gone round my head for the past few months escaping. "I was outside your room and I heard her inside. Laughing."

"Laughing?" He mocked me with the word. "Perhaps I said something funny."

"It wasn't that kind of laugh."

"Then perhaps I just enjoyed seeing a girl smile. I can barely remember the last time my own wife smiled at me."

"It was late at night. What was she doing in your room?"

"Well, I don't know. Maybe I needed a blanket, or a warming pan. Perhaps she brought me more candles. She is a maid, after all."

"But she does not sleep in the maids' room!"

"According to whom?"

I did not answer.

"Ah." Elias nodded. "The lady's maid. The one who just told me about your secret patterns. Yes, she seems very trustworthy and, if I'm not mistaken, pregnant as well."

I felt foolish, confused.

"Is that what this has been about? Some petty revenge for what you imagine I've done based on a girl's giggle and the gossip of a shameless servant?"

"No. It's about me, what I want to do. What I have a talent for."

"You have a talent for destroying things, Mrs. Thorel. That is all."

29

Sara

From the parlor window I watched Lambert leave, a shape in the graying light, coming round the corner from the tradesmen's door. He shouldered into his coat and trudged along the pavement, hands thrust into pockets, the boy running behind him, trying to keep up. When they had left the square, I picked up Madam's embroidery hoop and put it away in a cupboard. When I could find nothing else to pretend to do, I went to her room.

She lay on the bed with one arm flung behind her head, her face half buried in it. Her skirts frothed around her legs. The pose was so dramatic, she looked like a painting.

"What have you done?" she sobbed, into her sleeve.

I came into her room and began to tidy trinkets that did not need tidying. I tucked a pair of tiny scissors and a fruit knife into their embroidered case and stabbed her bodkin back into the pincushion. Anything rather than look at her.

"Stop it!" she exclaimed. "Stop doing that."

I put the things on the dressing table and tried not to look at the splintered drawer beneath it.

She propped herself up on one elbow and stared at me. Her hair had come loose and hung down her back. The powder was gone from her skin. Everything about her was raw and exposed. Guilt was spreading through me, as palpable as the constant ache in my belly.

"He's gone. My husband told him to go."

"Madam, I had no idea the master would do that. I never wanted—"

"What did you think he would do when you told him? Do you ever think about the consequences of the things you say? Are they even true?"

"What do you mean?"

She stared at me intently, as if searching my face for answers to questions she hadn't asked. Then she collapsed back onto her pillows. "He knows you are pregnant. I have tried to help you, Sara, but you are determined not to be helped. Well, try to live by your own hand, if you must, and may God help you do it. You are destined for a life on the parish and nothing more! Make sure you are gone by nightfall."

She rolled away from me and buried her head in her arms. A sick feeling crept up from my stomach, such as I had not felt for months, and there was a constant dragging ache from the base of my belly to the small of my back. What had I done?

୬ · ଶ

I gathered a few of my things and left Spital Square as soon as I could. Flurries of snow caught in the pools of light from the windows of the houses lining the square. I walked through them, covering my head with my shawl and breathing into the small pocket of air to warm my face. I knew even then that something bad was going to happen. Disquiet seemed to trickle through the streets. Then there was the strange knot in the pit of my stomach. A twisted clench that made me stop every so often and lean one hand on an icy wall to catch my breath. When I felt ready to go on, I found myself hurrying, my bag banging and swinging round my legs.

As I turned left out of Pearl Street into Grey Eagle Street, I saw a group of journeymen walking toward me. I stepped back into the shadows and watched them pass. Each held something in his hands. I couldn't see what it was until one raised his arm to wipe his sleeve across his face and I saw the blade of a cutlass beneath his greatcoat.

I followed them to Buttermilk Alley. There seemed to be journeymen everywhere. The door to Bisby Lambert and John Barnstaple's cottage was open and more journeymen spilled into the street. They huddled in groups and spoke in low, urgent voices. I pushed past them into the house, dropping my bag near the door so that I could move more easily through the crush of men inside.

You might have thought that John Barnstaple was made of honey, the way the other weavers swarmed around him. He sat at the table and so many heads leaned in toward him that it was only when they parted that I could see what he had in front of him. Six flintlock pistols, laid out on the table.

He took one in his hand, cradling it almost lovingly, rubbing his thumb along the polished wood as he stuffed the muzzle with powder and shot. Once he had finished, he put it down and reached for the next.

"Where did you get those?" I said.

He looked up, surprised by my presence and the sharp concern in my voice. "What are you doing here? This is no place for a woman now."

"The pistols," I insisted, nodding at them. "What are you planning to do with them?"

It was a foolish question. Some of the men sniggered and exchanged mocking glances.

Barnstaple shrugged. "Thorel hasn't paid his subscription. The men won't put up with it any longer. It's time they made their point." He rotated the pistol to half-cock, then placed it next to the others. "We are all ready," he said.

Laughter swelled behind me. I turned around and saw Ives pushing through the other men toward Barnstaple. He carried a stuffed sack in front of him. It had been crudely gathered at the edges to give the impression of arms, legs, and a head. Scraps of silk had been stuck all over the body so that it appeared comically overdressed. Barnstaple let out a howl when he saw it.

"Ives, you've done a grand job there," he said, clapping the boy on the back so hard that the effigy's head lolled forward.

"What is that?" Lambert's voice cut through the boisterous laughter, silencing the men around him.

"Not so much what, Lambert, as who. Don't you recognize him?"

Lambert looked thunderous, but Barnstaple just laughed and grabbed something from behind him. Then he leaned forward and stuck it on top of the misshapen figure, now sitting like a baby on Ives' lap. "What about now?"

There it was again, the searing knot in my gut that made me grab the edge of the table for support. I let out a low moan. It was Thorel's hat. The elegant upward sweep of each side was edged with Persian blue velvet and a small rosette was secured to one side.

"Where did you get that?" demanded Lambert.

"No matter," replied Barnstaple. "He will not miss a hat by the time the mob has finished with him."

Lambert brought his hands down onto the table with such force that even Barnstaple jolted back in surprise. "Stop this."

Barnstaple rested his forearms on the table and pushed his face as close to Lambert's as a lover's. He had only to whisper his response: "Or what?"

"Or I'll call for the parish constables."

Barnstaple reared back, snorting with laughter. "The Petticoat Police?" He folded his arms across his chest and stared at Lambert. Slowly he shook his head. "You don't know much about the English mob, do you? It's not a dog I can call to heel. It's a force, like the tide or the wind, and it's coming for Thorel, whether you like it or not."

"Why are you defending him?" asked Ives, bouncing the stuffed Thorel on his knee. "He was unpleasant enough to you this afternoon."

"There's things you don't understand, Ives. You're just a child."

"I'm man enough to understand you're sweet on Mrs. Thorel."

Barnstaple sucked his teeth. "What's this, Ives?"

Ives sat up straight in his chair. Near every weaver in Spitalfields was packed around them, yet all eyes were on him.

"Thorel just gave him his marching orders for spending all his time weaving for Mrs. Thorel instead of finishing his master piece."

Barnstaple tutted with exaggerated disapproval. "Who'd have thought it of you, Lambert? Go on, Ives."

"Don't know any more. Every time she turned up, they sent me away."

A gleeful Barnstaple banged his hand on the table. The pistols gave an alarming jump. "You scoundrel, Lambert! You rogue!"

The other weavers laughed as if they were at an alehouse and one clapped Lambert on the back so hard he fell forward.

Then Barnstaple was serious again. "All the more reason for you to join us. So, are you with us, Bisby Lambert, or not?"

My hand went to my belly. The tightness had begun to ease, only to be replaced by a sickness that brought my other hand to my mouth. Something was happening to me. I edged closer to Barnstaple and put my hand on his arm. I must have been digging my fingers into him because he looked up at me in alarm. I bent toward him until my face was close enough to his ear for him to hear my words, even though they came out in faint gasps. "Please help me. I'm not well."

Barnstaple glared at me. "What would you have me do, woman?" he said in a savage whisper. "Boil some water and rip up a muslin while the real men go out for Thorel? Find a woman to help you." He pulled his arm away and picked up another flintlock, holding it with more care and tenderness than I could ever remember him showing me, and busied himself tapping powder from the flask into the muzzle as if I had not spoken. I turned and pushed through the journeymen to get to the door.

Outside I drew in a lungful of air so deeply it made me cough. I leaned against the wall, resting my head on the bricks. I tried to focus on the chill of them against my face. It was a connection to reality when my mind kept clouding and wavering, as it had on that first afternoon at Mrs. Swann's. Then I started to slip down the wall, sinking into my own skirts until a hand gripped me from behind and broke my fall.

And as I fell, I thought, *It must be him*. It must be him catching me because otherwise he has abandoned me completely.

Esther

I did not rise to take supper. It was all I could do just to sit up in my bed when Moll brought me a cup of sweet tea. She did her best to pat air into my pillows and settle me against them, but all she succeeded in doing was catching my hair and jabbing my back with her elbows. I let out an exaggerated sigh.

"Sorry, ma'am," she said. "Shall I close the shutters?"

It was evening already. I had been so preoccupied that I had hardly noticed the creep of the dark into my room. Now I wanted to shut it out, along with the thought that I might never see Bisby again.

I nodded and Moll walked over to the window. She stood there so long that I grew waspish. "What are you doing?" I snapped.

"There's something going on outside."

There was an edge to her voice that made me throw back the coverlet and inch my feet along the rug to find my slippers. I rubbed at my arms and tutted about the cold all the way to the window.

Spital Square wasn't empty. Despite the bitter weather and the late hour, groups of men loitered. Then more began to appear. They came from Lamb Street ahead and milled, directionless, in the center of the square.

"Whatever could their purpose be?" I thought aloud. Moll said nothing, staring down and chewing her lip. Then I saw someone hurrying across it. She was trying to run while clutching at a shawl slipping down from around her shoulders. Her gait was cumbersome, ungainly, as if she were carrying something heavy. Then she stumbled forward and fell to her knees, curling up like a woodlouse on the freezing street.

"Oh, sweet Lord, it's Sara!"

Moll and I collided as we turned at the same moment. I allowed her to go first and she fled through the door and down the stairs faster than my heeled slippers would allow me to follow. By the time I got to the front door, Moll was already out in the square bent over Sara, trying to help her to stand.

"Bring her in," I said, scattering snow flurries with my windmilling hand.

Inside Sara gripped the newel post of the stairs with both hands. She was panting after her exertions and, despite the cold, beads of sweat flecked her hairline. After a moment she straightened, keeping one hand on the banister. "They're coming, madam," she gasped.

"Who, Sara? Who's coming?"

"I've come to warn you."

"Calm yourself," I said, stroking the hair away from her face. The anger I had felt earlier had dissipated at the sight of her. "Moll will get you some water." I nodded at Moll, who set off down the hall.

Sara swallowed hard and stared at me with wide eyes. "The journeymen, madam. They are coming for the master."

"But Mr. Thorel is not here," I said. I did not want to tell her that he had slammed out of the house barely an hour before without telling me where he was going. "What business do the journeymen have with him?"

"It's the combination. He hasn't paid them their money and now the mob is out to get him. You must leave!"

A mob? Was that what those men wandering outside like sheep were meant to be? I almost wanted to laugh, but then I remembered the vicious hiss of the weavers who had thrown ink at me. "Come, Sara, you are upset. It's been a difficult day for us all. I will send Monsieur Finet out to those men with some soup and bread. They will go home when their bellies are full."

"And me, madam?" Her voice was small, like a child's.

I looked at her sternly, but how could I turn her out onto the street at this hour? "You may stay here till the morning."

We had not even reached the end of the hall when a crack rang out so loudly that it stopped us dead and made me grip Sara's shoulders so hard she yelped.

Sara

I knew they must be near when the pistol shot rent the air. I pulled myself away from Madam's terrified grip and went into the front parlor. Men were snaking through the streets, holding aloft lit torches, which gave the square an eerie glow and occasionally threw their faces into sharp relief. Madam came up behind me. "Oh, dear God," she murmured. We stood there, watching, but I knew we were not searching for the same face.

Then someone threw a stone. It hit the bricks near the window and bounced back onto the pavement.

"We must close all the shutters," Madam said. "Get Moll and Monsieur Finet from the kitchens. We can each take a floor."

I went to do her bidding, but as I moved there was a tiny pop, then a flood of warmth all over the inside of my legs. I took a few steps forward in surprise, as if I could walk away from the strange sensation, but each time I moved more fluid trickled out of me. My petticoats stuck to my legs as I walked. I stopped and turned. Madam was staring in horror at the puddle on the parlor floor.

She screamed for Moll.

When Moll appeared at the door, she was talking so fast that I could hardly follow what she was saying. Then she saw the parlor floor and the words evaporated from her mouth. She looked from the floor to Madam and made a silent O with her mouth.

"Moll," said Madam, her voice deliberately measured now. "We need to call for help."

Moll blinked back at her. "Help, ma'am?" Her voice wavered. "Who can help us now?"

"Don't you know anyone who has ever had a baby?" Madam clipped back.

Moll shook her head. "No, ma'am. The only babies I've seen born were to the cows back home."

"Mrs. Anstis," I said. They turned to look at me as if they'd forgotten I was there. "The widow at Coats Lane, she'll know what to do. She's a midwife and apothecary."

Madam looked relieved. "Moll, fetch Widow Anstis from Coats Lane."

"Coats Lane?" exclaimed Moll, clearly quite forgetting herself. "I couldn't get her from the other side of Spital Square. Have you not looked outside?"

We all turned and stared at the window, which was now glowing orange against the dark wall. For a moment I felt disoriented, as if it might be dawn before the night had even started, but then I realized that a fire was burning in the middle of the square. Madam marched to the window and slammed the shutters closed. As she slid the iron catch into place, there was a hammering at the front door. "Upstairs, quickly." She herded Moll and me, like small children, to her own room and sat me down on her bed. As I watched her close the shutters, I felt very strange. I was no longer in control of my body. Instead I was being carried along by something quite apart from myself.

I could hear Madam instructing Moll to boil water in the kitchen and fetch linens, but their voices seemed to come from far away. A pain gripped me, so intense that I struggled to breathe. I was floundering, my hands searching for something to grab.

Then Madam was there, her hand outstretched for me to take. I pulled down hard on her arm while she tried to hold it firm as my body convulsed in pain. When I began to resurface, I heard the banging start again on the door, only it became rhythmic and persistent until I could hardly tell it apart from my own heart beating.

Esther

Moll and I hovered by Sara's bedside. Every so often—in the moments that Sara was quiet—one of us would wring out a piece of linen in the basin on the washstand and mop her brow. Moll kept the fire burning brightly in the grate, with a pot of scalding water next to it. I had immediately called for boiling water but, once it was there, I hardly knew what I was meant to do with it.

Beneath the window the crowd was simmering as well. We had refused to open the door and the mob swelled around us, like turbulent water. I climbed onto my dressing table stool and peered over the top edge of the shutters to see what was happening. I was not the only one. Across the square, lights appeared in other windows, blinks of an eye as shutters were opened, then hastily closed.

A group of men had surrounded the fire in the center of the square. Suddenly they broke apart and a boy was pushed forward. When he came nearer to the fire I could see that it was Ives, frightened and excited at the same time, clutching something to his chest as a child might hold a toy. Then one of the men crouched in front of him and the boy clambered onto his shoulders. The man staggered as he got to his feet, and as Ives checked his balance, the thing he was carrying swung limply from his hand. It looked like a stuffed mannequin, or a scarecrow perhaps. Something had fallen from it. One of the crowd bent to pick it up and handed it to Ives, who put it on the thing's head. It looked more like a man with its hat on ... The blood turned icy in my veins.

Ives tossed the stuffed man onto the fire. It went up with a satisfying whoosh, which made the crowd cheer. Someone handed the boy a pistol and he pulled back the hammer and pointed it up to the sky. The mob quieted in anticipation as the fire spat and roared in front of them.

Nothing happened. Ives lowered his arms and peered down into the barrel, prompting someone to grab his arm and pull it roughly away from his face. The pistol fired with a bang and a spark of light, which propelled the boy backward off the man's shoulders and sent the crowd scattering. The same man who had pulled the pistol away from the boy's face helped him to his feet again. I tried to see his face, but he was swallowed into the crush of men around him.

Behind me Sara let out a guttural scream. I stepped off the stool and ran over to the bed. She was moaning like an animal, and Moll stood beside her wringing her hands, saying, "It's coming, ma'am, it's coming!" over and over. Downstairs a window shattered. For a moment all I could hear was Sara, then a creaking sound from downstairs, like the shifting timbers of a ship. The creaking turned to splintering as the shutters split apart.

I ran out of the room to the top of the stairs, leaving Moll wide-eyed with terror behind me. I could see straight down the stairwell into the parlor. Men were climbing in through the open window. Once inside they crawled over the room like ants, fingering the velvet of the cushions and stroking the backs of the chairs. One picked up an ornament from the mantelpiece and weighed it in his hand before slipping it into his pocket. One by one, they started coming up the stairs.

31

Sara

"Oh, my eyes," muttered Moll, as she fumbled with my stays to loosen them. I was just wishing that Madam had not left me alone with her when she flew back into the room. She slammed the door behind her, then wedged the back of a chair under the handle.

I wanted to ask what she had seen that had made her face flush and her hands tremble, but even if I had tried to speak, I would not have been able to. The only noise that would come out was an animalistic groan. Moll helped me to lie back on the bed and I rested there a while.

Madam armed herself with a piece of damp linen, then pushed up my skirts. Shame spread through me, hot and searing, like the pain. But I was helpless. I had lost control of my body and mind, and my dignity had disappeared with them.

There was a dog that used to roam around Spital Square. He belonged to Mr. Proby, a mad old merchant from the house next door. I think he used to forget to feed it, because whenever I emptied the kitchen scraps outside, there that dog would be, panting and slobbering all over them. It was a strange thought to come into my mind then, but I thought of that animal as I lay there panting. I couldn't stop. The racking pain had abated, and I was left in a strange limbo, the baby neither in nor out, myself neither awake nor unconscious, and strange thoughts of old Mr. Proby's dog drifting through my mind.

"Oh, sweet Jesus."

Madam's exclamation pulled me out of myself. She would never normally use those words. I raised my head a little and saw her staring down as if the Devil himself was clawing his way out of me.

"What is it?" Moll asked. Madam just gave a small shake of her head. Moll left off sponging at my forehead and went to stand next to her. She tried to hide it, but I could see horror all over her face.

"Oh, ma'am," she breathed. "I've seen this before."

"Before?" said Madam. "I thought you had never seen a baby born?"

"No, ma'am, the cows." She hushed her voice, but I could still hear her—there was nothing wrong with my ears. "Back home, before I ever came to London, one of our cows delivered this way. Nothing but the little mite's tail hanging out there was. Went on like that for hours until it finally dropped onto the straw in a sticky heap. The cow bent down and tried to lick the life back into it, but it never so much as opened its eyes."

All the time Moll was talking, Madam was looking at me. I held her gaze, between the panting and the groaning, and I saw her give that determined little jut of her chin. The one that meant she'd decided something that will happen, no matter what.

"We need help," she said.

Moll rolled her eyes as if she were talking to the village idiot. "Have you clean forgot that there is near every weaver in Spitalfields outside baying for the master's blood?"

"Monsieur Finet," said Madam. "Where is he? He can find someone."

"He jumped out of the kitchen window at the first sign of trouble, ma'am. And I'm beginning to wish I'd done the same." For an instant, the image of Finet heaving his great frame out of the tiny kitchen window filled my mind and, had my body not been racked again with pain, I might have laughed.

Madam came to the head of the bed and knelt beside me.

"Sara, who is the father? You must tell me, so I can go and get him. He must help you or find someone who can."

I couldn't have answered her if I had tried. In that moment, I could hardly think myself who the father was. Even the pain had begun to dull, receding like a wave ebbing back from the beach. I was taking leave of my senses. I searched my body for the pain, willing it back. It was the only thing anchoring me to this world.

Madam turned back to Moll. "You must go and find Bisby Lambert. He will help us, surely."

"Go and find him?" squealed Moll. "You cannot mean it, ma'am. I will die out there and no mistake!"

"And Sara and the child will die if we stay here doing nothing." I saw Moll's eyes flick down toward me and, even in my addled state, I knew what lay behind them. She cared not a jot whether I lived or died.

She leaned in toward Madam. "Would that be such a bad thing? I mean, what hope is there for a babe born to an unwed servant? We could save him, and he will still end in the poorhouse."

"Which is exactly where you will be if you don't fetch help."

Moll flinched as if Madam had clipped her ear. She should have known that if there was to be a choice between her and me she did not have a strong hand to play. She gave me a glance as she reached for her shawl. Words were beyond me, but I glared at her with a look that told her I would not forget what she had just said.

Madam pressed her ear to the door. When she judged that it was as safe as it would ever be, she unlocked it and pushed Moll out onto the landing.

Esther

Sara gave a low moan, quite unlike the screams of even a few minutes before. Her whole countenance had changed. She no longer looked as though she was even trying. The fight, like the color in her cheeks, seemed to have leached out of her. I brought a cup of water to her lips and bade her drink, but she shook her head and dropped back onto the pillows.

As I looked at her I was reminded of the first time I had seen her outside the Wig and Feathers. I heard the same voice in my head telling me to walk away. What would my life have been like if I had done just that? What if I sat on the edge of the bed now and did nothing more to help her? Sara was as cantankerous as a crab, but there was something about her that had always drawn me to her. I went to the pot by the fire and dipped a muslin into the hot water. Then I wiped my hands with the steaming cloth.

Sara had started to pant again, but her breaths were ragged, coming out as little gasps followed by periods when I thought she had stopped breathing altogether. I looked again at the infant's foot protruding from her. The other seemed to be tucked beneath him, as if he were scrabbling to climb back inside. In the few minutes that had passed since Moll left, the foot had started to turn gray and waxy. Even if Moll managed to find Bisby, there was no time to get help now.

"We are going to get him out, Sara." My voice was firm, the same voice I had used countless times before, telling her which gown I wished to wear or when dinner should be served. She did not respond, but it did not matter: I was telling myself as much as her. I reached up to that crumpled little foot and tried to grab the ankle. Then Sara gave a piercing cry and I could feel her try to expel the infant from her. At the same time there was a frantic rattling at the door. Was it Moll come back, or one of the rioters trying to get in? I waited for Moll to call out if it was her, but then the door handle stopped twisting and everything was quiet, save for Sara's ragged breaths.

I worried at the baby's bent leg again as Sara pushed, and suddenly it came free. I cried out in delight as more of the child slid out, readying myself to catch it. But it stopped halfway out with its little arms still inside. There was no way that the baby's head could be born with the arms alongside it.

I felt tears of frustration prick my eyes and I swiped the back of my hand across my face. Sara must not see me cry, I chided myself. I must try harder. When my sister had been in childbed, the midwife had not given up so easily. She had pulled and twisted at the creature inside Anne as if she was uprooting borage from the garden. I was scared to hurt Sara, but when I looked at her clammy face, her gray pallor against the white of my pillows, I took a deep breath and held that tiny body more tightly. Then I twisted it round, hoping to slide the arms away from its ears. Sara cried out, but I kept twisting. I hooked one finger up as far as I could and felt for the little arm. When I found it, I curled my finger around it and pulled it down. Then I twisted the baby in the opposite direction to dislodge the other arm. I felt around for that arm too and managed to slide it out.

"Sara," I said, supporting the infant in my hands. "Try again, we are almost there." But she was silent, so silent that I could hear a great clattering of hooves in the square outside and the distant sound of a bugle.

"Sara," I said, through the tears now rolling freely down my cheeks, "it's over. The King's men must be here—I can hear them."

I saw Sara open her eyes, then close them again. I was losing her. I might have been gripping the new life she had produced tight in my hands, but she herself was slipping away from me. In the distance, I heard the bugle sound again. I fancy that Sara might have heard it too, as her body tightened again and then that little child came away from its mother and into my hands.

It was bloody and greasy as a Christmas bird covered in goose fat. I thought it would slither right out of my hands as I turned it over and slapped it. The baby gave an indignant mewl, proving itself as outraged by the slap as its mother had been earlier that day. I took my fruit knife from its little jeweled case and used it to cut the last rubbery bond connecting Sara to her new child. Then I wrapped the baby in clean linen and handed it to Sara, who was looking around her with almost the same questioning gaze as her newborn.

I left them for a moment and opened the shutters to see what was going on outside. The square was swarming with mounted cavalrymen and foot soldiers. They were looking around them as if unsure what the fuss had been about. Most of the would-be rioters had disappeared, slipping down the side streets at the first sound of a bugle, no doubt. The soldiers were rounding up anyone left and loading them into carts. And in the center of the square, Elias was mounted on a horse, tugging back on the bridle to quiet the panting animal as its breath clouded in the cold dawn. Then our own front door opened below me and two men came out, each with one arm bent behind his back, marched along by a soldier. The relief curdled in my stomach as I saw one of them was Bisby. When they got near the cart, the soldiers pushed both men up into it and signaled for the driver to move off. I watched them go, their forearms resting on their knees and their bent heads dipping as the cart jolted over the cobblestones.

32

Sara

I stared down at the tufts of matted hair on the baby's head. The puffy eyelids fused by a line of tiny lashes, the traces of my own blood left from when we were still one person. The little mouth opened to show blunt pink gums and the baby started to mewl.

"You must feed her, Sara." Madam was sitting on the edge of the bed, watching me gaze at my newborn. The shutters were wide open behind her and the wintry sunlight flooded into the room, haloing Madam's reddish-gold hair around her face.

"Her?"

Madam smiled. "Yes, her."

Balled fists began to battle with the linen as the baby's cries grew more insistent and she began to root blindly, like a mole. She made me ache for her.

"How long have I been asleep?"

"A few minutes," said Madam. "Moll has gone for Mrs. Anstis, but in the meantime we must do what we can on our own." She leaned forward and loosened the ties of my shift. I sat there mute and passive as a child while she helped me hold the baby to my breast. This was the woman who had seemed unable to lift so much as a powder puff to her own face. This was the woman who had turned from the sight of her own bloodied shifts each month.

I did my best to feed the baby. She tugged at me in frustrated bursts and pounded me with her little fists until she fell asleep. It was then that the previous night pieced itself together. I looked at Madam and saw the strain etched on her face.

"What happened last night?" I asked.

She swallowed hard and turned her face away from me.

"They took him away," she said. "The King's men came and arrested Bisby Lambert and another weaver. I don't know where they were taken."

"And the master? Moll? The house?"

"Shush, Sara," she said, placing a hand on my arm. "Rest until Mrs. Anstis gets here."

She left then, slipping out of her room as if I were the lady propped up on feather pillows. I allowed myself to sink into them and feel their softness against my back. I wriggled my toes under the downy coverlet and enjoyed the sight of the fine houses of Spital Square out of the window. It was a moment of borrowed time. I was snatching at a life that was not mine. Soon it would be taken from me, like the child pressed against my chest.

Esther

I walked through the house as if it belonged to someone else. The parlor was the worst. The window was smashed and the shutters split from the walls. Workmen had already arrived and were busy fitting wood panels over the empty frames to keep out the bitter cold. The room was so altered that it took me a moment to see what was missing. A vase my mother had given me, some silver plate and even an occasional table must have disappeared out of that yawning gap last night. Someone had punched right through Elias' favorite painting over the hearth so that a flap of canvas now flopped over his ancestor's face.

The damage in the rest of the house was not too bad. Once Moll had cleaned everything and the broken windows had been replaced, we would be able to put this behind us. I could not believe that Bisby had been part of this petty looting. Once tempers had calmed, he could help us find who was responsible and then he would be released. I sat down heavily on the stairs. I was feeling the beginning of relief, and with it came a wave of tiredness that made my legs buckle beneath me.

☙ · ❧

The last place to look was the garret. Nothing could have happened up there and I had decided not to climb the rickety stairs, when I heard footsteps thudding above my head.

As I lifted the trapdoor, Elias loomed toward me, a sinister shadow against the pale long lights.

"There you are," he said. "Where have you been?"

"Helping Sara Kemp with the baby."

Elias drew his lip into a sneer. "Waiting on your own maid? By God, the world really did turn upside down last night. I hope she is out on the street now."

"Husband," I said, putting a hand on his arm, "we cannot do that. They have nowhere to go and it is so cold. I beg you to let them stay a short while." I searched his face for some flicker of compassion.

"Did you know about the child?" he asked, accusing.

"I had thought she would be at the lying-in hospital before it arrived."

Elias glared at me. "So you did know. What in God's name has been going on under my nose these past months?"

"She will be gone in a few days. The lying-in hospital will take her as soon as she is strong enough to move."

I had expected him to glower at even that small inconvenience, but he did not. Instead he said something almost more surprising than anything else that had happened that night. "No," he said. "Keep her here. Much went on last night and I may yet have a use for her."

I had no idea what he meant, but such was my fatigue that I did not probe him further.

"The damage is not as bad as I feared," I said, my voice falsely bright.

"Not bad?" He turned my words into a question, incredulous. "Those journeymen will hang for what they have done to me."

"For smashing a window and stealing a vase?" My tiredness was getting the better of me. I had spent the night with Sara as she and her baby hovered between life and death. Everything else now seemed trivial. Elias' face hardened.

"No, Mrs. Thorel, not for that. For this."

He stood back and I could see the loom behind him. Bisby's master piece hung in ragged shreds from the heddles, like badly cut hair, and the layers of silk had been cut right through with a single slash running from one end of the roller to the other.

Elias seemed to be enjoying my reaction. "You see," he said, nodding at me, as if it were obvious that I must. "Silk cutting is a hanging offense, so he will go to the gallows."

"Who did this?"

Elias smiled. "Your dear friend, of course, Bisby Lambert. He was caught up here by the King's men, the cutlass still in his hand."

Fatigue clouded my thoughts and made everything seem illusory. I wrapped my arms around myself as if I were cold, but really I sought to protect myself from Elias' words.

"Why would he do that? His own master piece!"

"But it wasn't, was it? From the moment I turned him out it was never going to be his master piece. It belonged to me, woven on my loom, with all the thread paid for by me. He destroyed it out of vengeance when he knew his chance to be a master was gone!"

"But another weaver was taken away with Lambert. I saw them. It must have been him."

"That would please you, wouldn't it?" said Elias, stepping closer to me. I tried not to, but I couldn't help tightening my arms across my chest. "Mrs. Thorel, I don't care which of them cut my silk, but I care very much which one hangs for it."

Then he left, already shouting instructions to the workmen from the top of the stairs. When he had gone I turned slowly toward the back of the room. I hardly dared look at the loom in the corner, but when I did I saw the pale silk stretch undamaged from the warp to the take-up beam, as glorious as it had been the day before. Whatever had gone on last night, my own silk had been left intact, bearing silent witness to whatever else had happened.

33

Sara

Madam put an old cradle in my attic room and banished Moll to the cubbyhole behind the stove. The cradle was made of oak, with delicate scrolls carved around apples, cherries, and flowers. All symbolizing new life and fruitfulness, although perhaps not the fruitfulness of an unwed maid. I wondered whether Madam had ever imagined that the bastard of a whore would lie there instead of her own child. Still, my baby looked bonny in it, swaddled into a little white tube, like the larva of some strange insect. I left her there sleeping and went downstairs to the kitchen to eat.

Moll and Monsieur Finet were there, busy clearing up the Thorels' dinner. I ignored their reproachful glances and went to cut myself some bread. Moll picked up a platter scattered with pie crusts and pieces of ham fat, then blew out her cheeks.

"Is that too heavy for you?" I asked.

"Nothing I couldn't manage with a bit of help," she muttered, then set about scraping the scraps into a bucket while the cat rubbed hopefully round her skirts.

Monsieur Finet finished wrapping the leftover pie, then went to put it away. "You'll be finding somewhere else to live soon, I suppose," he said, into the cool darkness of the larder.

"Is Moll moving on, then?" I asked drily, when he turned. Moll glared at me and Finet clicked his tongue in annoyance. I refused to take their bait. Why should I be the one to leave? How many times had Moll betrayed her mistress and laughed as she did so? What kind of loyal member of the household had Monsieur Finet proved to be when he ran up the steps in the wet kitchen and rolled out of the window, leaving three women to fend for themselves against a mob? But I knew better than to hold up a man's failings before him. I had learned that at Mrs. Swann's. So I just smiled at Monsieur Finet and cut myself a slice of cheese from the leftovers.

Moll wiped her hands on a dishcloth and sat down next to me at the kitchen table. I had not left the house in days. Much as I didn't want to make her feel any more important than she already did, I relied on her for information.

"What news of Bisby Lambert?"

Moll smiled. "Why are you so worried about him? Don't you know who was arrested with him?"

"Who was it?"

My voice was urgent, but Moll relished the moment, taking the opportunity to brush some crumbs from the table before she said, "Why, it was your friend John Barnstaple. They're at Newgate jail, I'm afraid, and from there they'll be going to the gallows." Moll gave a little stretch and a delicate yawn. "Unless Newgate kills them first."

I turned away from her and jabbed at some ham with my fork. I thought of Barnstaple with his flintlocks and rash words. Look where they had landed him. In Newgate. I did not feel sorry for him, I felt angry that he had cared more for his cause than he had for me and our child.

I didn't want to carry on talking to Moll, but she seemed reluctant to leave me to my dinner. There was something sly about her pretty, pointed features as she watched me eat.

"They won't let you keep it, you know."

The cheese curdled in my stomach.

"I heard Madam talking to Mrs. Arnaud. The Foundling Hospital can't be doing with feeding their babies pap through a cow's horn. They need you to feed it, but once it's weaned they'll still take it away."

For the past few days I had been left alone with my baby. That little attic had become womb-like, protecting us from the grim reality that I was no more than wet nurse to my own child.

"The baby's crying," I said, although it was silent in the kitchen save for the sound of the clock on the mantel and the lazy purr of the tomcat. I scraped back my chair and took my plate to the dresser. Out of the corner of my eye, I saw Moll glance at Finet and smirk.

Esther

The turnkey grinned as he unlocked a huge wooden door run through with metal bolts. "Been here before?" he asked, as his keys jangled in the numerous locks.

I shook my head, mute with apprehension.

"Prepare yourself," he said. "It ain't pretty in there."

But nothing could have prepared me for what I saw as the heavy door swung open to reveal Newgate jail. Straight ahead of me was a narrow corridor running parallel to the enclosure for the male felons. I tried to keep my eyes straight ahead as I followed the turnkey, but I could still see them. Hundreds of men packed into one vast room, shouting and calling to each other, unkempt and emaciated. I fumbled in my sleeve for my lavender-scented handkerchief and held it against my face, but still every human stink imaginable crawled through that thin material. Wild faces appeared alongside me, pressed like lunatics against the bars, calling sweetly to me, then laughing and fading away. Their screams and moans burrowed into my head, like woodworm.

At the end of the corridor two metal grilles, spaced a good yard apart, separated me from the inmates of Newgate jail. I stood behind one and waited. The turnkey disappeared through another door into the throng of the enclosure. After a minute or two, I saw him walking toward the inmates' side of the partition with Bisby. How altered he was. How different from the man who had sat with me all those evenings, so in command of the loom. Close up to the partition, his face was like a jigsaw puzzle, hatched by the bars of the grille and put back together into some tragic semblance of himself.

"You shouldn't have come," said Bisby. "This is no place for a woman like you."

"But I wanted to. I needed to."

"Does Mr. Thorel know you are here?" He was practically shouting, but still I could barely hear him. I said nothing, letting my silence be sucked into the chaos of Newgate.

"Please go," he said. Then he turned as if he would walk back into the melee of humanity behind him.

"No," I shouted, gripping the bars and rattling them in furious frustration. "Don't walk away from me. You owe me that much." It was an extraordinary display. Anywhere other than in that place, it would have stopped people in their tracks and prompted whispers behind fans. But inside Newgate every human emotion was laid bare. I could have screamed from the rafters and my cries would have floated like dust into the pit below.

But it stopped him. He rotated back toward me and placed his own hands on his side of the grille.

"What do you want from me?" he asked, his voice cracking.

"I want the truth," I said. "I want to know what happened that night in the garret."

"I didn't cut the silk, Esther. You must know I didn't."

I nodded, kept nodding, because I wanted him to know I believed him and there was no other way to tell him among the sickening clamor of that foul place. "Bisby, you must tell them who did it. If you do, they will set you free."

Bisby smiled, a wry, futile smile, then shook his head. "If only it were that simple."

"What do you mean? Just tell them!" I was shouting again, but Bisby was being pushed to the side by other inmates. On my side of the grille, mothers and wives of incarcerated men were jostling for position, forcing me backward. I lifted my hand to him in a final gesture and he tried to lift his in return, but heavy chains circled his wrists. In a moment, he was swallowed into Newgate's teeming belly.

⌇ · ⌇

The keeper of Newgate looked at me over his spectacles. He was a large man and gave the impression of having sat there so long he had expanded into his chair. I wondered how quickly he might be able to get up again.

"He is in chains," I said. "He does not have enough to eat. How can this be right? Please take the chains off."

The keeper swiped his spectacles from his nose and rubbed at his face. When he had put them back on he regarded me with a bored expression. "There is a fee for the easing of the irons, just like everything else."

"A fee?"

"There is a fee for everything. If you don't pay, you stay in chains in the main enclosure."

A thought occurred to me. I had not seen Barnstaple in chains among that pitiful throng.

"Where is John Barnstaple being held?"

The keeper sat back in his chair, and let out an exasperated breath, which clouded the bottom of his spectacles.

"Now I cannot tell you that, can I, Miss?"

"It's Mrs., and why not? Is there a fee for that too?"

The keeper chuckled and leaned toward me, putting his elbows on his desk and steepling his hands under his chin. "I see you're beginning to understand how things work here."

I searched in my skirts for the drawstring purse that hung from my waist. Inside there was about three shillings. A shilling for each of the things I was going to ask him to do.

"Here," I said, pushing the money toward him. "I want you to tell me where John Barnstaple is, and I want you to take Bisby Lambert's chains off and give him a good meal. Is that enough?"

The keeper eyed the coins. Then he twisted his mouth and looked at me. He nodded. "It's enough …" he said.

I sighed in relief.

"… for this week. You'll have to bring more next week." He cupped his fat fingers together and reached for the coins.

I put out a hand to stop him. "John Barnstaple?"

"Ah," said the keeper. "He seems to have his own benefactor, although not, I should say, one as fetching as you." He grinned at me, then gave his hand a flick as if dismissing the importance of his own information. "He has his own room and regular meals."

"Who pays for the room?"

"That, ma'am, I couldn't tell you. Even for a fee." He put his hand over the coins and slid them off his desk.

34

Sara

My daughter completed me. When I put her to my breast it was like fitting a lid to a pot or stopping a bottle with a cork. We were connected. Airtight. This was my purpose now. For as long as I fed her, she would stay with me. But I could not bring myself to name her. A name is ownership and she was not mine to keep.

I cradled her with one arm and with my free hand made little swirls out of her impossibly fine hair. It was darkening already, turning an earthy brown. It was the same color as the mice that crept out of holes in the skirting board into a room so quiet they thought it was empty. Nothing from the outside world reached us in that little room. Even the endless chatter of the loom had quieted since Bisby Lambert had been arrested. In those moments, I dreamed that we could stay like that forever, but the fantasy was as fragile as the tiny fingers that pawed and kneaded at my flesh as the baby suckled.

"*Rock-a-bye, baby, On the tree top …*" I sang softly.

Until the baby is weaned. That is what they have told me. I had spent weeks with nothing to look at save the almost translucent whiteness of my own breasts and my daughter's midnight blue eyes beyond them, fixing me with an unblinking stare.

"*When the wind blows, The cradle will rock ...*" The baby's eyes were closing, the tiny lashes fluttering as she sucked.

She was already needing me less. Madam had started expecting me to be there to dress her in the morning, to clean her and help her into bed at night. As if I now wanted to do that for any human being other than my daughter. And all the while, the existence of my child hovered between us, unspoken amid the chatter about dinner and gowns and church.

"*When the bough breaks, The cradle will fall ...*" I was still singing even though she was asleep. I stroked her cheek with the back of my finger until she started sucking again.

No one told me exactly when I would have to give up my child. I carried on as before, sweeping and sewing and cooking, then escaping up to her when I could. It was easy to pretend that this could go on forever, but how long is a mother alone enough for her child? Weeks or months? A day of reckoning was coming, even as I sought to ignore it. Not just for me, for us all.

"*Down will come baby, Cradle and all.*"

Esther

"The blue, perhaps? Or the green?"

I stood in front of Elias with a sheet of wallpaper over each arm. I raised each in turn, trying to interest him in either the green flock with a pattern of stylized flowers, or the blue and white hand-blocked chinoiserie. The riot had provided the ideal opportunity to redecorate the parlor—if only Elias would make a decision.

"By God, woman, can't you see I'm busy?"

His anger took me by surprise. Even for Elias it was an uncharacteristic outburst. I lowered my arms. The wallpaper hung over them like ridiculous sleeves, making me feel even more foolish.

Elias sighed and put down his quill. He glanced over at both the sheets then said, "They are both lovely. I would be happy with either and so really it is your decision."

I nodded, but he had already picked up his quill and bent back to the page, which he was rapidly filling with words. What was there to write about silk that would fill pages?

"What preoccupies you, husband?"

"The trial," he said flatly, without looking up.

"What trial? Why have you not told me about this?"

"Because, Mrs. Thorel, I do not bother you with the concerns of men. Unlike you, who seems to think that I should be involved with the trivial matters of women." He gestured toward the wallpaper and a small drop of ink landed on his page. He tutted and blotted angrily at it.

"When is the trial?"

"Next week, so clear your days of wallpapering as I expect you to attend. The whole household must be *seen* to be there with me." He was looking right at me now, searching my face for any kind of reaction. But I had learned to paper over my emotions as if they were the parlor wall.

"You might even enjoy it," he continued, putting his quill down and leaning back in his chair. "Most of Spitalfields will be there. Who can resist the prospect of a man being sent to the gallows?" He let the thought linger a moment before he picked up his papers and shuffled them officiously. "Now, if you don't mind, I need some time to prepare my case."

—

35

Sara

On the morning of the trial we dressed Madam in plain blue damask with white lace edging. She asked me to draw her hair away from her face and put on her finest wig. I curled the ends into ringlets and added dark blue ribbons. She looked very beautiful, if a little severe.

She had hardly spoken of the trial, while Moll and Monsieur Finet had talked of little else. I tried to ignore their gossip. They cared as much about the lives of the journeymen as they did about the chickens whose necks Monsieur Finet wrung, then handed to Moll to pluck.

Madam held up her pot of rouge as a question. I gave a slight shake of my head. "You're right," she said. "It would not do for me to look so brash. I am a good Huguenot wife, after all."

"Is the master ready?"

"He should be," said Madam. "He has spent enough time preparing."

"What has he to prepare for?"

"Why, the whole case, of course," she said, peering closely at her reflection in the looking glass and brushing loose powder from her face.

"The allegations are his so it is for him to make the case against the journeymen. He is both the victim and prosecutor."

"It sounds very personal."

She glanced up and caught my eye in the mirror. "Indeed," she said.

We followed them out to the coach and horses, the master holding out his arm for my lady, dutiful and solicitous. She, elegant and gracious, the kind of wife you might see in a painting, sitting with her silk skirts spread around her, surrounded by wealth and children. A year ago, just the sight of them would have been enough to twist my guts with envy—but that was before I knew what lay behind their charade. They climbed into the coach and sat down facing the horses. Monsieur Finet struggled up next, the coach tilting under his weight, and sat down opposite them. I clutched the baby to my chest and followed him in, while Moll swung herself up as if she rode in coaches as often as she scrubbed pans.

We sat in uncomfortable silence, unused to being pressed together, thigh against thigh, in this manner. It was odd to think of the intimacies and confidences that might have passed between any two of us and yet could not be spoken of in front of the others. The only noise came from the rattle of the coach wheels over the cobblestones and the baby's occasional startled cry. I held her against me and bounced her in my arms, whispering shushes and nonsense into her ear. Moll sighed and shifted closer to the window as if even my arm against hers was a great inconvenience. I did not care: I enjoyed being my baby's creature. No one had needed me before. My father had left and even my mother had sent me away. Not one of the men at Mrs. Swann's had needed me above ten minutes, and Madam could have her nose powdered by anyone. I felt a raw love for my child that I had not felt for her father. I was a puppet on a string for my baby, her every whimper sending me this way and that. What terrified me was what would happen when those strings were cut and I crumpled into a heap without her.

Those thoughts went through my head every day. Now that my baby was here, I could not contemplate life without her. I had tried to stop thinking about my mother over the years. Indeed, every man at Mrs. Swann's had pushed the memory of her further from my mind, but this tiny being, nuzzling at my neck and chewing at her fists, had opened the memory like an old wound. If I could not bear to part with my daughter, how could my own mother have parted with me?

Esther

I had never been inside the Old Bailey before. It was like the nave of a church. Huge white pillars flanked either side of the vast courtroom. I sat beside Elias in the central seating in front of the bench. Behind the pillars, a gallery was wrapped around the walls of the court. It was full of people, chattering and fidgeting, rustling papers and sharing food, as if they were at the theater. Sara, Moll, and Monsieur Finet were among them, but I did not crane my neck to try to spot them. Most of the rest were journeymen weavers. I wondered how many had been part of the riot that night. Who among them had forced their way into my parlor? Whose pocket jangled with coins made from selling my trinkets?

The judge's seat remained empty and the courtroom was restless, waiting for him to enter. A large sword was mounted on the wall, pointing down toward his chair as if reminding him where to sit. Above it the lion and the unicorn of the royal arms stood on an elaborate architrave, their tails curling elegantly up the walls. Elias was reading a pamphlet, *The Proceedings at the Sessions of the Peace, and Oyer and Terminer*. It claimed to be the truest news about the sessions and an exact account of the trial and condemnation of some fellow for murder. Would Bisby's life be reduced to a sixpenny yarn?

The people in the court rose as the judge walked in. Black-robed and stern, he was wearing a wig bigger than anyone else's. He took his place under the pointing sword and looked out to the jury before him, seated around a large table draped in green cloth as if they might be about to play cards.

There was murmuring and nodding as the clerk scurried between the judge and the jury foreman. The rustling from the gallery above and behind me grew less, then stopped altogether, as a door at the opposite end of the courtroom opened.

Bisby Lambert and John Barnstaple were led out of a passage connecting the Old Bailey to Newgate. They followed the clerk to the dock. The clerk nodded to Bisby and he mounted the wooden steps to a raised platform in front of the judge and jury. My breath caught in my throat at the sight of him. Newgate had stripped the fat from his body and the color from his cheeks. He stood proudly in the dock, but the drag of his chains hunched him like an old man. A sounding board supported by a wooden structure hung over his head. Something about its sparse timber frame made it appear as if he already stood under the Tyburn Tree. The clerk tilted a mirror, mounted opposite the dock, so that the sunlight flooding in from the floor-to-ceiling windows at either side of the judge was reflected into his face. Illuminating the features of the accused is meant to shed light on the truth, allowing judge and jury to see every facial expression the prisoner makes as the evidence unfolds. It made Bisby squint as he pulled at his chains, trying to shield his eyes.

The clerk asked him to state his name.

"Bisby Lambert."

His voice was amplified strangely by the sounding board, as if he was a ventriloquist projecting his voice onto an image of himself.

The clerk read the charges: "One, that you did assemble together with others in the night armed with pistols and cutlasses; two, that you did enter into the dwelling house of Mr. Elias Thorel, master weaver, and did put his household in fear of their lives; three, that you did feloniously and maliciously cut and destroy a quantity of fine brocaded silk from Mr. Thorel's loom. How do you plead?"

"Not guilty." Bisby's voice had a rough edge to it, a shadow of something behind his words that I had not heard before.

"Do you have a lawyer?" asked the clerk.

"No." He spoke the word with some of his old strength, then paused for a moment. "I will let the truth speak for me." The journeymen ranged around the gallery broke into whoops and cheers.

The clerk called for order and the judge stared sternly at them as if they were errant children. "So be it, then," he said.

Next came John Barnstaple, sauntering into the dock to hear the same charges read against him. His plea of *not guilty* was almost incredulous, as if he had never heard such nonsense in his life. The judge nodded. "It is now for Mr. Thorel to make his case," he said.

Elias leaped to his feet, straightening his waistcoat and running a hand over his newly trimmed beard before he took his place in front of the judge and jury.

"My lord, good gentlemen of the jury," he said, with a bow to each. "You have heard the charges. That night, a great crime was committed against me and against right-thinking men everywhere. A crime that the King, in his wisdom, has deemed punishable by death. And rightly so. What—I beg you to consider—would happen to our country if the working man were allowed to run riot without censure, as these men did that night? What if journeymen were allowed to form organizations purely to force change to their working conditions on their masters?"

A couple of the jurymen started to nod. Above and around me the gallery felt like a malevolent presence, a black cloud threatening thunder.

"I will tell you," said Elias. "Anarchy, that is what. The kind of anarchy that spilled like sewage through the streets of London toward my home. Gentlemen, my silk is my life. To cut the silk from my looms is to cut the heart from my chest. The law has deemed silk cutting so serious that it is a hanging offense." Elias raised his finger and pointed it deliberately toward Bisby and Barnstaple. "These two men were arrested in my garret with my silk lying cut at their feet. Each claims not to have cut the silk and it is for you, gentlemen, to determine whether this can possibly be true."

There is optimism at the start of a trial, a sense that there is still hope. The charges sounded alien in my ears as I looked upon a man whose integrity I had experienced in the most visceral of ways. I did not fear for him then. I believed in the truth, in the rule of law and in the absolute certainty of justice.

The clerk called Bisby back into the dock. As he went up the steps, he started to cough, and once he had started, he couldn't stop.

36

Sara

Jail fever.

That was what all the coughing and spluttering was about. The judge reached for his nosegay and clutched it to his face so that he could breathe its protective scent, rather than the contamination from the court below. Everyone else had to make do with breathing into their sleeves.

It was hardly surprising. He was so altered that, had I seen him on a street corner, I would have tossed him a ha'penny and not given him a second thought. I pulled my baby closer, worried that those foul vapors might float up to the gallery. In the seats below, I saw Madam turn her face toward the sound of Bisby's racking cough, almost reluctantly as if she feared what she might see. Her own skin seemed to blanch in sympathy. Stricken by each other now, when once they had been enchanted.

The court was a somber place, as if we were all halfway to the gallows already. Black curtains were ruched over the top of huge windows to each side of the judge's chair, staring blankly down to the jury below. What chance did the working man stand before these men? They were merchants, constables, and surgeons. What did they know of empty bellies and the sting of an icy floor on shoeless feet? I saw one catch the master's eye and nod a fleeting acknowledgment. Had they laughed together in a coffee shop somewhere? It hardly mattered. They looked at Elias Thorel and saw themselves reflected. The master puffed and preened, readying himself to speak, but he had already told them all they needed to know by the cut of his jacket and the elegant curl of his fine horsehair wig.

Bisby's breathing returned to normal. The judge reappeared from behind his bunch of lavender.

"What is your business?" asked Thorel.

"Why ask?" replied Bisby. "I have worked for you since I was a boy."

Laughter rippled through the gallery. Someone balled up a piece of paper and threw it down into the court below with a jeer.

"To assist the court, Mr. Lambert," intervened the judge, "please state your business."

"Journeyman silk weaver, my lord."

The judge sat back in his chair and nodded at Thorel, who stepped forward again and said, "Mr. Lambert, look upon the other prisoner."

Bisby dropped his gaze to John Barnstaple sitting below him. Newgate had been kinder to him. His eyes were still bright as they regarded Bisby in the dock. No doubt a shilling in the right pocket had seen to that.

"Is this man known to you?"

"Yes. I shared lodgings with him in one of the weavers' cottages next to Buttermilk Alley and we both worked our looms there in the garret."

"And you were part of the same combination, were you not?" stated Elias.

The judge removed his spectacles from his nose. "Combination, Mr. Thorel?"

"Yes, my lord. It is the name for the illegal groups the journeymen formed. It is my case that both the prisoners were part of such a group."

The judge nodded. "Answer the question, Mr. Lambert."

"I was not part of any combination, my lord. I'll own that they exist, and one even met sometimes at Buttermilk Alley, but I wanted no part of it."

"Did you not sympathize with the weavers' plight?" asked Thorel, unable to keep the sarcasm from his voice.

"Of course, but Barnstaple is a plain weaver and I weave figured silk. Each branch of the industry formed its own combination. But even if their combination had all been figured silk weavers, I would not have joined them. I supported other ways to protect the journeymen's wages, like an Act of Parliament to set the piece rate for the silk." There were boos and mocking jeers from the gallery. Bisby ignored them. "I never condoned or encouraged violence. Never."

"Violence? So you admit that the combinations are violent?"

"Too right we are," shouted someone from the back of the gallery.

"They met at your lodgings," persisted Thorel. "Surely you knew what they were about."

Bisby shifted in the dock. His chains made a dull clanking sound, as if he were a ghostly apparition. "I told you," he said, "I wanted no part of it."

Thorel gave him a sly smile. "But you were part of it, Mr. Lambert, weren't you? How else do you explain that the King's men found you up in my garret with a roll of cut silk at your feet?"

"Perhaps," interjected the judge, "you should take the court through exactly what happened on the night of …" he rustled his papers until the clerk whispered in his ear, "… ah, yes, the twenty-first night of February, 1769?"

The eve of my daughter's birth. The night that gave her life but could mean the end of her father's. The baby began to cry, a persistent wail that earned me hard stares and tuts. I scooped her up and carried her away.

Esther

"I had been at ten Spital Square," began Bisby.

"Tell the court what you were doing there," insisted Elias. He wanted the jury to be fully aware of his patronage.

Bisby nodded, happy to acknowledge his master's benevolence. "Mr. Thorel had been allowing me to use his drawloom to weave a figured silk. When it was finished, I was hoping to use it to apply to the Weavers' Company to become a master. With Mr. Thorel's support."

"Why not use one of the silks you were weaving at Buttermilk Alley?" asked the judge.

"My master piece had to be a work of great technical skill. There are so many mercers buying silk imported from abroad that demand for really complex figured silk has dropped. I was having trouble finding a commission that would show the necessary level of weaving skill. Mr. Thorel suggested that I weave the right kind of silk in my own time. He was sure that once the silk was finished, he would have no difficulty selling it. He let me use his spare drawloom."

"'Spare drawloom'? You mean the loom in my home that my family has used for generations?" It was almost as if Elias had forgotten he was in a courtroom. The way he rounded on Bisby was as if he had accosted him in a tavern, drunk on ale and bravado. "And I commissioned the design for this silk myself, didn't I, Mr. Lambert?"

"You did, sir."

"And I bought the silk thread?"

"Yes."

"And I allowed you into my home?" There was the faintest break in Elias' voice, perceptible only to those who knew him.

But Bisby noticed it. I was certain that it was the hurt in Elias' voice rather than the question that muted him. He just nodded, never taking his eyes from Elias'.

"You must say yes or no," said the judge.

"Yes. Mr. Thorel did allow me into his home."

"And I was going to pay the fee to the Weavers' Company for you, wasn't I?"

"Yes, but you would also then have had a fine figured silk to sell, woven for you for nothing. That was the agreement we had."

"Oh, yes," said Elias. "That was our agreement, but you betrayed me, didn't you?"

I tensed, bracing against the humiliation that was to follow. My jabot seemed to stick to my neck and I felt apprehension prickle under my arms. Did Elias want revenge so much that he was prepared to parade my misdemeanors before a courtroom of people?

"That afternoon, when I came to see how you were getting on, I saw that you had not finished your master piece. In fact, you had made hardly any progress at all, had you?"

If words are weapons, then silence is defense. Bisby said nothing, building a wall of words unsaid.

"We argued about that, didn't we?" Elias insisted.

It was a risk. Bisby might easily have shamed me, decided that in the moral balance his reputation would weigh more than mine. He could have told the court that there was more to this argument than simply the misbehavior of an idle journeyman. But he left the accusation unchallenged.

"Words were exchanged, and I told you to leave my house, did I not?"

"Yes."

"Tell the court what happened after that," said the judge.

"When I returned to Buttermilk Alley, Barnstaple was talking to a few of the journeyman weavers there. They had weapons. I asked one of the weavers what was going on and he said he'd spent all day at the Eight Bells waiting for Mr. Thorel to pay his contribution to the combination. He'd been given a week, you see, to pay. Now that the week had run out, the men wanted to take matters into their own hands."

"Take matters into their own hands? What do you mean by that?" asked the judge.

Bisby looked uncomfortable. He glanced at Barnstaple, who was staring fixedly ahead of him, seemingly more interested in the splendor of the court than anything Bisby had to say. Bisby took a deep breath and went on: "I'd been trying to contain them for months, but that night the weavers were like a pot boiling over. More and more appeared. Word spread around Spitalfields that Thorel's time was up and he hadn't paid. It was like a fire catching hold and, all the while, Barnstaple was fanning the flames."

A slow smile spread over Barnstaple's face, but he didn't shift his gaze from the middle distance. Elias stepped toward Bisby and said, "But where were you, Mr. Lambert, when all this was happening? Right in the middle of it, I presume."

"But that's where I lived." The protest strained his voice and he started to cough again. The court seemed to shrink back. "How could I leave? I had been turned out of Spital Square and it was snowing outside. I had no choice."

The judge took his spectacles from his nose and rubbed at his forehead. Once he had replaced them, he peered at Bisby and said, "Yes, Mr. Lambert, the court is clear on that, but it does not explain how you came to be back at Spital Square in the thick of the riot."

Bisby nodded, as if acknowledging that he would have to say more. "It was because of the Thorels' lady's maid. She appeared at Buttermilk Alley, tearful and panting, as if she had run all the way there. Buttermilk Alley was no place for a woman then. There were pistols and cutlasses on the table. She seemed shocked by what was going on. I was worried about her. It was clear she was with child. She became agitated, as if she was having some sort of turn, and rushed outside. I followed her out in time to see her faint. She'd have fallen right onto the freezing street, if I hadn't caught her."

"Quite the hero, then, Mr. Lambert," drawled Elias. Some of the jurors smirked and exchanged glances. Distaste curdled in my stomach. As if it were not enough that Bisby stood there in chains, Elias had to ridicule him as well.

"It was what anyone would have done," said Bisby, evenly.

"Perhaps," said Elias, "if indeed that's what you did. But you still have not told us how you went from saving ladies in fainting fits to standing in my garret with a cutlass in your hand."

"The girl needed help. I could see that her baby was coming even though she told me it was too early. Mrs. Thorel is a kind and God-fearing woman. I knew she would not turn her back on her maid at such a time."

"So you took her back to Spital Square?" said the judge.

"Yes, my lord. I walked with her as far as the entrance to the square and then she left me and stumbled toward the Thorels' house. Someone must have seen her approaching, as the scullery maid rushed out and took her in. That's when I should have left, and I wish to God that I had. Journeymen had already gathered in the square and lit a bonfire. There were chairs and all sorts being burned, looted from houses along the way. Windows were being smashed. Even honest folk who had nothing to do with the weavers' plight were in fear that night. I could see that matters were out of hand and I wanted no part of it, but then I spotted my nephew, Ives, on Barnstaple's shoulders near the fire. He had a pistol in his hand and was waving it about as if it were a flag. Who in their right mind would give a flintlock to a child? Ives tried to fire it into the sky, but it misfired. Good God, when I saw him peer into the barrel, I thought he was going to blow his own head off. I ran over and pulled it away from his face."

"Would you describe the men as riotous in disposition?" asked the judge.

"Very, my lord."

"But even then, you did not leave?"

"How could I leave any child alone among a riot, let alone my own flesh and blood? My sister died of consumption not two years past. The only thing she ever asked of me was to look after her boy. Barnstaple had some kind of hold over Ives, I don't know why. It was as if Ives wanted to impress him, so I begged Barnstaple to send the boy home, thinking Ives would listen to him, but he refused. Then I saw someone smash a window at ten Spital Square. For a moment I clean forgot the boy as I was more worried about Mrs. Thorel. I thought she might need my help and so, when the rioters forced the shutters, I ran in after them."

So, he had gone into the house looking for me. A hundred times I had asked myself what had possessed him to run in there like that. Now I knew. He was trying to protect me. I should have been pleased to hear it, but instead I felt as though I had withered in my seat. He was in prison because of me, as surely as if I had gone out that night and dragged him into Spital Square myself. I could hardly bear to hear more, but I forced my attention back to Bisby.

"The journeymen seemed more interested in looting trinkets than anything else, so I left them downstairs and tried to find Mrs. Thorel. I looked in the kitchens and all the rooms, until I found one upstairs that was locked. I banged on the door and rattled the handle, but no one would open it. I knew the women were in there because I could hear the maid screaming inside. I don't blame them for not opening the door—they must have been scared for their lives. Just then Barnstaple came up the stairs with Ives behind him. They walked right past me and carried on up to the garret. I knew what Barnstaple was going to do."

"How did you know?" asked the judge.

Bisby took a deep breath. There was plainly more to this than that single night. There was a history, something deeper and more complex informing who did what to whom. "Barnstaple," he said carefully, trying the name on, seeing if he could find a fit between what he knew of the man and what went on that night, "always resented me. We were apprentices together, but when I moved on to figured silk, he stayed with the plain weaves and the velvets. It wasn't that he couldn't do it, he's skilled enough. Laziness, perhaps. Either way, when Mr. Thorel invited me to weave my master piece, Barnstaple was angry. I truly believe that when he went up into that garret, he was looking for my master piece."

"You are suggesting he cut it out of spite?"

"No, my lord. Barnstaple didn't cut the silk."

"Of course, he didn't." Elias stepped in front of the judge. His case had been veering off course, Bisby steering it in an unexpected direction. "You cut it, didn't you?"

"No, sir."

"You are the one who is full of spite. You cut the silk because I turned you out of my house. You cut it because I would not allow you back to finish it. You cut it because if you could not have the silk as your master piece then you would not allow anyone to have it!"

"No, that is not true."

"And once the silk was cut from the loom, you sliced through every layer of it on the roller, so that weeks of work was destroyed completely."

"Why would I destroy my own work?" said Bisby, his voice deliberate.

The whole court was silent now, listening to this exchange. Even the near constant chattering from the gallery had stopped.

Elias' voice was quiet: no need to shout in the pristine air of the courtroom. "Because you realized that you would never be a master. You couldn't bear the thought that without me you would stay a journeyman for the rest of your life. So you destroyed my silk, the single thing that defined your place in the world and mine."

"No, I did not."

"Then who did?"

It was a strikingly simple question and it seemed to bounce round the walls of the court while Bisby stood there, silent.

"Well?"

"I cannot say."

"Mr. Lambert," said the judge. "Surely I do not need to impress upon you the gravity of this offense. I ask you, with due thought to the seriousness of your situation, who cut the silk?"

"I cannot say, my lord."

"Then that concludes your evidence." The judge's voice was curt, annoyed. I glared at Bisby in frustration as if I could stare the words out of him, but he was already picking his way back down the wooden steps. Barnstaple rose too, and the clerk took them back to the doorway at the far side of the court, and the passage that would lead them into Newgate jail.

Sara

He peered at his daughter, while she blinked up at him over the edge of her swaddling. Her eyes had darkened from inky blue to deep brown. She sought out his own dark eyes and locked him in mutual contemplation.

"Aye, she's bonny, all right," said Barnstaple, sitting back in his chair as if that brief glance was a sufficient experience of parenting.

"She's the spit of you," I said.

I was glad they had had a chance to meet, even under such strange circumstances. I'll own I had been surprised when Elias Thorel himself had told me Barnstaple wanted to see me and given me twopence for the stagecoach to Newgate. I looked around the room. A small bed, washstand, the table Barnstaple was sitting at, and little else. Still, it was a world away from the rest of the jail.

"Why did you ask to see me?"

"Why?" He blew into his black hair so that it lifted from his forehead. "Does a man need a reason to meet his own daughter?"

"You have not wanted to meet her before."

"By God, woman, how could I?" He held up both hands and glanced

221

around him, as if those four walls were the answer to everything.

"But before," I said, keeping my voice level, "when she was coming, and I had no one to turn to, you wouldn't help me." I spoke as simply as I could, but each word twisted inside me.

He seemed to recoil from the truth of what he had done. "Why must we look back, Sara? Is it not better to look to the future? Our future."

"That is strange talk from a man who faces the gallows."

He smiled. "That will not happen. Do you know why?"

I shook my head.

"Because you will help set me free."

"How can I do that?"

"You'll see," he said, with a strange look. Then, "Tomorrow at court I will give my evidence. All you need to do is to listen carefully to what I say. If I walk free, we can be together, start a new life in another parish."

There was nothing convincing about this rosy portrayal of a life we'd never have.

"Thorel himself gave me your message," I said. "Seems odd, that."

"Does it?" Barnstaple kept his expression blank. "Perhaps he's beginning to see my worth. Maybe now he knows it was me all along, not that milksop Lambert, who can be trusted."

The guard opened the door. He walked over to Barnstaple's table and banged down a metal tray with food on it. Bread and some kind of stew. The smell made my stomach turn, but the baby twisted in my arms to look.

Barnstaple hunched over his meal and broke off a chunk of bread, jabbing it into the gravy. The guard stood by the door, holding it ajar, looking at me pointedly.

Barnstaple nodded toward it. "You best be off," he said, through his mouthful.

"But you haven't explained yourself."

He shrugged. "It's them that make the rules, miss," he said, grinning at the turnkey. Then he went back to his dinner, the scrape of his spoon on the metal plate echoing in his bare-walled cell.

꒰ · ꒱

He did not knock. Why should he? He was master of the whole household. When he came into my little attic room he looked around him as if he were almost surprised that such a place existed in his own house. I got up quickly from my bed, casting aside the tiny cotton shift I had been sewing for the baby. Elias Thorel held up a hand as if he bade me to remain seated.

He stepped toward the cradle and ran his hand over the polished oak, more interested in the craftsmanship of the woodwork than the infant asleep inside.

"Such a shame," he said, almost whimsically, "that I do not have my own child to fill this."

It was an intimate thought to express to me. I had never really considered how the master felt to be childless. Yet if he were so concerned, why did he not spend more time with Madam and less with Moll?

"You are blessed," he said, matter-of-factly. "Whatever the circumstances, a child is always a blessing."

The smile I attempted soon evaporated from my face, for when he turned back toward me, his face was grim.

"But you cannot care for this child. Better to send it to the Foundling Hospital. You can make a new life for yourself." He reached inside his waistcoat pocket and pulled something out. When he opened his palm, I saw that a guinea lay on it. "Take it," he said, extending his hand toward me.

And I did. I took that coin and felt the solid weight of it. I rubbed my fingers over the faint outline of George III and admired the dull gleam of the gold in the candlelight.

"It's yours," said Thorel. "You will need it for your new life."

"What do you want from me, sir?"

Thorel's laugh was empty and mirthless. "My goodness," he said, "you are cynical. No, no, all I want from you is your cooperation. That is a fair exchange, is it not?"

"My cooperation with what, sir?"

"In court, of course. Barnstaple will give his evidence and it will be the correct version of events. If you are asked, you may confirm that. It is all very simple."

I had wondered why I had not been packed off to the lying-in hospital, but all Madam had said was that the master wanted to keep me here. The guinea began to feel heavy in my palm. I tightened my grip on it and the edge dug into my skin. "And if Barnstaple doesn't tell the truth?"

"The truth? All of a sudden you are concerned with the truth? You have come into my house and thought nothing of telling stories. Is there a word of what you have told your mistress that is true?"

When he got no answer, he pressed on: "Tell me, did you have any idea of the truth when you took your tales about me and Moll to your mistress?"

Despite the low, even pitch of his voice he was still terrifying. I heard my own heartbeat pounding in my head. "I told her what I believed to be true, no more, no less."

"Yes, and the damage is done now. Just make sure that tomorrow you say what you need to say and Barnstaple's evidence is believed."

"But that would mean Lambert goes to the gallows."

Thorel said nothing, just looked at me levelly.

"You want me to scrag him?" I whispered the words, as if they might taint the air my daughter breathed.

Thorel made a face as if he had found gristle in his pie. "*Scrag*," he said, "is an unpleasant word. The outcome is not your concern. Just think of what you could do with that."

He looked down at my hand to where the guinea burned against my palm.

Esther

Surely he spoke the truth.

I had gone over every detail of that night until the memory was raw. I had seen him grab the pistol from the boy. I had heard someone rattling the door of my bedroom as Sara cried out in pain. The thought that it was him was almost unbearable. If I had just opened the door, he would never have seen Barnstaple and Ives go up to the garret. If I had let him in, I could have stopped all this happening.

"What's the matter with you?"

Elias had been watching my face in the mirror as I sat at my dressing table, getting ready for bed. I had almost forgotten he was there.

"Nothing," I replied, tying the end of my hair with a ribbon. "I'm just tired."

He walked up behind me and put his hands on my shoulders. "You look as if you've got indigestion," he said curtly. "Try not to grimace like that in court tomorrow. People will be watching you."

Was he joking? It was always so hard to tell with Elias.

"It's been a long day, husband," I said, rising from my stool and turning to him. "I thought I would retire early."

"Indeed, wife, I had thought the same." Elias was standing so close to me that I could smell the sandalwood on his clothes. His face was flushed, and it was not with drink—I knew him better than that. Success was flooding his veins. He thought he was winning.

"Did you see him today?" he asked, almost whispering. He put his hand on my forehead and smoothed the hair from my brow. "He had nothing to say for himself. He couldn't even answer the simplest of questions—who cut the silk?"

"Is there not honor in silence, husband?"

"What do you mean?"

"It is not that he cannot say who cut the silk, it is that he will not. Even in the face of death he will not condemn another. That is valiant indeed, to my mind."

The edge of Elias' mouth lifted. "Well, let's see how *valiant* he looks when they string him up."

"Why are you doing this? What purpose could there be to seeing either of those men hang?"

"I know which one is going to hang. The one who lied to me. The one who accepted my help and my charity, then made a fool of me with my own wife."

"Then the wrong was mine, husband, not his."

"Do not try to protect him. That only makes it worse. This is between men. I cannot allow another man to come into my household and treat me with the contempt he has."

I saw him then as a man of his own people. Like the community of his birth, he offered support to those who followed the unwritten moral code. But to those who transgressed, there was no forgiveness, only vengeance. He had seen it himself when he had refused to take a Huguenot bride, and now he intended to inflict that righteous wrath on someone else.

He trailed his hand over my hair, taking hold of my plait and drawing it toward him across my shoulder. He thumbed its ridges, one by one, lower and lower. At the end, he took the black ribbon between his fingers and tugged until it loosened and fell to the floor.

I closed my hand over Elias'. "I really am tired," I breathed.

"But I am not," he said. His eyes were bright pools of triumph. He began to undo the plait, working his way back up, unraveling all that I had done.

It had been a long time since my husband had lain with me. His rage at Bisby had driven him away, and now his satisfaction at destroying him had brought him back, more urgent and forceful than before, as if chicanery were an aphrodisiac. He twisted his fingers into my hair and pulled me toward him. I stayed rooted to the spot, resisting the impulse to turn away. I took no pleasure from the feel of my husband's mouth warm and determined against my own. I felt like an animal being branded.

38

Sara

Carrying his chains more lightly than Bisby had worn his, Barnstaple stepped up to the dock. He had been given a clean shirt and breeches, his wayward hair tamed by a ribbon tied neatly at the nape of his neck. The voice that the sounding board projected to the court was a confident drawl.

I sat at the very front of the gallery, looking down on the court below, following his every word. What would I have to say to the court with the same conviction that Barnstaple was projecting now? I had not been in the garret that night: I had been lying in Madam's bed barely aware of my own breath. What could they expect of me that it would be wrong to say?

There had been nothing untoward so far. John Barnstaple had taken the court through the preliminaries with perfect candor.

Then, "What do you know of the combinations, Mr. Barnstaple?" asked Thorel.

"I know they exist. Bisby Lambert is part of one. The Conquering and Bold Defiance, I think they call themselves. They like to give themselves grand names, or name themselves after ships, like the Rebellion Sloop." The gallery tittered. Barnstaple twisted round and looked up, grinning, turning his face to the sun.

"But you were not part of one?" asked the judge.

"The men looked to me for leadership, my lord. To be sure, there was no one else who could give them any direction. There were often journeymen at Buttermilk Alley. I spoke to them, drank with them, but what does sharing a pot of ale with a man really mean?"

What could I say to that? There was no truth or otherwise to it. Trying to find the point in his words was like picking up egg yolks.

Thorel moved round to face Barnstaple.

"That day then, the twenty-first of February, where were you?"

Barnstaple preened, sensing his moment. "I was up in my garret in Buttermilk Alley, weaving a plain velvet for you, sir. It was getting late, so I was just finishing, thinking about my supper and whether to go to the chophouse or eat the bread and cheese I had in the pantry."

Thorel looked impatient. "Just what's relevant to the issues, Mr. Barnstaple."

"Well, I decided on the bread and cheese and went downstairs. That very minute Lambert flew through the door and came into the front room where I was cutting myself a slice of bread. He was fair spitting with rage. That's the only way I can describe him. Saying things I would not want any lady in this court to hear."

He paused for a moment until the judge raised his eyebrows. "I'm afraid you will have to repeat those words to the court. What did Mr. Lambert say?"

Barnstaple feigned reluctance. He chewed his lip and cast his eyes about the courtroom as if searching for another solution rather than say what he had to say. Then his eyes met mine. For a moment I felt as if he and I were the only two people in the courtroom. Everyone else fell away. Even though he was far below me, his pitch eyes seemed to hold me so that I had the sensation of being a fish hooked on a line, captured and about to be dragged, gasping, out of the water.

He turned back to the judge. "Of course, my lord," he said, with a slight bow. "It is just that it is a sensitive matter."

I pulled my daughter to me, that same sensation flipping in my stomach.

"He had had an argument with the master, Mr. Thorel. There had been an … indiscretion in the household."

"Speak plainly, Mr. Barnstaple," said the judge, sounding impatient. He had half an eye on the defendant and half an eye on the clock mounted on the wall, which crept steadily toward midday.

"I shall, then," continued Barnstaple, slightly petulant.

"So," said Thorel, keen to draw Barnstaple back to the point, "we have heard from the other prisoner that he and I had a disagreement that led me to tell him to leave. He has agreed that much. How would you describe Lambert's demeanor when he came back to Buttermilk Alley?"

"Beg pardon, sir?" said Barnstaple, blinking at Thorel.

"How did he look and behave? What did he say?"

"Ah, right," said Barnstaple, looking relieved. "He were angry, sir."

"Direct your answers to the judge, please, Mr. Barnstaple."

"Sorry." Barnstaple shifted slightly in the dock, angling himself toward the judge. The clerk popped up and scurried to the mirror, adjusting the angle so that the light gave Barnstaple's face a perfect sheen. The woman next to me whispered something to her friend, who giggled into her gloved hand.

What was the purpose of this show of naivety? Was he trying to portray himself as too simple to be capable of deceit? The sounding board amplified his voice and the reflected light illuminated his features, but the court had nothing that would reveal the guile flowing through his body.

"Angry, you said?" prompted Thorel.

"And worse," said Barnstaple. "He threw his bag down on the table and told me that Mr. Thorel had turned him out. I asked him why, and at first he wouldn't tell me, but I guessed why. There'd been a girl, a maid up at ten Spital Square, who had been around Buttermilk Alley a lot. It was obvious there was something going on between her and Lambert. After a while, it became plain she was with child. That was what the argument was about. Once Lambert had calmed himself and I'd given him a pot of ale, he told me that the master had finally noticed he'd been spending more time at Spital Square with the maid than working on his master piece. Thorel told him he felt betrayed, as well he might. Mr. Thorel had shown such confidence in Lambert that for him to bring shame on his household … well, it's not right, is it?"

The world was spinning, a topsy-turvy place with no reality. The noise from the gallery was a distracting buzz that clogged my ears and muddled my thoughts. Was that what I would be asked to say? That Bisby Lambert was the father of my child? I stared at Barnstaple, trying to get him to look in my direction as if I could challenge his terrible deceit with my glare. But why would he look at me? I was the inconvenient truth, sitting in the midst of this warped version of reality he was creating. Then Bisby lifted his eyes to mine, filling the gap Barnstaple had left, and I was forced to look upon his confusion, his despair, for as long as I could bear to hold his gaze.

"And then," continued an almost jubilant Barnstaple, "the maid herself turned up at Buttermilk Alley, not long after Lambert. She'd been sent on her way as well!"

There was a clank of irons as Bisby stumbled to his feet. He rose so quickly that he misjudged the limit of his chains and they pulled taut, reining in his protest. "That's not true, my lord!" His voice was broken, coming from somewhere deep within his chest, forced out, as if each breath cost him dear. Then the coughing started again, and he sat down heavily and yanked at the manacles in hopeless frustration.

"But you admitted that we had argued in your evidence," said Mr. Thorel, when the coughing had stopped.

"Yes, but you did not suggest it was about that!"

Thorel shrugged. "Then what was it about?"

Silence. Bisby did not say that the argument was about the patterns Thorel had found. That it was about the time he had spent in the garret with the master's wife doing goodness knew what. But if those were the reasons, then this—the judges and the jury, the watchful lion and the unicorn, the undercurrent of desperation and the echoing cough—was all my doing.

Bisby rested his forearms on his knees and sagged. Lies have a weight that ends up being borne by someone.

The judge looked over at Thorel. "May I remind you that this defendant is not giving evidence. You should not address him, Mr. Thorel, and nor should he address the court. Continue, Mr. Barnstaple."

"Lambert was saying Mr. Thorel wouldn't get away with sending him off like that. He said he had as much right to the silk he was weaving as Thorel did. But it wasn't just about his master piece, there was much more than that. Thorel had been told to pay a subscription to the combination and he hadn't. Lambert said that the men wouldn't tolerate the masters lording it over them and behaving as they pleased. Then he said something that stuck in my mind."

Barnstaple chose to pause there, his face angled against the light in a perfect profile, like the King's face on the guinea in my pocket.

"Well, what did he say?" Thorel was impatient and unconcerned with the way the light glanced off Barnstaple's cheekbones.

"He said, *Thorel's time has come.*"

Slumped in his chair under the dock, Bisby slowly shook his head.

"What did you take that to mean?"

"I couldn't say, my lord, save that it struck the fear of God into me."

The judge nodded. "Go on."

"Ives, Lambert's nephew, had come back with him. He was at Buttermilk Alley a lot, ever since Lambert's sister died, God rest her. Most often Lambert ignored him, but then he took the poor boy by the arm as if he'd caught him with his hand in a purse. He knelt down in front of the boy and told him to fetch all the weavers in Spitalfields he could find and be quick about it. Once word got around there was no stopping them, such was the tide of feeling against the master weavers. That was the beginning of it, my lord. The start of everything that happened that night."

The court broke into chatter and comment. The judge, sensing he had lost order, glanced hopefully at the clock. There was a rustle of paper as the woman next to me unwrapped a pie. When she broke it open the smell of mutton made the baby squirm in my arms. She watched the woman eat with bright, interested eyes.

"Are you hungry, little mite?" whispered the woman.

It would not be long before she was weaned.

Esther

Afternoon drew the sun down in the sky so that light flooded through the courtroom windows straight into my eyes. I shielded them with my hand, watching the clerk scatter fresh herbs over the jury's table and put a new nosegay out for the judge. I wondered how we could have been unaware for so long of the resentment building against us. I felt exposed, sitting beneath the journeymen weavers in the gallery, as if they stared down at me with the same malevolence that had ripped through my house that night.

The gallery was even more packed with people than before. If the plight of their fellow journeymen had been enough to bring the weavers out in droves, it was the prospect of a salacious story that kept them there all afternoon.

The door leading from Newgate opened again and Barnstaple walked through it. Bisby must have been behind him, but for a moment Barnstaple eclipsed him. It was the same with his evidence. Barnstaple was a showman, a charismatic charlatan. He had manipulated the weavers to riot, used their hunger and their want to make them violent. Now he was playing on the court's desire for moral condemnation to secure the outcome he needed. I had no doubt that Barnstaple was the father of Sara's child. In a strange way, watching Barnstaple in court had only made me more convinced of that. As repugnant as I found him, I could see how that charm might have drawn Sara to him, in another setting entirely.

The two prisoners took their seats. They were two sides of the same coin, those men. A coin that was spinning in the air and could land only one way, heads or tails. Their fates were intertwined, yet opposite. You could almost see that from looking at them. Barnstaple seemed to be gaining strength at Bisby's expense, sitting taller and prouder even as Bisby shrank and withered in the seat next to him. I wanted to scream at the jury, demand that they see these men for who they really were, but I could only sit mute below the dock, gagged by a laborious system that I was fast losing faith in.

Barnstaple seemed keen to take the stand again, as if he knew he held the interest of the court in his hand. He had fidgeted through the judge returning to his seat and the daily rituals of the court, like a child having to sit still at the dinner table. When he was allowed to speak again, he was even more eager than before.

"They started coming from all over the parish," he continued. "Weavers I hadn't met before were at our door with cutlasses and the like. And Lambert ushered them in. Then he got out a flintlock—only the Lord knows where from—and put it on the table. That was when I got worried. I told him to put it away as no good could come of it, but he shoved me to the side and carried on loading the barrel. That was when the maid arrived, the one with the baby. She'd come to find Lambert. Poor wretch had nowhere else to go after she had been turned out of Spital Square." Barnstaple shook his head in a show of ruefulness. "But Lambert didn't want to know. He was more interested in having his revenge on Mr. Thorel than facing up to his responsibilities. He sent the poor girl stumbling back to Mrs. Thorel. Once she'd gone, he rallied the men and took them over to Spital Square. It wasn't hard. Thorel had done himself no favors with the journeymen by refusing to pay the subscription. But for Lambert it was personal. He wanted to get back at Thorel for denying him the chance to be a master. And there's nothing more personal between a master and his journeyman than the silk."

"You mean my silk?"

I had almost forgotten that Elias was there, such was the power of Barnstaple's speech.

"Yes, sir, your silk. I saw him do it. While the other weavers were busy in the parlor doing nothing more than petty looting, Lambert strode up the stairs. I followed him, desperate to stop him, knowing what he was about. But I was too late. By the time I got into the attic, the silk lay on the floor, cut from the loom and sliced through to the roller. Lambert just stood there, smirking at me, clutching his cutlass at his side."

Someone in the gallery booed and something else—I think it was a piece of bread—sailed down from above me and landed next to the jury's table. One of the jurymen, sitting ramrod straight in his chair, taut with his own self-importance, turned in his seat and glared up at the gallery.

The judge leaned forward. "So you did not actually see him cut the silk, Mr. Barnstaple?"

Barnstaple flustered. "But I did, my lord, with my own eyes."

"But you said that the silk was already cut at Mr. Lambert's feet when you entered the garret. So therefore you did not see it. Which is it, Mr. Barnstaple? It cannot be both."

If Barnstaple had been fairer of complexion than he was, I think we would have seen him color then. But, as it was, he merely cleared his throat and nodded at the judge. "Beg pardon, my lord. What I meant was, if he did not cut it himself then I cannot see who did as there was not a soul there but us two."

"Except for Ives, Lambert's nephew," said the judge with a frown. "Unless you say he was not there."

Barnstaple grew agitated. "He was there, my lord, but he was following up right behind me. So there, yet not there, if you see what I mean."

The judge raised his eyebrows. "Thank you, Mr. Barnstaple. Unless Mr. Thorel has any more questions, that concludes your evidence." He glanced toward Elias, who gave a small shake of his head.

"Does the prosecution have any witnesses to call tomorrow?" asked the judge.

"Just one," said Elias. "The lady's maid, Miss Sara Kemp."

39

Sara

I turned the guinea in my hand. What would it buy, this quarter-ounce of gold? A gown as fine as the ones Madam wore? A year's worth of mutton dinners from the cookshop? Lodgings of my own with my baby? But I would not have my baby, and what use were gowns and fancy things to me, a whore and a servant? I pushed open the door of the master's withdrawing room.

"Beg pardon, sir," I said dipping a curtsy in front of his desk. "But you left this in my room."

I dropped the guinea onto his desk, where it landed flatly on his papers.

He looked up at me, confused. "What do you mean?"

"I mean, that this is yours, sir."

Thorel scowled. "You are making a mistake, Kemp." There was an edge to his voice, the first bubbles in a pot about to boil over.

"Sorry, sir, but no mistake." I turned to leave.

"What if I let you keep your child?"

His words stopped me, anchoring me to the spot. I stayed motionless, staring at the door.

"I will let you live in Buttermilk Alley," he said to my back. "With Barnstaple, if you really want that feckless good-for-nothing. If you don't, I will make sure he pays the Bastardy Bond before they let him out of prison. That is what I will give you if you do as I ask."

I did not turn back toward him. I just walked toward the door, my steps slow as if I were now weighed down by much more than a quarter-ounce of gold.

Nameless.

My own daughter did not even have a name. I had not felt able to give her an identity. I was the vessel. Nursemaid, not mother. But Thorel's words had changed that. It was as if he had thrown open the shutters, so I could look out on a life I never thought I'd have.

Anna.

I hardly dared speak the word aloud so instead I breathed it into her hair as I held her close. "That is what I would call you, my sweet."

I felt Madam's eyes on me as I moved around the room. I smoothed her clothes and folded them into her wooden chest. I took out a fresh petticoat for her to wear the next day and laid it across her chaise. When I tried to fold her pannier, a bent cane sprang free of the linen and jabbed into my hand. Her scrutiny had made me clumsy.

"Madam, can I help you with something?" I said, rubbing at the scratch on my hand.

"You did not tell me that you would be giving evidence at court." Her gaze was level and unblinking.

I took a deep breath. "I did not know until yesterday."

"But why, Sara? What can you tell the court when you were laboring with a child while all this happened?"

"The master has some questions for me. That is all I know."

"You will at least be able to clear up that nonsense about the father of your child." She stated it simply. One of the absolute certainties of her world.

I went back to the pannier, trying to push the cane rod back into the tunnel of material. Out of the corner of my eye I saw Madam purse her lips. "Won't you, Sara?" Her voice was severe, compelling.

I could imagine what the master's questions would be. I had turned them over in my mind again and again, lining them up, like stepping stones, and following each one to see where they might lead. *To damnation if they are not the truth*, was what my mother would have said. But I could keep my daughter for the price of my soul. What mother would not think that that was a fair exchange?

But would she ever know, my sweet child, that I let a man hang to keep her with me? Would she grow up thinking that there was already blood on her tiny hands? I set down the pannier on the bed.

"Madam?"

"Yes?" She was eager, as if I was going to tell her how I would set that journeyman of hers free. But why was his liberty of more value than my own? Were we not both a kind of prisoner? Elias Thorel had offered me a life with my daughter in return for sending Bisby Lambert to the gallows. It was up to Madam to match his offer. Give me back my baby in return for setting her lover free.

"Mrs. Arnaud ..." I faltered. I had thought I knew what I wanted to say, but even the sound of her name made my throat tighten.

Madam's face hardened, and she turned back to her ointments. She knew what I wanted to ask. "She has arranged everything with the Foundling Hospital," she said, wiping the powder off her face. "Mrs. Arnaud will be coming next week. If she does not take her in soon, she may lose her admission."

"Next week? But she is still so small! And she feeds every few hours. She must stay at least another month."

"Sara, she can be weaned now."

My heart started racing. I focused on the tick-tock of the clock on the wall, trying to calm myself with its relentless rhythm. When I could speak again, I said, "Madam, I should like to ask you something."

"What is it, Sara?" She sounded tired rather than unkind. There were shadows under her eyes where she had wiped away the powder.

"I want you to help me keep my baby."

"Oh, Sara." She put her hands on her dressing table and caught her powder puff under her hand. Dust clouded onto the polished wood. She tutted and wiped at it with her sleeve. I knew her annoyance was not with the powder. She rose and dusted it from her hands in an exaggerated fashion. It was almost biblical, Pilate washing his hands in front of the crowds.

"There is nothing I can do. Mrs. Arnaud has been more than kind already. We cannot tell her now that the child is not going!"

So, it would not do to offend Mrs. Arnaud, but *my* forgiveness— for stealing my own child—was as disposable as the broken cane of her pannier. I picked it up and began to force the rod into the stitched fold of linen. She came over to me and rested her hand on my shoulder. "Think of the child, Sara," she said softly into my ear.

And then it snapped, that little rod. Splintered into two under the pressure of being pushed into a place it could not go.

Esther

The final day in court. If Elias had had his way, even the woman who delivered our warm rolls in the morning would have been there to see his triumph. Finet sat with Moll in the gallery, but Sara sat in the row in front of the jury's table.

Was Bisby's fate now in the hands of a maid? As I looked at her, I thought how little I really knew her. Do you know a person just because of the intimacies you share? In their different ways, my husband and my lady's maid had seen me at my most exposed, shared the workings of my mind and body, yet they were as good as strangers to me in that room. I should have been able to trust them both, but I could predict neither.

Last night, in my room, I had expected Sara to share my horror at the lies Barnstaple was telling. I had expected her reassurance to be swift and emphatic. She would set matters straight. She would bar the path that Barnstaple was trying to lead us down. But instead her eyes had slipped away from mine and she had busied herself with the petty work of a maid, this woman who only months before had been something else entirely. She was not the person she seemed to be. I did not know who she was.

In those idle moments before the judge entered, I let my eyes and my mind wander. I had grown strangely accustomed to the court, its rhythms and rituals over the days we had all sat there. Every morning, I saw the clerk shake out the judge's velvet cushion and place it on his chair, smoothing the surface free of wrinkles. I knew that the juror who sat at the far left of the table did not care for lavender and preferred his place strewn with rosemary. I knew that the door to the passageway leading to Newgate opened at precisely nine o'clock every morning.

That day, a woman in the crowd caught my eye. I knew that I had seen her somewhere before, but I could not place her. She was quite elderly, and others stood up respectfully as she made her way, along the row of people already seated, to an empty place at the far end. She settled herself and took off her shawl. There was precious little else to look at in those tedious minutes, so I kept watching her. And she was watching too, with bright black eyes, her hands neatly folded in her lap. Her gaze followed Sara as she was taken by the clerk to the witness box. Even when the whole court rose and fell with the entry of the judge, she kept watching Sara, a slight curve to her lips, something between a smile and a sneer.

Sara

Everything looked bigger than it had before, as if magnified through glass. I could see the folds of skin of the judge's face and the strands of horsehair in his wig. When the clerk approached me to adjust the mirror, I could see that he had had the pox and his face was pitted with scars. In the gallery, I had looked down at players on a stage, but this was real.

The clerk handed me a Bible. It was the Old Testament, bound in aged leather and worn by the thumbs of a thousand witnesses. I took it gingerly, like the first time Madam had handed me my newborn. It felt heavy in my hands.

"Have you learned your letters?" asked the clerk.

I nodded, and he handed me a piece of parchment with the oath written across it. I could read better than most of the people in that courtroom, but I still stumbled over the words. Everything that had seemed simple from the gallery was like astronomy down there. There was the sound of a baby crying. I snapped round to look, conditioned to the noise, but it was someone else's child. I could see Moll near the front of the gallery with Monsieur Finet, holding my own baby on her knee. The sooner this was over with, the sooner I could get back to my little girl.

Mr. Thorel approached me with a smile that he must have intended to be reassuring. But masters do not smile like that at servants. *Just say what he wants you to say,* I told myself.

The first few questions were easy, the answers falling out of my mouth with perfect sincerity.

"So," said Thorel, stepping nearer to me, "turning to the night of the riot."

I did not want to, but in that instant, I looked at Bisby Lambert, sitting in the dock. I had thought him quite handsome once, with his easy grace and gentle ways. But he was not that man now. He was empty somehow, as if Newgate had hollowed him out, then filled him back up with straw. It did the same to all of them.

What price, my little girl?

"Just a few questions, if I may?" Thorel's voice was curt, as it had been in his withdrawing room. There was always the sense of something more to come with Thorel.

"On the night in question you returned in the afternoon to Buttermilk Alley, did you not?"

"I did, sir."

Then Bisby Lambert lifted his eyes to mine and gave me a faint smile. He was close enough that I could see the cracked skin on his lips. My gut already twisted with remorse and the deed was not yet done.

"You had been turned out of your place of employment because your mistress had discovered your pregnancy, had you not?"

"Well, sir, it was not quite like that."

Thorel gave me a hard stare. "Just simple answers, please, Miss Kemp. That is all I require." He said each word precisely. *Just listen carefully. Just do as I ask. It is all very simple.*

"You are unmarried, correct?" he stated.

I nodded. "Yes."

"And you spent time at Buttermilk Alley, did you not?"

"I ran errands there sometimes."

Mr. Thorel smiled. "Indeed, but you spent more time there than that. Alone. In the company of the journeymen who lived there."

One of the men on the jury shook his head and took up his quill to make a note on the paper in front of him. Whispered disapproval floated down from the gallery.

"On occasion, you were even at Buttermilk Alley when the combination met there, weren't you?"

"I may have seen some other journeymen there from time to time. I don't know about them being part of a combination or otherwise."

"Mr. Lambert led the combination, didn't he?"

Bisby Lambert tried to clear his throat and it brought on his racking cough. No one could speak until he had quietened. In those moments, while I watched him labor to breathe, I wondered what wrong can be done when life is taken from a man already dying. My baby's whole life, in exchange for a few weeks of his.

"He did, sir," I said, and as I spoke those words I felt horrified and thrilled in equal measure. It was as if I were catapulting myself into a place I'd never been before. Somewhere I was wretched and beyond redemption. Somewhere I was free.

Thorel smiled and nodded, encouraged by my response.

"And, from what you observed that night at Buttermilk Alley, John Barnstaple is correct when he says that it was Lambert who spurred on the men to riot?"

I could hardly speak, so I left the answer to creep into the silence.

"Is that yes, Miss Kemp?"

I nodded and whispered, "Yes," a tiny movement as if even the air around me had become heavier than I could bear. And all the while he was looking at me with his sad, kind eyes.

"And is the first defendant, Bisby Lambert, the father of your child?"

"What is the purpose of asking?" I said. "Fathering a child is not the same as cutting silk."

Some of the journeymen sniggered. Thorel grew impatient. "It is plainly relevant to the moral character of the man."

The judge interrupted: "Miss Kemp, I understand that all this is difficult for you—a servant and a woman—to understand, but you must answer Mr. Thorel's questions. It is Mr. Barnstaple's contention that

Mr. Lambert was dismissed because he was the father of your child, and that Mr. Lambert sought revenge for that dismissal by cutting Mr. Thorel's silk. It is a question of motive. Do you understand?" The judge peered at me over his spectacles until I gave him the nod that he sought, then he sat back in his chair.

"So," insisted Thorel. "Who is the father of your child?"

"I came back to Buttermilk Alley to find him—the father, I mean. I asked him to help me, but he wouldn't, that much is true. I felt faint, so I went outside and when I fell it was him that caught me."

"You mean, Mr. Lambert?"

How I wished it had not been. I remembered the hurt and disappointment I felt when I had come to my senses and seen Lambert kneeling beside me instead of Barnstaple.

"Yes," I said.

"And he followed you outside and caught you when you fainted because he is the father of your child, isn't he?"

I said nothing. Up in the gallery my baby had heard my voice and leaned down toward me, extending her arm as if she could somehow grab me from all the way up there. "Wah," she cried, swiping toward me. If I did not say what he wanted, would they take her from me right now? Would Moll be asked to carry her from the court straight to the doorstep of the Foundling Hospital?

Madam stared at me from the seats to my side, her face blank but her eyes infinitely sad. Then I saw a woman only a few seats down from Mrs. Thorel. Birdlike and watchful. She was wearing her special wig for the occasion, an elaborate thing stuck with ribbons and combs. But underneath it, she was still the same person. The sight of her drained the blood from my head and brought it back to my face in a flush. She seemed to be enjoying my reaction and gave me a wide smile. She had lost a tooth since I had seen her last. Her watchful gaze was like a mirror held up in front of me. Was this the person I had become? Whore to liar?

"You must answer the question." Thorel was agitated: a muscle worked in his jaw.

I looked Thorel full in the eye. "No, he is not." A suitably simple answer. "John Barnstaple is."

Thorel looked as if he might explode. He strode back to his bench and grabbed a handful of his papers, staring at them as if what to do with me might be written down in them somewhere. He looked up at the judge. "I have no more questions for this witness," he said.

"And what is more," I almost did not recognize my own voice, ringing clearly round the courtroom, "I take back what I have already said. It was not Lambert who led the combination, it was Barnstaple."

"I said I have no further questions," spat Thorel.

"And it was not Lambert who rallied the men to riot, it was Barnstaple. That is, if they were not riled up enough already by their hatred of Mr. Thorel."

For the first time in three days, the court was truly silent. Even my own child stared down at me, quiet and alert. I realized then that she would never even remember her own mother. But at least, at that precise moment, she looked down on an honest woman.

Thorel approached the judge. "My lord, given the circumstances, I would like permission to call a further witness."

"Whom do you wish to call?"

Thorel straightened and looked out across the court. "I call Mrs. Margaret Swann."

Esther

Mrs. Swann, that's who she was.

She looked different with that ridiculous headpiece. The last time I had seen her she had been drenched with rain, her straggly gray hair plastered in strips down the sides of her face. But there was certainly a familiarity about her. Perhaps it was the smug smile with its cruel twist.

Sara rose so that Mrs. Swann could take her place in the witness box. At one point the two women passed each other so close that Sara had to turn sideways to allow Mrs. Swann and her elaborate skirts to pass. When she did, I saw Sara's face clearly. She looked as fearful as a rabbit with a fox coming near. Mrs. Swann merely nodded to her as if they were old acquaintances passing in the street.

Mrs. Swann settled herself into the witness box. She had brought a fan with her and swiped it briefly back and forth in front of her face, then flicked it shut and took the Bible the clerk handed to her. She examined it with mild interest as if it was not something she was familiar with. I could well imagine that mine was the only Bible to have been in the Wig and Feathers. Once she had read the oath, she turned pleasantly to Elias. He approached her somewhat warily, as if she were a cat twisting around his legs, appearing friendly but capable of lashing out with hidden claws.

"I have just a few questions for you, Mrs. Swann."

Mrs. Swann inclined her head, gracious as a queen.

"You are the proprietress of the Wig and Feathers tavern, are you not?"

"I am indeed, sir," said Mrs. Swann, giving a gap-toothed grin. All over the court flurries of whispering went up. Mrs. Swann seemed not to mind. She might have announced that she ran the bakery on Quaker Street.

Elias cleared his throat. "And tell me, is this woman known to you?" He rotated and pointed at Sara.

Mrs. Swann followed his gesture with her eyes. For a moment Sara and Mrs. Swann stared at each other, until Mrs. Swann nodded slowly and said, "She certainly is, sir."

"What name do you know her by?"

"Miss Sara Kemp, of course. Same name everyone knows her by."

"And how do you know her, Mrs. Swann?"

"Why, she was one of my best girls, sir. When she behaved herself, which was not often, I can tell you."

The whispers became catcalls. Sara sat rigid in her seat, the vortex of the storm gathering around her.

The judge frowned and addressed Mrs. Swann. "I'm afraid you must clarify exactly what you mean by one of your girls."

"She were a whore!" shouted someone from the gallery.

Mrs. Swann gave a sad smile to the judge. "I'm afraid that's true, my lord. Miss Kemp is a prostitute."

Behind us someone hissed and threw something at Sara. It hit the side of her face. I saw her body flinch, but she didn't turn round. After a second, she slowly raised her hand and wiped away the smear that it had left across her cheek.

Elias took a step closer to Mrs. Swann. It gave the impression of conspiracy between them, intimacy even. "Would it be fair, do you think, Mrs. Swann, to say that Miss Kemp is a woman almost completely lacking in morality? In basic decency?"

"Well, I don't know, sir." Mrs. Swann shifted in her seat. "All my girls are decent. It's just that some of them have had a hard life. They can't be blamed for the hand they were dealt."

Elias shook his head. "There is no blame here, Mrs. Swann. It is the defendants, not Miss Kemp, who are on trial after all. My only question is, would she lie, do you think?"

"Oh, she'd lie just as soon as turn a trick with a sailor, that one!"

The journeymen burst into jeers and laughter. Barnstaple had blanched at Mrs. Swann's revelation, but the color was returning to his cheeks. Anger, perhaps, or excitement. The relish men can feel at the humiliation of women. Only Bisby looked at Sara with compassion. She had tried to save him. She had gambled her own future against his and they had both lost. What now for either of them? A year ago, they had not even been part of my life, but now I could not bear the thought of losing them. Especially not him. Sara's past was her own, whereas Bisby's misfortune was the one to which I had led him. How do you say sorry from across a room?

What use are fragile sentiments to a man who may hang? He shifted his gaze from Sara to me, drawn to meet my eye as if my desperation were a kind of vacuum. I searched his face for some indication that he understood, but I couldn't read his expression.

"Go on," said Elias, when the court had settled.

"There was a gentleman—esteemed within this parish and so you'll forgive me for not mentioning him by name—who came to the Wig and Feathers one night. He came to see me after he had had to do with that girl there. His pocket watch was missing, he said. Then lo and behold,

Miss Kemp has three pounds, eight shillings, and sixpence jingling in her pocket."

"Could there not have been a perfectly innocent explanation for that, Mrs. Swann?"

"Might 'ave been, but she ran off quick as a wink before I could ask her."

"So Miss Kemp is a whore and, quite likely, a thief as well?" Elias turned to the jury and said, "This is a woman who came into my house and kept all this hidden from me. She sat at my table and ate my food. She took wages for a job she had absolutely no right to do." His voice escalated with every point he made. By the end he was almost shouting.

Just when Elias must have been thinking he had won, the judge leaned toward him and spoke, his voice loaded with quiet authority: "Why have you brought this woman into my court?"

"My lord, I am trying to establish that the evidence of the previous witness cannot be relied upon."

"She was your own witness, Mr. Thorel."

Elias fidgeted in front of the judge. "Indeed, my lord, but when she gave untrue evidence, I felt that I had to make the court aware of her background. The simple fact is, the court cannot believe the word of a woman of such ill repute."

"But it can believe the word of her madam? The keeper of this disorderly house?"

Elias floundered, searching for a reason why a caricature of womanhood like Mrs. Swann could be believed, but not one of her girls. The judge did not give him a chance to answer. I was beginning to warm to this reserved and austere man. He did not seem to be taken in by the posturing before him.

"Mr. Thorel, I will give you one last opportunity to present evidence that might be of assistance to this court. Otherwise, I will consider your case to be concluded." He nodded to his clerk, who rose and hastily ushered Mrs. Swann out of the witness box.

Elias' case was in disarray. No one had stuck to the same story. The only thing the jury could do was stack half-truths against each other and see which pile was highest. For the first time in all the days I had sat in court, I began to believe there was a chance that they would look at Bisby and see what I saw: an honorable working man brought low by the vicious retribution of his master. When I looked at Bisby the pallor of his face seemed to be lifted, as if the chance of freedom had flushed through him like a physic.

Sara

I knew she would be waiting for me. Mrs. Swann had flounced straight out after her evidence and now loitered in the hallway outside the door to the courtroom, her fan swishing back and forth in front of her face. She snapped it closed when she saw me.

"Once a whore, always a whore, eh?" she said, stepping toward me.

I looked at the floor and tried to move past her toward the small staircase that would take me back to the gallery, but she grabbed my arm. The fingers that held me were as bony and insistent as they had been the day I had met her in Spitalfields market.

"I'm just trying to get back to my baby," I said, still staring at the floor.

"That squalling bastard up there?" She grabbed my chin with her other hand and twisted my head up to look at her.

Her fan dug into my cheek. It smelled of sweet musk and lye, the essence of the Wig and Feathers caught within its folds.

"I told you you'd never be able to get away from me, didn't I? Now you see that I was right." I studied her wig, dusted with powder and edged with a smear of face paint. She gave my face a frustrated shake. "Look at me," she said.

I dragged my eyes to hers. They were set like beads of onyx in her whitened face. Her lips were a vermilion streak beneath them. She made Lucy Carey look like a wholesome farm girl. "How did you know I was here?" I asked.

"Maybe you haven't made as many friends in your new household as you think." She smiled, revealing the gap in her teeth again. "They all know what you are," she continued. "Now you can't pretend to be a lady's maid—or whatever it is you think you are." She let go of me and began to stroke my cheek with a shaky hand, affectionate suddenly. Her face softened, and the skin lay in powder-creased folds either side of her mouth. "Come back to us, Sara. We'll even take the little one."

I grabbed her wrist and pulled her hand away from me. "Leave me alone."

"What a thing to say to your only friend in the world! I'd try to keep me sweet, if I were you. It's only me that's keeping the constable from your door. I should have thought you'd had quite enough of courtrooms as it is!"

I turned to walk up the stairs, but above me small feet in neat shoes were stepping their way down, kicking out frothy skirts with each tread. It was Moll in her best dress, the one she wore to church to sit next to the master, daydreaming no doubt that she was his wife.

"What have you done with my baby?" I said, trying not to sound concerned.

Moll rolled her aquamarine eyes. "It's with Monsieur Finet," she replied, her words coming out in impatient little taps, like her footsteps.

I did not stay to ask her where she thought she was going. I just waited for her to get off the stairs and went straight up to my daughter.

"Good day to you, pretty little girl," I heard Mrs. Swann say to Moll as she passed.

My baby was far more interested in Monsieur Finet than he was in her. As I pushed along the row of people to get to them, she was grabbing handfuls of his fleshy jowls and squeezing them. I would have taken her home then and there, but as I plucked her from his hands, I saw something that surprised me. Moll was now sitting in the witness box, tidying the curls away from her face and smiling at the jurors. And they all sat up, those men, and looked at her. Moll behaved as if she barely noticed. She was so used to the attention of men that she simply accepted it, like the sun shining on her face.

Then she started speaking in her quiet elfin voice, taking the oath like a solemn child. The eternal rustling and fidgeting in the gallery stopped. Even the women leaned forward in their seats to hear what the little doll had to say. I lowered myself onto the bench.

"If it pleases your honor, I am able to tell you exactly what happened in the garret that night. I was busy all the time the riot was going on, helping my mistress, Mrs. Thorel, with her lady's maid. Having a baby, she was, but it was not going well. The baby was stuck fast, like a cork in a bottle, and no amount of tugging or pulling was getting it out. Well, the wee thing was turning gray—at least its foot was. That was all we could see. Madam didn't know what to do so I said I'd go and get help. It was dangerous outside that room, what with all the rioting and the like, but I wasn't thinking about myself, just about the babe, who was as innocent in this world as it is possible to be."

Some of the jurors nodded and smiled at her. Even through the haze of my pain and bewilderment that night, that wasn't my recollection of what she had done.

"We had all guessed that the father was one of the journeymen. I had seen Miss Kemp go off to Buttermilk Alley with my own eyes, after all, and more than once. So I went to fetch them. Out in the hall, it was quiet. There was plenty going on down in the square, but the house itself seemed to be empty. I was about to run downstairs, when I heard voices from the garret, male voices that sounded like Mr. Lambert and Mr. Barnstaple. I wasn't sure whether to go up, because it sounded like they were arguing, but I did, for the baby's sake."

Moll paused a moment, toying with her handkerchief as if wondering whether to go on.

"And what did you see when you got to the garret?" asked the judge, more kindly than he had spoken before.

"I saw him cut the silk, my lord."

"Him?" prompted Thorel.

"Mr. Lambert, sir." Moll turned her almond eyes on Elias Thorel for just a moment longer than she needed to. Then she shifted her gaze back to the judge and jury. "I opened the door and Mr. Barnstaple was shouting at Mr. Lambert saying, 'Put it down,' or something like that. They were in a bit of a tussle and Mr. Barnstaple was grabbing at the cutlass that was in Mr. Lambert's hand. But Mr. Lambert just shoved him aside. Then he grabbed the silk and sliced it right off the loom with that cutlass."

The judge looked grave. "Do you have anything else to tell the court?"

Moll shook her head. "That very moment the King's men arrived and, well, they could tell you as much as I from then on."

The judge nodded and bent his head to speak to his clerk. Moll sat there patiently during their whispered exchange, demurely inspecting her hands, while the jurymen cast her occasional glances and pretended to write notes. She must have looked pretty as an angel to them.

And angels don't lie.

Esther

Despite all the memories it held, the garret was still one of my favorite places in the house. By the time we had gotten back from court, it was about five o'clock in the afternoon before I could get up there. It was April and the days were longer. Too long. The same light that had been so precious when Bisby and I were weaving was now just time that had to be endured before I could end another day separated from him.

My petticoat lay crumpled on top of the silk where Elias had thrown it. There was no one to hide it from now. I pulled away the material and let it fall onto the floor. I stood there for a moment, struck again by the luminescence of the silk. I trailed my fingers over the flowers as they arced across the gathering roller. *Blackberry and Wild Rose.* It made me think of myself and Sara to see the wild roses' steady progression through the silk, with the blackberry, tart and prickly, among it.

Bisby had been right. The run of white threads through the weft lifted the piece and gave definition to the intricate flowers meandering across the warp. I would never have thought of putting them together, assuming that the pale yellow would seem faded against the bright white. Instead it enhanced it and gave it a life it would not otherwise have had. Just as Bisby had done for me.

I walked to the other end of the loom. I had always been the one pulling the lashes while Bisby controlled the rigid limbs of wood and cord. I sat down on the weaving bench. Bisby was in Newgate and Elias had let his obsession with convicting Bisby take over his life. The looms had lain dormant since the riot, lending an unnatural quiet to the house. Mine was the only silk left now. I inspected the edge as it met the heddles, expecting it to end partway through the final repeat, but I saw that it had been neatly finished. He must have done that with Ives after I had told him my visits to the attic had to stop. True to his word: *I promised you I would help you weave this silk and I will do it.* He had done everything he said he would do, fulfilled every promise, and what had I done in return? Prevented him from finishing his master piece and earned him the wrath of his master. I could not even bring myself to think of the final step, that it might be me who sent him to the gallows. And for what? My love of silk? My love of him?

I picked up the shuttle and raised the heddles. I had not been able to weave before because Bisby had been standing behind me, secure and reassuring, yet maddeningly distracting. It took a few attempts to time the throw of the shuttle with the lift and drop of the heddles, but after a while I fell into a rhythm and the garret was filled with its familiar *clack-clack-boom* again. One inch of plain weave was all that was needed before I could remove the piece. No need for a drawboy, no pattern mechanism to set, just the simple build of warp on weft.

I finished as the light was fading. There was just enough time to release the tension of the warp threads and gather them together to knot. Cutting it from the loom was like severing the birth cord, both an end and a beginning. There was nothing left to bring Bisby and me together, but what I now held in my hands was something new and precious.

42

Sara

She didn't even hear me come in. She was too busy singing a little song to herself under her breath as she spun the coin on the kitchen table. Every so often it would hit a knot in the oak and clatter flatly on the wood. She didn't seem to tire of picking it up again and watching its dull golden sides flash in the candlelight.

"I always knew that if you throw a penny up high enough, it'll land in someone's pocket."

Moll looked up at me standing in the doorway, then slapped her hand down over the guinea, quietening its metallic clang.

"Where did you get that?" I said, approaching her.

Moll slid her hand, palm down, across the wood until the coin fell off the table into her lap. "Get what?" she said.

I laughed. "You must think me a fool."

Moll tipped her head to one side. "I might call you many things, but a fool wouldn't be one of them."

"I'm surprised he had to pay you to lie. I thought you would've done it for nothing, given what else you do for him."

Moll gave me an overly sweet smile. "I have no idea what you mean. Don't make the mistake of judging me by your own standards."

Her words didn't sting me. There was nothing this girl could say to me that had not been offered up to the whole parish this afternoon.

"Anyway," Moll stopped trying to hide the money and cupped it in her hand, "who says I was lying? How do you know what I saw up in the garret? Far as I remember, you were flat on your back at the time, snorting like a sow in muck."

I dragged out a stool from under the table and sat down. She glared at me, but I ignored her and laid my forearms on the table. "You'll go to Hell for what you've done," I said.

"Better to go to Hell in a fine gown and a new bonnet than rumble off in a cart to sift cinders at Tottenham Court, which is what you'll soon be doing."

"Do you really think he'll prefer you to her once you're wearing a fine gown?"

Moll's eyes left the coin in her hand and searched my face.

"What do you mean?"

"You're just a scullery maid and she is the quality. Even a hundred guineas won't change that."

"You wouldn't be so nice about her if you knew what I've been doing just now." Moll got up, slipping the guinea into the pocket of her apron. She walked over to the kitchen dresser and brought back a piece of material draped over her arms.

"Beautiful, isn't it?" she said, laying it out before me on the table. "Madam said that she and her sister were christened in it. It's to be your baby's token."

"Token?"

"Yes, the thing your little foundling will take with her to the hospital so that she can be identified later if anyone ever comes to claim her." Moll gave me a vicious little glance. "Should anyone ever want to claim such a base-born thing."

On the table was a cream silk christening shawl, edged with intricate lace embroidered with flowers and scrolls. It was so beautiful, I felt compelled to touch it, but Moll whisked it from the table when I reached out my hand.

"Best not have the likes of you touch it, not after I've spent so long making it nice. I must say, I'm glad the poor mite will finally be christened. She's been a nameless bastard far too long as it is."

If there had not been a yard of oak between us, I would have taken that dainty shawl and twisted it round her neck, and well she knew it. When Monsieur Finet walked in, she scuttled over to him like a dog called to heel and busied herself wrapping the shawl in tissue. Finet sat down heavily in his chair and began to ease off his shoes. "I'm exhausted," he said, holding them up so that Moll could put them by the hearth. "It'll be good to get back to normal after all this unpleasantness." I watched him as he sat back in the chair and reached across his chest to rub at his shoulder. The cat sprang onto his lap and circled round, following its own tail until it was comfortable.

"It was a difficult day in court for you, Kemp," said Finet, idly stroking the cat's copper fur. "That's the thing about a past like yours. You can't escape it. It marks you forever—like the pox." Behind him, Moll gave a snigger as she snipped off a length of string to tie round the tissue-wrapped shawl.

I had spent all the time since leaving court wondering how Elias Thorel had known of my connection to Mrs. Swann and where to find her. There was something pointed about Finet's words, something so deliberate that it made me think of Mrs. Swann's remark outside the courtroom. She was right: I had made no friends in this household. I got up and walked over to the hearth as if I were about to put on a pot of water to boil, but instead I stopped in front of Finet's chair. When he saw my skirts in front of him his hand stilled. The cat half opened an eye.

"What is it, woman?" His voice was low and resonant with warning. What did I care? I had nothing to lose.

"How did you know about me?"

Finet thought for a moment, then looked up. "Didn't do you much good, did it?"

"What?"

"That Bible Mrs. Thorel sent you. If you'd spent a bit more time reading it, and a bit less time at Buttermilk Alley, you wouldn't be in the trouble you're in now."

In the corner, Moll had stopped preparing the parcel and was watching us with eyes as round and gleaming as the fat guinea in her pocket.

"How did you know about the Bible?"

Monsieur Finet chuckled. "Mrs. Thorel asked me to deliver it to the Wig and Feathers. Even then I didn't know who you were when you turned up on the doorstep. It was young Moll who found the book and brought it straight to me."

"Found my Bible?" I spoke through gritted teeth, staring at Moll. "You've been going through my things?"

Moll ignored me and lowered her gaze back to the christening shawl, tying a neat bow with purposeful fingers. The cat stood up and stretched on Finet's lap, then jumped onto the floor. Finet got up and pulled out a slab of mutton, hacking it into chunks while the cat looked on with watchful amber eyes.

Esther

You might have thought it would take longer to decide whether a man lives or dies than it would take to drink a glass of port. But that was exactly how long it took. The jury retired for their refreshments after Moll gave her evidence and were ready with the verdict the next morning. There was land to be managed, after all, tea and sugar to be imported and sold, silver to be wrought into trinkets to adorn the wives and houses of those fine men. No more time could be spent sitting in court deciding the fate of common working men.

The defendants were asked to stand in front of the judge one by one. They took Barnstaple first, pulling him by the arm so hard that he stumbled. But those chains did not hang heavy on him for long. The clerk was already unlocking them before the foreman had finished delivering the verdict. Barnstaple brought his newly released hands in front of his face, inspecting them as if someone had just put them there. In the gallery, crowds of journeymen cheered and shouted his name, as if he were a fighter in a ring. Then he tilted his head back and raked his fingers through his thick black hair. Relief filled his cheeks with air and made him nicker like a horse.

Bisby watched Barnstaple intently, as if he were a parody of himself acting out what might be. When it was his turn to stand, Bisby leaned heavily on the clerk's arm as he walked the short distance to the judge and jury.

Heads you win, tails you lose. But why could they not both be set free? If the jury couldn't decide who had cut the silk, then surely they could convict neither man. I was wrong to imagine that this trial was some kind of duel to the death between these men. Their fates were linked whether they liked it or not. Barnstaple's freedom predicted Bisby's own. It had to, because there was no more evidence to convict Bisby than Barnstaple.

Apart from that pretty little girl, her words spoken like pearls of truth from the mouth of a paragon. Apart from her.

The jury foreman cleared his throat and readied himself. Just that tiny affectation was enough to strip the warmth from my blood. It shifted the center of my being, so that the world seemed to deconstruct around me. Why did the foreman need a clear throat and a straight back to free a man? Elias seemed to tense beside me, becoming more alert, the optimism I had felt moments before being sucked from me into him.

The judge asked him for his verdict on all three charges. The foreman read with perfect clarity. "Charge one, guilty. Charge two, guilty. Charge three, guilty."

Each one a hammer blow. Each time the word was repeated, a fresh insult, hope receding with every breath.

The judge asked Bisby if he knew of any reason why the sentence of death should not be passed. He shook his head in mute despair. He was neither a woman nor a clergyman, what hope had he to escape the noose? The judge placed the square of black silk on his head, but it sat too far forward so that the corner pointed down almost to his nose. He pushed it back up, dislodging his wig as he did so, exposing an edge of brown hair flecked with gray. A glimpse of the real man underneath all this ceremony.

Then he told Bisby he would die. He said that he would be taken back to Newgate and, on the seventeenth of April 1769, from there to a temporary gallows erected in Bethnal Green so that all who lived there could learn from his example. He told him he would be hanged by the neck until he was dead and that thereafter his body would be buried within the precincts of the prison. By this time, the court was so silent that the judge's final words were spoken with absolute clarity.

"May the Lord have mercy upon your soul."

My husband leaned back in his chair. He took the glass of malmsey wine I handed him without remark, or even looking at me. He was staring into the empty grate as if it were a miniature theater. I tried to slip from the room.

"Do you know what the best part of all this is?" he said, just as my hand was closing over the door handle. I stood there silently: he did not want an answer. "It is that he will be hanged outside the Salmon and Ball. Not at Tyburn, but here in Bethnal Green, where everyone we know will be there to see it." He twisted in his seat to look at me. His eyes were strangely incandescent. "Where *you* will be there to see it."

He took a swig from his fourth glass of wine. "Why did you bring a whore into my house?" My hand tightened on the door handle. "Do you think I am stupid, Mrs. Thorel? Did you think I would not find out that there was another whore in my house?"

"I am not a whore."

"Whore, daughter of a whore, what's the difference? *If the foundations are destroyed, what can the righteous do?*"

"I wanted to give her a chance to lead a better life," I said.

"Then you are a fool," he said, swilling the wine round the glass. "Whores never change. *Draw near seed of the adulterer and the whore. Against whom make ye a wide mouth and draw out the tongue? Are ye not children of transgression, a seed of falsehood?*"

"You quote the Bible, yet there is nothing Christian about you or your actions. You, too, have sinned and fall short of the glory of God."

"Me?" He hung his arm over the back of his chair so that he could move further round to face me. "What have I done but make sure that justice was served? You call me a sinner, but the other master weavers are calling me a hero. They are saying I have saved Spitalfields. Think of the riots that will never happen because of what I have done. The property that will not be destroyed and the silk that will never be cut. Why, I have probably even saved someone's life, just by calling those weavers to account and making an example of Bisby Lambert."

"Have you finished, husband?" His face darkened. I walked back round to stand in front of him and bent over his chair. "With the wine? Shall I take it away?" I picked up the half-empty bottle by his chair and held it up to him.

He laughed and swiped it from my hand. "Indeed I have not, Mrs. Thorel. I am celebrating, and you will sit there to celebrate with me."

"No, I will not. I have nothing to celebrate with you." I remained standing in front of him.

He poured a glass of wine, which he held out to me. When I didn't take it, he returned it to the table. "As you wish. You see," he said, "people like you and Lambert always think you are doing good turns, but you'd be better off leaving well alone. I can't imagine Lambert's best pleased he helped you now, is he? And soon you'll be thinking the same about that Kemp girl."

"What do you mean?"

He took a sip of wine, able to take his time now he held my interest. "Did you think I would let her get away with humiliating me any more than Lambert got away with it? I allowed her and that bastard to stay here and she repaid me by making me look a fool. Of course, I knew it might happen. That was why I made sure I found out all about her. Now she'll pay for what she's done."

Did he mean that Mrs. Swann was coming for Sara?

"She will suffer enough when the child goes to the Foundling Hospital."

"No," he shook his head, "the bastards of loose women don't go to the Foundling Hospital. Now that everyone knows what she is, the place has been withdrawn."

"I don't believe you! Why would you do that to a child?"

"It is not my doing, it's hers. Anyway, Bridewell will be good for her. She'll be a new woman after a year spent beating hemp and having some morals whipped into her."

I felt disgusted by him. When he looked at me for a response, I had only one to give. "Remember, husband, the harlots will go into the Kingdom of God before you."

43

Sara

"What are you doing?"

He shrugged nonchalantly, tossing shirts and breeches into a cloth bag. Outside the window the milkmaids sang on the street corner to the sound of their clanking pails, calling the town to buy their morning buttermilk. I barely noticed them now. Their melodic chatter had become as unremarkable to me as the pulse of Bisby Lambert's loom at Spital Square. John Barnstaple straightened up. "There's nothing left here for me now. Better I go back to Bermondsey."

"I didn't know you were from Bermondsey."

"And I didn't know you were a strumpet." Barnstaple sighed and folded a waistcoat over his arm. "Anyway, I'm not. My wife is."

"Your wife?" He might as well have told me he was off to join the navy. "You're married?"

Barnstaple smiled grimly. "I'm afraid I am. It seems there is much we didn't know about each other."

He searched my face, hoping for a reaction, but my emotions had been stripped away by each falsehood I had heard him tell. Lying on his pallet, our baby tugged one of his shirts out of the bag and stuffed the end of it into her mouth.

"You are leaving because you fear the other journeymen weavers," I told him. Among all the lies, I wanted there to be one moment of truth, when he would know the man he was and know that I knew it too. "You are a liar and a coward. The journeymen know better than anyone the lies you told! They know you made Lambert into your whipping boy."

Barnstaple's face was set hard, eyes narrowed. He turned and shoved the waistcoat into his bag, then pulled his shirt away from the baby. She started in surprise, tiny arms flailing.

"The mob will watch Lambert hang and then they'll come for you," I went on, not wanting to stop, "and when they do, you'll be begging them to take you to Tyburn instead. And I'll be there, watching them do it."

"Will you?" He took a step toward me. It was the closest I had been to him in months. Close enough to see the texture of his skin and the stubs of hair around his jaw. "What are you doing here, then? If you find me so despicable, why do you keep turning up, like a bad penny, just like you've always done?" He looked at me with that same gloomy intensity and for a moment I didn't know if he might strike or kiss me. Then he bent toward me. "You still want me, don't you?"

"No," I whispered. "I want my Bastardy Bond."

He jerked back, mouth curling in distaste. "Of course you do. I've had my fun and now I need to pay for it!" He picked up his bag and swung it over his shoulder. "They'll never make me pay a Bastardy Bond when you've lain with near every man in the parish," he said. "Still, I'm happy to pay my fair share." He dug into his pocket, then tossed a ha'penny onto the mattress.

I picked my baby up from the pallet, not wanting her to be anywhere near where that man had been. Then I left him standing in the garret, taking a last look around, his eyes lingering on the loom standing silent by the window.

I remember his last words to me, called out from the attic as I stepped carefully down the stairs with our child in my arms: "If you really loved her, you would let her go."

ॐ · ॐ

It was lying on Madam's dressing table when I got back to Spital Square. Wrapped in tissue and tied neatly with string. Without Moll's meddling, I might have thought it some new lace sleeves for one of Madam's gowns, but I knew what it meant. They must be coming for my daughter today. I turned and fled up the stairs to my room, half expecting the cot to be standing empty, even though I knew I had only just put her down. When I saw that she was still there, I fell to my knees and covered her sleeping body with my own, my tears dampening her downy hair. I had tried everything I could to keep her and now they were coming for her. I had no idea what kind of life I could give her. All I knew was that I would rather die than be parted from her.

From far below there was the rumble of carriage wheels over cobblestones. I went over to my little window and watched as the Arnauds' carriage drew into Spital Square.

Esther

Elias was upstairs lying down, feeling the effects of the bottle of malmsey wine he had drunk the night before. I'd been watching for Mr. Arnaud's carriage, and when he stepped through the door of the workshop, I was waiting for him.

"Mrs. Thorel," he said, surprised.

"Mr. Thorel is unwell, I'm afraid."

"No matter," he said. "I have other errands to run." He made as if to return to his carriage.

"Before you go, Mr. Arnaud, I was wondering if I could ask you what you thought of this?"

I lifted the bolt of cloth and placed it on the wooden counter. Mr. Arnaud came over and watched as I held the end of the silk in place and rolled *Blackberry and Wild Rose* over the full length of the counter.

He stared at it for a while, then nodded slowly. "It's very fine," he

265

acknowledged. "But an unusual design. I've not seen such natural-looking flowers before. Who is the *dessinateur*?"

"*Dessinatrice*, Mr. Arnaud. I drew the pattern for this silk."

Mr. Arnaud smiled politely. "But you jest, Mrs. Thorel."

"No, sir, I do not. This is a silk of my own design and I am offering to sell it to you. Of course, if it doesn't interest you …"

I began to roll up the silk, but he placed a hand on my arm. "No, please. It is quite beautiful, and the quality of the weaving is superb. I'll give you eighteen shillings a yard for it, my best price."

"But it's worth more."

He shrugged.

"I will accept your price, Mr. Arnaud, but on one condition."

"Go on."

"I want you to take this silk to the Worshipful Company of Weavers. I want you to tell them that it was made by the finest weaver in Spitalfields. Then I want you to pay them the fee to admit Bisby Lambert as a master weaver."

He let out a breath, a sigh that was almost a laugh. "You can't be serious, Mrs. Thorel."

"I am perfectly serious."

"Well, I'm afraid I won't do it."

I nodded and began to roll up the silk. "You will have heard of my unfortunate lady's maid, Sara Kemp, I'm sure."

"Everyone in Spitalfields has heard about your maid, Mrs. Thorel," he said grimly.

"Such scandal! The Wig and Feathers indeed!"

He took out his pocket watch and glanced at it. "I beg your pardon, madam, but my other errands …"

"You would not believe the stories she told me about it. Why, there was this one particular man, I blush even to mention it to you, but she told me that he liked to—what is the phrase those girls use?—*bake his bread in a cold oven*."

He stood perfectly still, his hand tight around his shiny gold pocket watch. "I really wouldn't know what goes on in such places," he said.

"Indeed not, sir! Nonetheless, I would like you to go to the Weavers'
Company and ensure that Bisby Lambert is admitted as a master weaver.
In fact, I might say that I *insist* upon it."

He set his jaw and dropped his watch back into his pocket. Then he
gave a curt nod. "I'll send my footman for the silk."

Sara

I heard a light tread upon the stairs. Was she coming up herself, or had she sent Moll to take my baby from me? I picked up my sleeping daughter and held her so close that she snuffled and hiccuped into my shoulder. I walked over to the window and looked down into the street. The Arnauds' carriage was still waiting outside the house, the signature mulberry tree carved into its door. The sudden silence made my head snap round. She must be just outside my door. "*Rock-a-bye, baby …*" I started to sing.

The door creaked open slowly, almost respectfully. I was relieved to see that it was Madam. My grief was enough, without Moll there to enjoy it. I turned away from her toward the window, shielding my baby, still murmuring that song into her ear. Madam stood there for a moment, then started walking toward me. I huddled so close to the window that the baby's head was almost touching it. My breath misted the glass as I sang the last words of the song.

"Sara?" Madam was right behind me now. She brought up her hand and rested it lightly on my shoulder. I flinched as if it were hot as burning coal. The baby opened her sleepy eyes and blinked in the unexpected light from the window.

"Sara," said Madam again, more urgently than before.

I was shaking my head. "No, no," I said, over and over again. Madam gave her characteristic sigh. The one she used when I had knocked over one of her powder pots, or when the bath water wasn't hot enough. She reached across me to take hold of my other shoulder and twisted me round to face her. "I am going to help you," she said.

Madam was looking at me intently, searching my face with her eyes. Below the window I heard the front door slam shut and a coachman call out to his horses. Then there was the clatter of hooves over cobblestones. I glanced down into the empty street.

"It's just Mr. Arnaud," Madam said. The light from the window was shining full into her face. I could see the flecks of green and blue in her eyes and the fringe of pale lashes.

"I thought it was Mrs. Arnaud come to take my baby to the Foundling Hospital."

"She will not be coming."

"I don't understand. What about the baby's place there?"

Madam looked grave. "She has none. Mr. Thorel has seen to that. Sara, he's going to send you both to Bridewell. You cannot stay here. You must leave as soon as you can."

"Leave?" I almost laughed, I was becoming quite hysterical. "Where could I go? To the poorhouse to await Mrs. Swann and the constable banging on the door? I'd be better off in Bridewell! If I had somewhere to go, do you not think I would have gone there already? Who will have me with a baby? What work could I get? How will I feed and clothe us?" Madam reached out and pressed her fingertips against my lips. It was such an intimate gesture that I fell mute with surprise.

"Shush," she said. Then she reached into her skirts and drew out her purse. "This is for you." When she held out her palm to me, there were gold coins on it.

"Two guineas! Madam, I couldn't take that."

"You can," she said lightly. "Consider it a gift ... from Mr. Arnaud."

"Why did he give you money?"

"I sold him my silk."

"But my debt?"

She took my hand and pressed the coins into it. "You have more than repaid your debt."

"You are too kind, madam." She had always been kinder to me than I deserved. But she just smiled and gently squeezed my hand before she let it go. I must say that it felt good to hold Mr. Arnaud's money.

Madam's expression darkened so quickly that I thought she must have changed her mind. Then she said, "They will hang him next week." She looked stricken, as if just saying the words out loud would make it happen.

I nodded slowly. I had not been at court when Bisby was sentenced, but I had heard Moll and Monsieur Finet picking over the news as if it were a chicken carcass.

She looked at me urgently. "That is when you must go," she said. "The Justice of the Peace will not come for you until after Elias has made you watch Bisby Lambert hang. Everyone in Spitalfields will be outside the Salmon and Ball that day. We will say you are too ill to go and then you must be gone before we get back."

I was nodding at her, but I hardly knew what I was agreeing to. All I was aware of was the warm weight of my baby, squirming in my arms.

Esther

The close of a day. There should be no grief at the setting of the sun when you are confident in its eventual rise. But what if the waning light marks the end of your last day? What if the dawn will bring your death? I would have snuffed out each star that appeared that night, if I could have, and demanded that the sun return.

They let me see him. Even the keeper, for all his arrogant greed, just gave a curt nod and allowed me through the huge door as if he could not bring himself to meet the eye of loss. There was no sickening melee to fight through. Bisby had his own room and proper food. A paltry trade for a life taken.

He was opposite me. I had brought my chair up close to his so that we sat, almost touching, in front of a simple hearth surrounded by a plain wooden mantel. Above him a small circular window was set high in the wall. The lowering sun shone directly through it, sending shafts of light down onto a threadbare rug at our feet. It caught the top of his hair, brightening the sandy color to gold. His face was in shade. A blessing. It made it harder to determine the sallow tone of his skin and I could imagine that the shadows on his face were just some quirk of the light. But I could not ignore the bloodstained handkerchief gripped tightly in his hand.

There are no words for a man who is about to be hanged. I knew this, yet still I searched for something to say to him, started sentences that I could not finish. Eventually Bisby held up his hand in a plea for me to stop. We sat in silence for a moment, Bisby looking at the floor, while I watched dust motes drift through the shafts of light. Beside us, the pie that I had brought him sat wrapped in muslin, turning the air wholesome and meaty. It smelled of comfort and well-being, of security and home. I wished I had not brought it. In this place, it seemed only to mock us.

I did not need to ask him what he had done that day. I already knew that, like all the condemned, he had attended the chapel at Newgate. They would have made him sit next to a black coffin to hear the ordinary of Newgate preach. Then the ordinary would have taken down the history of his life and his descent into crime. From this, he would write his account. He would include his own sermon and, later, the details of Bisby's behavior and last dying words at the place of execution. This pamphlet, sold for sixpence after his death, would be all he left behind. I bit down on my own teeth, making my face rigid. The thought was more than I could bear.

"Be at peace, Esther," he said. "I am."

I almost believed him. There was no rage, or even bitterness, in his voice.

"How can you say that? You are not guilty."

"It doesn't matter now." He glanced down at the blood-streaked cloth and closed his hand around it, as if embarrassed by what it revealed.

"It does matter," I insisted. "Why did you not tell them who cut the silk?"

Bisby sighed and shook his head. "You know that I am ill?"

"You have jail fever. You would recover if we could only get you out of this place. You need to rest and eat, that is all."

"No, Esther. I'm dying. If I will die anyway, what purpose would it serve for another to be hanged in my place?"

"If they are guilty, they should hang," I said, surprised at my own vehemence.

"And what if they are just a child?"

I stared at him for a moment, not understanding what he meant. Bisby started to cough, wiping at his mouth with his handkerchief. I looked away. The daylight was dipping below the circular window, making it glow as if the room had its own miniature sun. It was precisely the time of day that Bisby and I had so often spent together, snatched moments before the light faded.

"What I ask myself," continued Bisby, when he had caught his breath, "is what my sister would have wanted. I know she would not want her son to die so that I could live out a few more weeks coughing into a cloth." He balled up the handkerchief and threw it into the fireplace where it hung on the edge of the empty grate.

"She would have wanted you both to live. You should have told the court what happened. They would not hang a child." Even as I said the words, I knew they were not true. Bisby lifted his eyes to mine, infinitely sad. "You must tell me what happened that night."

"I could not leave him," he said helplessly, "any more than I could have left you. Ives and Barnstaple went up the stairs to the garret and I followed them. I wanted to get Ives out of harm's way, that's all, I swear it. By the time I got to the attic, they were already standing by the loom and Ives had the cutlass in his hand. I went straight over to him to take the knife from him, but Barnstaple was too quick. I fought him for a while, but Barnstaple held me back. Then he said, 'We're making a man of Ives tonight, aren't we, Ives?' That was it. Ives sliced through the warp with the cutlass, then cut the silk on the roller, as if I might somehow try to tie each of the severed threads back together."

Bisby gave a mirthless laugh, which set him off coughing again. He patted at his waistcoat, looking for another handkerchief. I handed him mine. He took it carefully, smiling slightly at its delicate lace, as if he thought it a strange object to have in a place like Newgate.

"But how could Ives have done that? He had worked on the silk himself. It was your silk."

"He is a child wanting to be a man. He did what he thought the other weavers expected of him. He probably thought he was being brave, sacrificing his own work for a cause that Barnstaple had told him was noble and true."

"We should have made Ives give evidence. He could have told them that Barnstaple made him do it."

"Then they would have hanged us all. Esther, please, there's no purpose to this."

He was right. Nothing now could be changed. We could only say goodbye.

"You are going to die because I fell in love with you." That one statement was both the joy and the tragedy of my life. And his. "I made you set up the loom. I pushed you to weave the silk with my selfish whims and demands. If I had left you alone you would have finished your master piece and become a master weaver. But I couldn't leave you alone. I have brought you to this." It was my voice that cracked then, broken in two by a sob that made me slip from my chair to his feet.

"No!" I was surprised by the strength in his ragged voice. "Don't say that." He moved to the edge of his seat and grasped my hand, pulling it up, forcing my eyes to follow. "Knowing you has been the best thing in my life. I helped you because I wanted to. I helped you because every moment I spent in that garret with you was worth a lifetime anywhere else. I helped you because you are the most courageous, talented, beautiful woman I have ever known."

If I had tried to speak I would have wept, cried tears of love and grief at his feet, so I clasped my hands over his own and brought them to my lips, kissing his cracked skin.

"I don't want to have regrets," he said, resting his forehead on my hair.

"I want to die thinking of what I had, not what is being taken from me."

I lifted my face to his. For a moment we were as close as we had been that night in the garret. "You will be a master weaver, Bisby."

"Oh, Esther, how could that possibly be?"

"The Weavers' Company has seen *Blackberry and Wild Rose*. Mr. Arnaud took it to them. They said that they had rarely seen anything of such skill and complexity. They will admit you as a master."

For a moment he almost smiled, but the expression twisted on his face into unfathomable grief. He gave my hands a final squeeze, then released them.

The door opened and the ordinary stepped inside, clothed all in black. I began to rise, but he smiled and shook his head as if I had no need to be ashamed of my sorrow.

He walked over to us and knelt next to Bisby. "We must spend some time in prayer," he said.

I stood up, but Bisby's hand caught at my skirts. "My nephew," he said, his voice breathy with concern. "I know what he did was wrong, but he has no one now."

"I understand," I said. "I will do what I can to help him. For your sake."

He nodded. "Goodbye, dearest Esther," he said, looking up at me. The blue of his eyes had disappeared, swallowed into the unending darkness.

The ordinary took out his book of psalms and began to murmur:

"O death, where is thy victory?
O death, where is thy sting?"

45.

Sara

I stood in front of the bed I'd given birth on, then bent to smooth the sheets one final time. When I had finished, I placed Madam's favorite cushion on top. It was covered with our embroidery. Endless hours of sitting and sewing, the tiny stitches we had made joining our lives together. And now they were to be picked apart.

Madam sat humming at her dressing table, quietly defiant about what the day would bring. Her little melody was a bright thread through a somber moment. The grandfather clock struck ten, each chime bringing us closer to the appointed hour of Bisby Lambert's death. Madam's humming stopped when the clock did.

"It's almost time," she said. Her voice was fragile, wavering. When she tried to pick up her brush, she fumbled and it clattered to the floor.

I bent down next to her and picked it up. "Here, let me."

I uncoiled her hair, as I had a hundred times before, and drew the brush down its length over and over. Each strand was a different shade, from flaxen to copper. The color of autumn.

I picked up the lavender pomade, the glass bottom of the pot visible through the last of the cream. "We shall have to get you some more of this," I said, with forced brightness, even though I knew that my part in her life was over.

In the mirror, I saw her nod at me and smile. I scooped out the waxy ointment with my finger and gently rubbed it into her hair. She closed her eyes and at first I thought I gave her comfort. Then I saw her tears, even though her eyes were closed so tightly they wrinkled her smooth pale skin. A tear tracked down her cheek, leaving a shiny path through her face powder.

"Don't cry, madam," I said, my voice pitched high by distress. I had seen every side to her. Her petulance and vanity, her willfulness and anger. The sheer beauty of her nakedness and the coarse reality of her bodily functions. I had fought against her for so long that her weakness was the one thing I could not bear to see. "You have never cried, madam, not in all the time I have known you."

She opened her eyes and smiled. "You are wrong," she said. "I cried the morning your daughter was born." And I remembered her then: arms bloody up to her lace sleeves, hair plastered to her glistening forehead, wiping away tears cried for me and my child.

I pressed her damp cheeks with powder and pinned her hair in the style that flattered her most. Then I went to her wooden chest and opened it. Under the dried sprigs of lavender were her summer gowns. I lifted up layers of damask and linen until I found the gown I was looking for. When I held up the flowered cream silk tabby, she smiled and nodded.

❧ · ❧

The scent of lavender. It is enough even now to take me back to her. The slip of her heavy hair through my fingers and the marble whiteness of her skin as I bathed her. Her lingering presence in a room, long after she had gone.

Esther

"Just threepence to you, my sweet."

The old woman gave Moll a crinkled smile and held the pamphlet out to her. Moll dropped the coins into her hand and plucked at the paper.

His "last dying words," yet he was not even dead.

"How can you buy that nonsense?" I snapped at her. "You must have money to burn."

She flashed me a look from under her feathery lashes, something between shame and defiance. A look I had seen before, many times.

More people were beginning to arrive, the crowd thickening around the makeshift scaffold. Tutting and perspiring in the spring sunshine, a man hammered nails into wooden struts while the sheriff looked on, giving directions with a flick of his wrist. A woman ambled through the spectators with a large tray hung around her neck, inviting them to buy her freshly baked buns, her singsong voice a playful contrast to the somber ring of the hammer blows.

When the gallows were finished, there was something about its jutting corners and vast wooden frame that reminded me of a loom. The sheriff draped the platform with a black cloth, then pulled out his pocket watch and checked it against the clock hanging outside the Salmon and Ball. A quarter to eleven.

Only fifteen minutes until the appointed hour of Bisby's death. So many people had arrived to see him hang that we were being pushed ever closer to the scaffold. A front-row seat to a show I could not bear to see. This was not how the story was supposed to end. It was the Idle Apprentice who ended at Tyburn, not the Industrious one.

"There you are," said Elias, pushing through the crowd toward us. Finet followed him, his arms full of the hawker's cakes, handing them out as if we were at a cock fight. I refused one. How could I eat when this whole spectacle disgusted me? Finet offered my cake to Moll who took it greedily, saying, "'Tis a shame Miss Kemp was too ill to come and see this." Indeed, it seemed that all of Spitalfields was out in carnival mood that day. No one was expected to work, not Moll or Monsieur Finet, or any other servant or journeyman in our parish or the next. Every so often some notable man in the community would come over to shake my husband's hand, congratulating him with a smile and a clap on the back, as though he had begun the movement to abolish slavery, not condemned an innocent man to die. I stood beside him like a marionette, a nodding Judy to Elias' Punch.

In the distance, there was the rumble of wheels over cobblestones, becoming louder. The ordinary of Newgate sat at the front of the cart, an enormous black crow obscuring Bisby from the eager crowd, who craned their necks and jostled for the best view. The constable rode alongside them on horseback, a large pike held aloft in one of his hands. In a moment, the cart drew up alongside the gallows, inexpertly at first, the driver overshooting where he was meant to stop, then backing up, amid shouts from the sheriff and men scattering around them.

Many journeymen weavers had been following the cart and clustered around it when it stopped, offering Bisby a pot of ale or an apple. Those men might have been there that night, carrying cutlasses and pistols into Spital Square, intent on looting and troublemaking. Yet here they were, paying homage to Bisby's tragedy with a measure of gin offered to the condemned, before they bought themselves a bag of gingerbread nuts and went on their way.

The ordinary rose, slightly unsteady in the cart, and began to sing. His low, resonant voice quietened the crowd as he chanted the verses of a psalm. Bisby sat at the back of the cart, wearing a white linen shirt over his clothes. He hung his head and touched a white lace handkerchief to his lips as the ordinary sang. Despite the horrified enjoyment of the crowd and the suffocating crush of the voyeurs of death, I felt connected to him. There was a part of me that was with him.

The last prayers. There was time for one more prayer, even as the ordinary helped him to stand and the rope was tied around him, thrown up and over the gibbet. Bisby spoke for a few moments but I barely heard his last words. They scattered around me, like leaves in the wind. But Moll started to cry, great noisy sobs and sniffs, which earned her a kindly glance from the sheriff standing on the platform. I hadn't thought the girl could do anything else to shock me, but her hypocrisy took the breath from my lungs. Next to me, Elias' face was still as a painting. I never saw so much as a crack in that expressionless veneer the whole time he watched Bisby die.

Bisby seemed bold, defiant even, as they pulled the cap down over his head. It was like snuffing out a candle, one moment burning brightly, then nothing. I closed my eyes tightly—without his face there was nothing left to see in the world. Elias' fingers dug into my arm, harder and harder, trying to force up my lids to look upon the life that my foolish vanity had destroyed. I would not open them. Silently I prayed.

The crack of the whip. I heard the startled horses lurch forward to pull the cart from underneath him. Then there was no sound at all, save the creak of rope on wood and the dull chimes of the clock outside the tavern. My own heart seemed to slow with his. Grief devours time: I could not measure seconds or minutes, or know when to open my eyes. The crowd grew restless, persuading me it must be over. I didn't realize that even dying becomes tiresome, that there is an eternity of dangling, kicking, and pedaling. A desperate search for purchase in the empty air.

When I thought I could not resist the urge to run to him any longer, a boy broke free of the crowd, wrenching his arm away from the constable when he tried to stop him. About twelve years old, hair a sandy brown mop. He jumped at Bisby and clung to him as if he were drowning and only Bisby could save him. The gibbet bowed under their joint weight and, for a few moments, Bisby and Ives hung there together.

"A blessing," said someone behind me. "Quicker that way."

Even as my own world seemed to stop dead, the relentless minutes still passed. Elias retired to a coffeehouse with some other master weavers, and Moll and Finet went back to Spital Square, but I stayed, unable to leave him. The crowd dispersed, and the hawkers packed up their wares. The sounds of the street rose up to fill the unnatural quiet. The surgeons came for the body and the last of the onlookers squabbled over who should keep the contents of his pockets. After a while, there was nothing left of what had gone before, save a sandy-haired boy sitting alone on the edge of a platform swathed in black.

46

Sara

It was like going back in time. Retracing steps that I had taken years ago. I sat in a cart trundling along the Old London Road, being sucked back toward my beginning. The baby sat on my knee staring at hills and houses and roads she had never seen before, but which were as familiar to me as the swirls of hair on the back of her head.

I was between worlds, neither leaving nor arriving. Stuck in transition, as my daughter had been on the night she was born. Madam's house had been my place of safety, but even the sanctuary of the womb does not last forever. It had not been easy to leave. I sat in Madam's room long after they had all left. I had never been in that house completely alone. The silence was an unfamiliar companion, usually chased from kitchen to garret and back again by the clanking boom of the loom, the scrape and clatter of pots and pans. I almost expected to hear Madam's shrill voice calling from the parlor below for a boiled egg or an extra log for the fire. I had stayed sitting there until the grandfather clock rang its eleven low chimes, reminding me that time runs out for us all.

Now I raised my hand and called for the cart to stop. The steady plod of the horse's hooves slowed and we drew up alongside the end of a long drive that stretched toward a fine house sitting on the crest of a hill. The man opposite me looked from me to the house and back again, perhaps wondering what business I might have at such a grand place. I climbed down, watching my step, pressing the baby to my shoulder with one hand and holding my bag with the other. I stood at the side of the road for a moment, watching the cart disappear into the woods at the edge of the fields, then began to walk up the drive toward the house.

As I got closer, memories started to build in my head, like the blocks children play with. One on top of another, piecing my childhood back together. I walked round to the kitchens at the back of the house and stood in the sunlight for a moment, watching from some yards away. My baby's patience with the journey was wearing thin and she rooted at my chest and muttered small complaints into my shawl.

I had such a short distance left to go. Only a few steps to the kitchen door, but it was as if I stood on the edge of a cliff. While I contemplated the jump, the door opened and a woman walked out into the little kitchen garden. She had a basket hung over one arm, which swung as she walked along the flowerbed, inspecting the rows of lavender and herbs. She was singing and the sound of her voice was like a familiar cloak wrapped around my shoulders. She bent to cut rosemary and sage and put the clippings into her basket. Once she had sung the first verse of the song, she paused and made do with humming the rest.

> "Then she pull'd off her silk finish'd gown,
> And put on hose of leather, O!"

She looked up, startled. She held her hand to her eyes against the sunlight, trying to see who had spoken. I stepped toward her. "And then she runs off with the gypsies. Isn't that how the song goes, Mother?"

❧ · ☙

My mother bustled around my daughter. She clucked at her and shushed her when she fussed. She picked her up and rocked her in gentle arms, singing songs to her that took me back to a place I had left long ago. I sat at the kitchen table and told her about the years that had passed. Or, at least, snatches of them.

"It is good to see you, Mother," I said.

She looked at me over the baby's shoulder. "Oh, Sara, I cannot tell you how much I have missed you. How I have thought about you every single day since you left."

There was a part of me that could not bear to hear this. The same part that I had left behind years ago when the cart I sat in trundled off, separating me from my mother. The part of me that had dissolved into a bloody bowl of water that first time at Mrs. Swann's. The part of me that Mr. Arnaud had almost choked out of me that cold March day.

"You sent me away."

My mother turned her face from me and took the baby on a jiggling walk to the kitchen window. She stood like that for some time, looking out over fields and land that belonged to someone far wealthier than she or I would ever be.

"Why did you do that?"

When she turned, her face was streaked with tears. The sadness aged her, and I looked at the floor, not wanting to be reminded of the time that had passed.

"There are things you don't know," she said. "Things a child would not have understood."

"Perhaps I would understand now."

My mother sighed into the downy top of the baby's head. "When you are a woman alone, there are men who take advantage of that. The master here was one of those men. He was starting to look at you. I was trying to protect you. I didn't know what else to do but send you away."

I nodded slowly as if I understood, but I was not sure that I did. I felt an overwhelming need to hold my daughter, so I walked over to the window and gently took her from my mother's arms.

"Sara," my mother's voice was insistent, "I would not have been able to stop him. What could I do but send you away?" Somewhere in the back of my mind, there were strains of a conversation that I would never have with my own daughter: *I had to give you away. What could I do?*

"Where is he now?" I asked.

"He died a year ago. Fell off his horse during a hunt." My mother put her hand on the top of my arm, rubbing at me as if checking I was real. "Look at you, my darling, you've done so well. A lady's maid, no less, and a cook too, by the sound of it. Your old father would be proud. You have had a life in London that you never would have had here."

"Yes," I said. "You are right about that."

The baby started to cry. I was relieved. The conversation was meandering toward a place I did not want my mother to go. "She's hungry," I said.

"She? Does this child not have a name?"

"Oh, Mother, I hardly dared name her."

"Well, then, let's do it now. What about Esther? Your mistress has been good to you, I believe."

I wrinkled my nose. The baby's chin wobbled, and she started to wail.

My mother laughed. "Perhaps not Esther, then. What else do you like?"

"Madam's sister was called Anne. She died having a baby, like I almost did. Maybe that name. Or Anna, perhaps? That is what I always wanted to call her."

"Anna." My mother rolled the name around her mouth, as if it were marzipan. "Yes, Anna."

My child had an identity then, just as I was regaining mine, piecing myself back together among the familiar landscapes of my childhood, while my mother stood at the hearth making stewed cinnamon apples for my little daughter.

Esther

Monsieur Finet was seated at the kitchen table. Moll stood behind him, one arm leaning on the table, the other resting on his shoulder. Finet was reading aloud from a pamphlet in deliberately pompous tones, causing Moll to giggle. Oh, that laugh, that tinkling laugh. When Finet finished, Moll made a gesture, as if she were wringing the neck of a goose, and it was Finet's turn to chuckle, grabbing at his stomach, as if the force of his mirth might pop the buttons on his waistcoat.

"What is that?"

Two heads looked up at me and stared. "'Tis nothing, madam," said Finet, gruffly.

"But I should like to see it. Give it to me."

I could see the man swallow, even in that thick neck. He folded the paper before he handed it to me, as if that would stop me reading it. Moll made to slip away to the wet kitchen but I glared at her.

I opened the pamphlet, handling it gently as if it were my last connection with him. I did not want to read it all, but the words would not release me.

T H E

Ordinary of Newgate's full and
particular account of the execution

O F

B I S B Y   L A M B E R T

A T

Bethnal Green, London.

With his last dying speech and Exhortations
and behavior at the place of Execution.

MORNING OF EXECUTION
17th APRIL 1769

ON Monday the 17th Instant, this Parish was presented with a spectacle as solemn as it was uncommon; the public execution of the criminal, Bisby Lambert. A platform and temporary gallows were erected near the Salmon & Ball public house, in Bethnal Green, all hung with black. Then, just before Ten o'clock in the Morning, Lambert was brought down from the Newgate Chapel to the Press-yard to have his irons knocked off. His Behavior at this time was in every way becoming to his unhappy situation. The clock striking ten, Lambert lifted up his hands and said, "I have not one hour more to live in this world," and being put into a Cart, was carried to the Place of Execution.

He arrived a little before Eleven o'clock, and immediately began to pray fervently, and with an audible voice; which he continued during the whole time the executioner tied him up. While the officers were preparing him, an acquaintance of his standing by, says to him, "Lambert, you little thought of this once." He wantonly answered, "No, I did not, and I will take care not to come to it again," for which he was sharply reproved, and desired to think a little more of the approaching Awful Moment.

He addressed the spectators boldly to the following effect: "I am now going to suffer an ignominious death and you are all gathered to see my untimely end. It would be of no service to me now to tell a lie, and so I can say to you that I am as innocent of this crime as the child unborn. Let my blood lie to that wicked man who has purchased it with gold, and that notorious wretch who swore it falsely away."

He then looked upon a woman weeping in the crowd before him and said, "If I were not strung up here, I would put my hand to your eyes to feel your tears as I do believe you have spit on your fingers to counterfeit them."

Then Lambert looked undaunted around on the crowded multitude about him, as if he bade defiance to grim death and all its terrors; Lambert thanked God for His goodness in thus mercifully calling him to repentance before he was too much indisposed with the jail distemper. He desired that his friends would not be troubled or concerned about him, for he was very happy to be leaving this sinful, vain world.

Then, after a short time spent in devotion and having recommended his Soul to the Almighty's Protection, he stood up straight and waited, saying only, "'Tis well you can do no worse."

Then the Cart was drawn from under him, and he was turned off.

"Is this how you spend your time, Monsieur Finet? Have you nothing better to do now that Sara Kemp is gone?"

The cook got up and turned pointlessly to the dresser, making a show of looking for something. I walked over and stood beside him. "I came down to the kitchens to tell you that Miss Kemp left her book for you." We both glanced up at *The Art of Cookery* still sitting on the dresser shelf. "She thought you might have more use for it than her."

Finet managed a thin smile.

"Now," I said, "I should like oysters before the season ends. Finet, go out and get them for me."

He stared at me. "Can she not get them?" he said, nodding toward Moll.

"No," I said flatly, "she cannot."

Finet gathered his jacket and left. Moll sought the sanctuary of the hearth, putting water on to boil for some unknown purpose.

I watched her for a moment, head bent, plaited hair falling forward over her shoulders, the heat of the range bringing a pink flush to her cheeks. Or was it shame? I still did not know whether the girl felt any shame at all.

"There is a woman," I said to her, "a friend of Mrs. Arnaud's. She has need of someone to help her around the house. I think that might be a better position for you than here."

Moll spun round. "What do you mean?"

"I mean that you should go and work there. Her husband has passed away, so there should be no *difficulties*."

Moll's sweet lips formed a little circle and her smooth brow wrinkled. "But the master," she said, after a pause, "he wouldn't allow this?"

"You don't understand, do you? You think the master cares what happens to you, but he doesn't. He finds it all ... tiresome. At any rate, the hiring and dismissal of servants is up to me, not my husband."

She said nothing. Just turned back to the hearth, cavernous and empty inside, blackened to its core.

❧ · ❧

"I have dismissed her."

Elias was in the workshop, yet more patterns spread out over the wooden countertop.

"As you wish," he said.

If I had thought his reaction would betray him, I was wrong. There was no hint of pain or loss in his features as he studied the patterns. Perhaps he was skillful in hiding his feelings, or perhaps he had no feelings to hide. But, of course, the absence of feeling is not the same as the absence of deed.

"Sweet Peony and Laurel," he said.

I looked at him quizzically.

"That is the one we should weave next." I realized then that my own watercolors were spread on the counter, the ones he had grabbed in fistfuls from my dressing table drawer. "If we shade the peony petals correctly, the effect would be quite striking. We could add a ribbed ground. What do you think?"

There are no apologies from men like Elias Thorel, no acknowledgments even, just small concessions.

"I spoke to Arnaud the other day," he continued. "He was most complimentary about your silk. He said that he will buy the next one we weave. He thinks there is a good market for—how did he put it?—"*your wife's elegant and natural designs.*"

I stood in the garret watching as my new apprentice strung fine silk thread through the heddles. It was the palest of greens, the weft shot with silver thread. Once the pattern was set, a meander of shell-pink flowers would begin to run through the emerging silk, traversing its perfect line of symmetry with each repeat.

The house had been strangely quiet for the past few months, as if the soul had been cut out of it when the silk was destroyed. A loom is the heart of a weaving household. It is what drives us all forward.

Our new apprentice looked up at me, questioning. I ran my hands over the threads, feeling the tension of the warp, just as he had taught me to do. I nodded at my little journeyman. He gave me a shy grin and raked his hand through his sandy hair, readying himself to begin. His look of concentration as he started the loom was so like his uncle's that my heart ached.

The point paper for *Sweet Peony and Laurel* lay stretched across the loom. As the silk is made, the point paper will be destroyed; an appropriate end for a new beginning. Ives started the loom and the house's lifeblood began to flow again.

NOTE

Esther's character is loosely inspired by Anna Maria Garthwaite, the foremost designer of Spitalfields silks during the mid-eighteenth century. She is credited with bringing the artistry of painting to the loom, although her success predated the industrial troubles of the Spitalfields silk industry by some years. Many of her patterns and silks have survived and can be seen in the V&A Museum.

The eighteenth-century Spitalfields silk weavers were a militant bunch and formed early trade unions, then called combinations. The industrial tensions between the journeyman weavers and the master weavers are accurate and culminated in sporadic riots, during which the "cutters" would cut and destroy the masters' silk as punishment for not cooperating with the combinations. After one of these riots, John Doyle and John Valline were hanged in Bethnal Green outside the Salmon and Ball Inn. John Doyle went to his death swearing that he had been scragged and some of his last words are incorporated into Bisby's Last Dying Speech and Exhortations.

Buttermilk Alley is shown as a small passageway running between Phoenix Street and Quaker Street on John Rocque's map of Spitalfields and its environs dated 1746, although there is no trace of it now.

ACKNOWLEDGMENTS

Thank you to my UK and US agents, Juliet Mushens and Jenny Bent, for being such an amazing dream team and realizing my long-held ambition to be published in the US, where my father lived for many years.

Thank you to the wonderful team at Blackstone Publishing for their enthusiasm and support. Particular thanks to Djamika Smith for designing such a stunning cover, Lauren Maturo for championing *Blackberry and Wild Rose*, and Courtney Vatis for her careful edits.

Lastly, thank you to the fascinating pocket of London that welcomed the Profitable Strangers this book is about, and to the silk weavers of eighteenth-century Spitalfields for entrancing me fifteen years ago and never letting me go.